THE STORY OF E

BOOK I

INNER EARTH

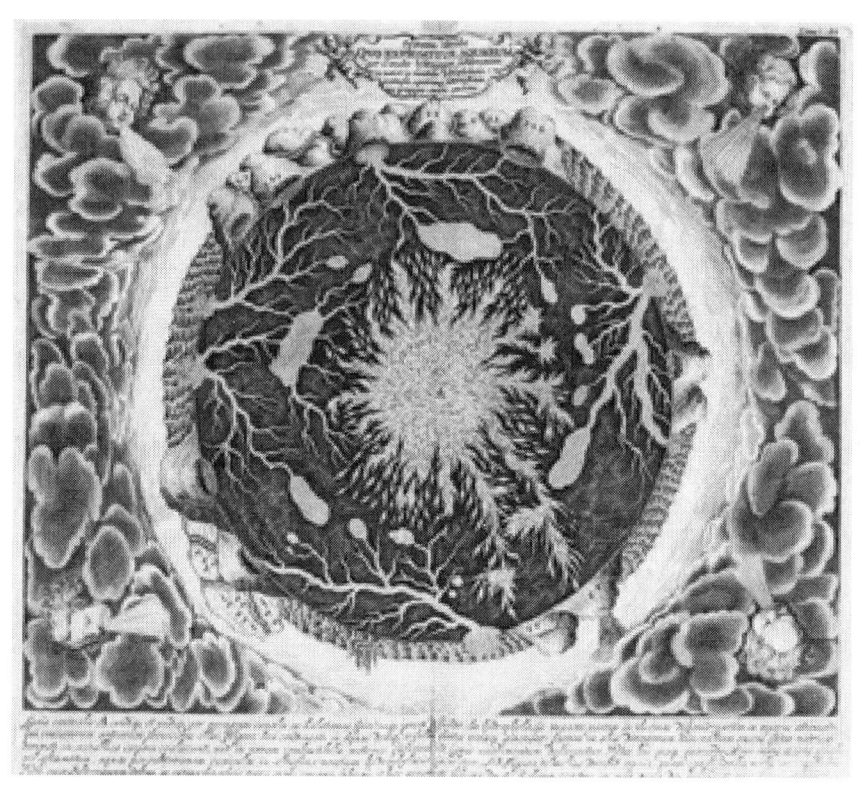

Athanasius Kircher 1602 - 1680

Dearest Chris,

May all your adventures

Be full of Light & Love —

Buried But Never Forgotten: A Journey through Earth by Elisa Chastaine is a spellbinding fantasy that will excite the imaginations of fans of the genre, a perfect escape for any reader who enjoys adventure and takes delight in navigating rich and beautifully constructed worlds. The story follows Lina, commonly known as E by those closest to her, who finds herself on uncharted paths after a flash flood hits them while hiking with Daniel, the man she loves. She is swept away by the flood that thrusts her under the earth into an unfamiliar world and a forgotten civilization. In this world, she will need more than courage to survive, face all kinds of creatures and challenges, and will make stunning discoveries, especially of a civilization that fascinates her. But the biggest question is: *Can she make it out of the bowels of the Earth alive?*

A work of rich imagination... It is a tale with a fully drawn and steely protagonist. E's adventure is exciting to follow, but the story provokes strong reflections in readers and makes them think differently about the world and civilization. Elisa Chastaine makes readers believe that there is a world beyond our own and that nature might be concealing far more than we can ever imagine. **The writing is gorgeous,** littered with strong descriptions and the kind of imagery that keeps the imagination awake. It is hard to identify just one element that stands out in this novel, but the **page-turning plot** with all its loose ends tucked in tightly appealed to me. It is tense and absorbing, and you can't just put it down.

- Christian Sia for Readers' Favorite

BURIED
But Never Forgotten

A Journey Through Earth

By
Elisa Chastaine

© 2020 ELISA MARIE CHASTAINE

All rights reserved. This book or parts thereof may not be reproduced in any form, stored in any retrieval system, or transmitted in any form by any means—electronic, mechanical, photocopy, recording, or otherwise—without prior written permission of the publisher, except as provided by United States of America copyright law. For permission requests, write to the publisher at the address below.

ISBN 979-8-4679643-7-9

Book designed by Wyatt Hill - Hill Creative

Interested in more information or to contact the author:

Elisa Chastaine
elisa@metaphysicaladventures.com

Published by OMIFY Productions
2020

Dedication

This book is dedicated to my beloved, Michael. His presence in my life has allowed me to relax into my own beingness, to accept myself exactly how I am and to provide a beautiful home where I can find refuge and travel to new worlds. He is my shelter and my joy. I am eternally grateful for his presence. Always have been, always will be.

A special note must be added to acknowledge Liise. Her love and encouragement combined with expert editing helped to make this, my first book, something I am proud to share with the world. Thank you, my dear friend.

Awards for
Buried
But Never Forgotten

2021 Best Book Awards
New Age Fiction – Winner
Fantasy Fiction - Finalist
18th Annual Awards Sponsored by American Book Fest

2021 International Book Awards
New Age Fiction – Finalist
12th Annual Awards Sponsored by American Book Fest

2021 American Book Awards
New Age Fiction – Finalist
12th Annual Awards Sponsored by American Book Fest

2021 Eric Hoffer Award
Da Vinci Eye Honorable Mention
Presented to books with superior cover artwork – judged on both content and style. Personal note: A big thank you to Wyatt Hill from Hill Creative for making my vision a reality and then some.
www.HillCreative.design

2021 Living Now Book Award
Bronze Medal – Spiritual/Romance Fiction
The purpose of the Living Now Book Awards is to celebrate the innovation and creativity of books that enhance the quality of life, from cooking and gardening to spirituality and wellness.

2021 Los Angeles Book Festival
General Fiction – Honorable Mention
Winners and Honorable Mention books are chosen for general excellence and the author's passion for telling a good story plus the potential for work to reach a wider audience.

2021 National Indie Excellence Awards
New Age Fiction Finalist

Winners and Finalists are determined on the basis of superior written matter coupled with excellent presentation in every facet of the final published product from cover to cover.

www.indieexcellence.com

2021 San Francisco Book Festival
General Fiction – Honorable Mention

Winners and Honorable Mention books are chosen for general excellence and the author's passion for telling a good story plus the potential for work to reach a wider audience.

Readers' Favorite 5 Stars Award

Winners selected by a review of other authors.

2021 New York Book Festival
General Fiction – Honorable Mention

Celebrates books that deserve greater recognition from the world's publishing capital.

2021 Hollywood Book Festival
Fiction - Honorable Mention
Genre Fiction – Honorable Mention

Based in the capital of show business, the Hollywood Book Festival aims to spotlight literature worthy of further consideration by the talent-hungry pipeline of the entertainment industry.

A message to you, my fellow adventurer...

As you embark on this journey with me, I want to set the right context for the words that follow. Some of this truly happened to me. Some is loosely borrowed from other people's stories. The rest is pure make believe... *maybe*. It will be up to you to figure out which is which.

It is my sincere hope that you are able to suspend what you think is real and what you think is fiction, at least for a long enough period of time that other borders start to bend. A flexible mind is a prize worth attaining, above all else. It is only through the honest entertaining of foreign ideas that our worlds can open to new adventures, new lands and new possibilities. We are in dire need of all of these. Without allowing new thoughts and concepts to enter, change cannot happen. My fear is that we are doomed to repeat the past. And that, my friend, has not worked so well for us.

I invite you to suspend your world for a time and enter mine. I promise that it will be well worth the interruption. And who knows, maybe you will come out the other side a different person too.

Elisa Chastaine

The Author

TABLE OF CONTENTS

CHAPTER I   1

    Playing Dead
    Adventure to Nowhere
    Something was Wrong
    Into the Abyss
    The Pearly Gates
    Dawning of Hope
    Out of the Rubble

CHAPTER II   37

    A New Ending
    Another Reckoning
    Caught Between Earth and Sky
    Growing up
    A Slice of Solace
    Good Vibrations
    Tinky and Me
    The Vigil
    Homage to Authenticity
    The Flow

CHAPTER III   79

    The Temple's Secrets
    Meet Thy Makers
    Freedom
    The Library
    Close Encounter
    Peace Out
    Into the Garden
    Exodus

CHAPTER IV   **115**

        The Claws of Life
        An Opening
        Urda
        The Kingdom
        Counterbalance
        Fundamentals
        Ripe Fruit
        A Lady Never Tells
        Grace of God
        The Choice

CHAPTER V   **177**

        The Three Visions
          ◇ Earth Story
          ◇ Homecoming
          ◇ Before Birth
        Overcoming Fear
          ◇ Fight or Flight
          ◇ Repatterning Dreams
          ◇ The Classics Rebooted
        Truth or Consequences
        Mission Ready

CHAPTER VI   **215**

        Point of No Return
        Darkness All Around
        Monsters at the Gate

CHAPTER VII   **231**

        Buried but Never Forgotten

EPILOGUE   **237**

        Daniel

LOST WATERWAYS IN EARTH
MUNDUS SUBTERRANEUS

Athanasius Kircher 1602 - 1680

CHAPTER I

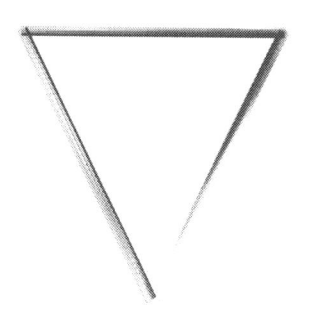

BURIED

Playing Dead

Animals play dead for a reason. It is a choice made deep within their limbic brain that tells them to move means to die.

When I first woke, maybe that is too generous, let's say when I first became aware that I still had a physical body, I regretted it. I felt like an ancient woman who had been mercilessly pummeled by the hands of time. There were no isolated areas of hurt. There was just pain everywhere. It was as if someone had worked me over with a small hammer, from head to toe, from inside to out, making sure not to leave any part unscathed. I opened my eyes, but nothing happened. I closed them. Still the same, nothing. In fact, I could not tell if they were even opening or closing. Either way, it was the same complete blackness. Beneath me the ground was hard, damp and cold. There was utter silence. Even my breathing felt like an intrusion into the nothingness. Surely, I must be dead. I did not know you could feel so much pain when you had passed over to the other side. Then pure unadulterated terror, primal uncontrollable fear, started creeping up from the base of my spine. I might still be alive. Just entertaining the thought was too much for my traumatized nervous system and I passed out again.

▽

Born as Ermalina, I was named after my great grandmother from Italy. All the women on my mother's side of the family had names that began with the letter 'E.' My full given name was too much for most Americans and too old school for my modern sensibilities.

When I decided to go by Lina I felt like such a rebel. To my close friends, the inside circle, the few that truly got me, I was and will always be known as "E." That name always seemed to fit the best to those I let in. At some point on this journey together, maybe you will start to call me by that name, but let's give it some time. There are many miles to travel yet and a lot of things can happen.

It was Sunday May 19th, 2019, a typical day in the adventurous life I shared with my best friend and soulmate, Daniel. We were married for two years but had known each other for many. It was the second marriage for him and the first for me. He had been a family man and I had been a wanderer. We had lived very different lives, but those divergent paths miraculously brought us together in the same odd time and place to meet. It was more than love at first sight. It was a deep sense of friendship, like we had known each other forever. You know that feeling. Some say such a deep sense of knowing surely spans many lifetimes. Whether that is real or not, I was prone to believe that way. But no matter, our friendship grew and blossomed over time until one day it fully revealed itself. Little did I know that on that warm weekend day, our carefully planned excursion would take us on divergent courses again, but this time might not ever bring us back together.

We were going to the slot canyons of northern Arizona. Even if you have never been there, you are sure to know the famous images of tight chasms and sleek cliffs undulating in graceful curves and flowing with bands of magnificent desert hues. The enigmatic photos taken in this area have been widely seen thanks to many talented photographers. They all seem to capture that moment when a well-placed beam of light breaks through and highlights a person standing at just the right place. Bathed in a beam straight from heaven, the images look other-worldly. It was those unearthly images combined with our unquenchable desire to explore that hooked us in.

Adventure to Nowhere

I trusted Daniel with my life. Always had. He was at home in the wilderness and adept at survival, having been an elite endurance adventure racer for many years. For those who are not familiar, adventure racing is an extreme sport that includes multi-disciplines from trekking, to biking, to mountain climbing, to white water rafting - just about anything you can throw at crazy people who thrive on pushing themselves to the extremes. Some races last a couple of days and others go on for weeks on end. Racers must be both mentally and physically tough since they are traversing through vast expanses of wilderness with just a map and compass, navigating strategically placed check points that must be reached and are, of course, not on any existing path. Supplies are limited to what you can carry, short naps replace actual sleep, weather is what Mother Nature decides to challenge you with – and we all know her unpredictable temperament! To top it off, you are racing with a team of four that must all cross the finish line at the same time. The challenge is putting a group of people under extreme physical and psychological stress and then expecting them to work together. That sort of test is not my style, on any level.

I had always preferred to be by myself, until I met Daniel. With him I liked to do just about everything – until alone time called. My friends were carefully chosen and few. For work, being an entrepreneur had always been my preference. I didn't like to answer to anyone or to have anyone answer to me. Daniel was a self-employed contractor, known for doing the difficult jobs that no one else wanted to attempt. He and his roughneck crew had no fear and always got the job done. No matter what. They were scrappy and so was I, just in a different way. But let us be clear, my past time pursuits did not include extreme outdoor sports of any kind. It did not before Daniel and still did not, even up to that fateful day. I was always active, loved hiking, skiing and biking but only for a few hours or one day. Multiple days would require an evening hot bath, a warm nourishing dinner and a nice rest in a soft bed. Oh, and a real toilet. You know, the kind you can sit down on and flushes. Nowadays I am considered an urban adventurer of sorts.

Daniel opened a whole new world up to me, in so many ways. Our various adventures included things I would never have done alone. They typically were in magnificent places that I had always dreamed of seeing. But let us be clear, they did not include a few things like spelunking and climbing mountains. No confined spaces and no sheer cliffs. If all my prerequisites were checked, I was willing! While this allowed for only minimal challenges on his scale, he loved being with me and so I think he genuinely enjoyed the tamer times in the wilderness because of us. The presence of another person always has a way of changing the matrix of one's experience. As the two mold and morph together, tastes and aptitudes change to accommodate. You do not even have to be aware of it. The changes just happen. The absence of that other person can do the same thing.

Together we made the perfect adventure pair. He made sure we had everything we would and could ever possibly need. He meticulously plotted out our course and packed all our food while I... well I packed my clothes but not until I badgered him on what to bring. *What will the weather be like? Will I get cold? Will I be hot? Will I get wet? Will I... Will I... Will I?* His answers were always the same and given with a modicum of frustration and incredulity at how someone so competent at so many things could be so inept at something as easy as what to wear while outside. He always replied with a simple - *look at the weather and figure it out!* Obviously, I was not capable of figuring much out when it came to the outdoors. Well, at least I thought I wasn't so capable. Guess you really do not know what you are capable of until you have no other choice.

▽

The day was perfect. A bit brisk as the sun was rising, but soon it would turn into a gloriously warm high desert day. It was just the two of us as we headed up the canyon around seven a.m. An early start was needed to be able to fit in the ten-mile hike we planned to accomplish that day. Each of us had carefully organized daypacks – thanks to Daniel. His contained the motherload of items since carrying a heavy pack was not my forte. We would require lots of water throughout the day and since that was the heaviest, Daniel carried most of it. My pack included, believe it or not, a small space blanket in case we took longer than expected. Evenings in the high desert can get quite chilly. He also had me pack a headlamp which again, amazing to me, Daniel always made me carry, even if we were not going to be out at night. His motto - *you never know when one will come in handy*, always won. I learned early on that this was his new version of racing, so I needed to cut him some slack as he loved the 'plan and prep' as much as he loved the actual adventure. And part of the plan was being prepared for anything, so I came to learn. The rest of my pack was rather mundane. A sandwich, a couple of granola bars, an apple and an orange, plus a small bag of trail mix. Plenty of food for just one day of exploring. There was the obligatory sunscreen and two tubes of Chapstick, since having chapped lips in the dry desert was not on my list as fun. My cell phone would have to go into a water-resistant bag. Always in a water-resistant bag no matter where we went because, as Daniel drilled into me – *you never know!* That was about it. Plenty for our day journey. Shorts, tank top, tech shirt, sneakers, thick socks and a bandana, I was ready to take on the average day.

Something was Wrong

The canyon delivered everything we expected. Gorgeous striations of perfect desert hues. Magnificent steep walls that wove their way through the unblemished surface like an elegant scar. And while it was hot on the surface, deep in the canyon it was delightfully cool. We made sure to keep a steady intake of water because sweat was evaporating before we could feel thirsty. Water - ok maybe I did have one specialty, that would be always making sure we had enough water. Due in a large part to my paranoia of dehydration. It typically kicked in after a mere ten minutes of activity with no bottle on hand. Daniel was the opposite, more like a camel than anything else. He could go a whole day without drinking anything, not that that was ideal, it was more that he could just roll with it. I did not roll so well with being thirsty.

It was about mid-day and we had arrived at the turn around point about five miles up the canyon. Stopping to enjoy the moment and to have lunch, Daniel decided to go off and explore while I went into documentary photographer mode. There was beauty everywhere. I always looked for the unusual angle or pattern of light, the things most people would just ignore. I was excited to catalog this journey in particular. There was a heightened sense of adventure from the very moment we had started planning. Maybe because it had been on my bucket list for so many years or maybe because I knew it would be life changing. To finally be there was a dream come true. It was then that I looked down and noticed a delicate stream of water snaking its way along the ground. Always keen on capturing the unexpected and artful designs nature has to offer, I was totally intrigued and utterly oblivious to its meaning. I yelled to get Daniel's attention, to try and get him to look down. I knew that he would never notice something like this on his own. His head was always up in the clouds, looking where to go next. Mine was always down looking for treasures in the here and now.

"Daniel, check out this stream of water. It's making a pretty winding track just like the canyon!" I was so totally amazed and absorbed with my artistic analogy that it shocked me when Daniel roared back.

"What are you talking about! Where is there water?" I could see him looking around the walls, trying to figure out what I was talking about.

"It's not on the walls silly, look down!" I shouted back with a bit of attitude. My keen observation skills were one of the few things I could contribute and that gave me the excuse to be a little condescending.

No sooner had I said that then Daniel was back at my side. Through heavy breathing from the sprint, he said in a tone that I had never heard him use before. It was direct and forceful. *"E, we have to go now and go fast."*

As I started to question him, he screamed, *"NOW!"*

I knew when to push my agenda and when not to. This was not a time to question. I quickly packed up my belongings and we started running down the canyon. Just then a strong ominous wind hit our backs. The temperature was dropping fast as the water was rapidly rising. Even though the stream was just a few inches deep at this point, I could feel its growing determination. No one was going to turn it away from its mission to get downstream as fast as possible.

Starting to get worried, I yelled at Daniel. *"What is going on? You are scaring me!"*

I think I knew what was happening but if the thought hadn't fully formed and if Daniel maybe, just maybe said something different, then just maybe it wasn't happening.

"FLASH FLOOD!" he shouted back.

"SHIT." I replied.

As we ran, Daniel kept looking back to make sure that I was close since there was no way I could run as fast as him or for as long. I was trying my hardest. My heart was beating so hard that it felt like it was going to explode right out of my chest.

"Can we make it out in time?" I desperately tried calling to him.

"WE NEED TO GET TO HIGHER GROUND FAST," he frantically yelled.

Well that was just great. The path was narrow and the walls went straight up. It had been like that for a while. There was simply nowhere to climb out. The water was rising even more rapidly now and was up to our calves. I understood our plight having read about people being swept away in canyons due to rain in some distant hills. There would be no warning. No forecast or sign to give you the heads up before it was too late. It would be a beautiful sunny day and everyone would be out having a grand old time until they weren't anymore. And there was never a good ending.

Thank god I had Daniel, he was a survivor. I knew he would think of something.

"Daniel please slow down for a minute so I can catch my breath."

I could not run anymore, even with the water aggressively pushing me forward. He stopped but the deep sigh and dropping of his shoulders before he turned around told me all I needed to know. But I still asked as I gasped for air.

"Daniel, are we going to be ok?"

He just looked at me. At times of heightened tension, I was used to him not speaking. Emotions and words did not go together in his world yet. His silence was not the sign I wanted. The water was now fast approaching our knees. As we started running again it was getting harder to keep my balance and stay upright. A glimmer of hope appeared as we rounded the next corner and saw a giant pile of strategically stacked rocks. YES!!! This was truly good luck. How could I ever doubt my guide, my love. He had always been my good luck charm.

Daniel yelled for me to follow him to the rocks. By the time we got there the water had reached my knees and was moving up swiftly. It had risen to the point where I could barely control what I did with my legs. He told me to hang on to the bottom rocks while he climbed up and threw me a rope – of course he had a small rope with him. While he was scampering up, the water was almost able to pull me away. I was scared and did not want to wait any longer, so I tried to climb towards Daniel all by myself. The boulders were large and slick and hard to hold on to. Daniel was about a body length above me when I shouted to him.

"I can't find a place to hold on to. Please hurry with the rope!" But there was not going to be enough time.

He quickly turned around and reached down to pull me up. The temperature had dropped precipitously making my hands numb. Combined with the cold wet rocks, I had a hard time feeling my fingers. With my right foot resting on a tiny ridge in the rock and my other pressing against another slick stone for balance, I reached up and grabbed on to his hand for dear life. We gripped hard. There was a moment of hope in my heart that we were going to make it out. Like always, Daniel would save the day. No sooner had the thought formed than my right foot slipped off the ledge. Our grip could not hold the unexpected weight of my body falling. The last thing I remember seeing was the expression on Daniel's face as I slipped out of his hand and out of his life. It was as if time stopped and transcended space to allow him to get one final message across. It was pure and raw. It was complete love and utter agony.

The water rapidly swept me away and out of his sight. Now it was just me and raging Mother Nature. Instinctively I tried to grasp at something but there was nothing. I started thrashing my body around trying to get my legs under me so that maybe, just maybe, I could stand. But each time I was about to get into a position to leverage my balance, the relentless power of the water knocked me over so that I was horizontal again. I tried swimming to shore except that there was no shore. The more frantic I got and the harder I tried to do the impossible, the more exhausted I became. Finally, I realized that I had only one choice. Go with the flow and hopefully pop out at the end of the canyon. To this day I do not know if that has ever been done or if it's even possible to ride out a canyon flood. But it was the only thing I had to hold on to.

▽

If you have ever been in a life or death situation, you will understand that time can behave strangely. It slows way down while your thoughts become crystal clear. I remembered Daniel telling me about a time he got knocked out of a raft in class five rapids (that is the toughest grade). He knew from experience that you always want to go downstream feet first with your hands crossed over your chest so that if anything hits first, it will be your feet and not your head. Bouncing around like a ping pong ball made it hard to get in that position. But finally, I did it and it gave me enough time to catch my breath and to gather my thoughts. The odds did not look good but at least I would not die of traumatic head injury. Guess that was some sort of blessing. My back felt relatively safe because of my daypack protecting the next most vulnerable body part, my spine. The crazy idea that maybe I could ride this thing out grew stronger… until I went around the next curve. My tenuous confidence would be shattered, along with my entire life. Never would anything be even remotely the same, ever again.

I was now fully engulfed and succumbed to the water's will. Around the corner was another big sweeping turn off to the right but to the left, to the left was a large black hole. It was very odd. I did not remember seeing it on the hike up or hearing about random holes in this canyon. But there it was. Big, dark and ominous. The water was being split in two. Half was racing around the corner and the other half was disappearing into the void. I don't think I ever had a chance to choose. I was going to the left and there was nothing I could do about it.

Into the Abyss

At record speed I flew downward and downward and downward. Maybe if this were in a theme park and maybe if it lasted only thirty seconds, like most thrill rides, it would have been exhilarating. This was not. I was struggling for every breath. The width of the tunnel varied from the size of a drainage ditch to being so narrow that I was sure to get stuck and drown. The scariest part of all was that there was nothing I could do but try to survive. It was pure animal instinct of staying alive at all costs and against all odds that kicked in. The swirling torrent of water continually slammed my body back and forth against the rock walls. I look back at that moment in time and marvel at the tenacity of the human spirit. At my spirit. I was a fighter, and right then I was fighting for a precious pocket of air. *Why did I struggle so hard to live only to die in another second?* I did not have a choice. My body did what a body does. Survive.

It was not until one eternity passed that I was unceremoniously spit out at the other end with a big splash.

When I woke a second time, the pain was still there as a crude reminder that I was very much alive. I was in the dark – figuratively and literally. To be really clear before we move on, when I say 'dark' I mean the complete absence of light. You could take your finger and poke yourself in the eye and not even blink in protection because you could not see your own finger coming. If you have ever been in a winter storm whiteout, you will understand. There is no seeing an up or a down, it all looks the same. When everything blends together, that is when your balance starts to play tricks on you... *but let's not get too far ahead!* I was still frozen in the fetal position and not willing to move a muscle yet, and at a loss for what had just happened or where I was.

▽

The human response to darkness is universal. It is in the dark that bad things come out to get you, whether they are monsters from the fairy tales of yore or the crazy mutated beings from modern cinema. No matter, it is under the cover of night that they are out, they are hungry and they are coming for you.

In the past, I thought I knew something about fear. For most of my life, every day felt like a juggling act of how to cover up its constant presence. My modus operandi was not to admit feeling any fear. If I ignored it then maybe it would not find me. But right then, there would be no covering it up. I had been swallowed by a raging monster and my whole world was gone. At last, the terror I had avoided my whole life was poised to engulf my entire being.

I tried to wrap my head around my situation, but how would that even be possible? It was just me, all by myself in some god-forsaken place. A place that was utterly quiet. At first the silence was deafening. Yes, deafening. I now understand what that turn of phrase means. The average mind does not appreciate a void of noise, especially not a traumatized mind. It will do anything to fill it. Quietness just emphasizes loneliness and fear. Whether it be with thoughts or noise, the space must be filled to maintain a sense of rightness. At this point my mind had nowhere to turn for stimulation so it simply turned in on itself and burst into a cacophony of inner voices. One part was shouting at another part, one was singing some stupid song. One, bless their heart, was trying to talk reason to the other voices but the loudest were the most aggressive parts trying to assume control of a very bad situation.

"You are going to die."   *"This is it!"*

"You have to fight back."

"You are doomed."

"Buck up."   "It's going to all be ok."

"Don't you dare move."

"Give up."   "Run!"

"Die."   "Fight."

Back and forth, my mind was torn by warring thoughts all trying to seize the day with their own self-serving logic.

Finally, my mind had enough and with one final implosion, everything came to a crashing halt. All the voices were obliterated in that one split second. My mind had enough and it had snapped. It was then and only then that I truly became aware of my surroundings. What I thought was complete silence was actually being filled with the most delicate sounds. There was a steady stream of little splashes. Some close by, some off in the distance... *drip drip drip...* with the slightest echo that played off the water and stones. I strained to hear if there was anything else. Like the footsteps of some predator as it approached. Some monster rising from the deep. But no, there was nothing. Absolutely nothing. Still, I lay there not willing to move a muscle, trying to control my breath so that it too made the least amount of impact on the surrounding air. All in hopes that maybe I would just fade away, disappear completely and then reappear back into the light of the surface, back to my normal life. I had practiced this technique many times in my past. Wishing myself into oblivion just so I could wake up in a new reality. Now I didn't have to play. This was for real.

▽

Daniel always saw the best and brightest in everything, everyone and every situation, and always with me. I was more war torn and jaded for someone so young and seemingly so fresh. In his mind I would have been the Amazing E, laying there quietly gathering her thoughts, developing a plan before she leapt forth and conquered! But I knew the truth about who I was and what I was doing. I was simply paralyzed with fear and wanting to die. Nothing heroic there. Never anything heroic. Always just surviving.

The first clear and logical thought that came through was that I had fallen into an aquifer somewhere in the bowels of the Earth. The amount of time I traveled and the pitch downward, would place me nowhere near the surface. I was buried deep. No one would ever find my body or know what happened. It wasn't going to be like the miners in Chile, where rescuers knew their location and could drill down to victoriously release them from their stone prison. Unlike them, I was long gone. I had disappeared to a location unknown to anyone. My dearest would look for days and days, maybe even weeks. He would not give up easily but alas, I would not be there, nor would any trace of me ever be found. No one wants to die much less to die alone, but to be all the above and have no one ever know what happened was a brutal thought. I would not wish that on anyone. And there was nothing I could do about it. I would not be able to climb my way out, even if I were lucky enough to find the chute that carried me away. I had traveled too far to clamber back out. I was trapped. I knew it. It was over.

▽

The reality of being buried alive is a rough one. I had only ever played dead before, never really died, so I was not sure what the process was going to be like. Growing up, God was never forced on my brother and me. Once we got to be teenagers, attending church was optional, except for the major holidays like Christmas and Easter. Putting on our best clothes and joining mom at those times was all she asked and, at least for a period of time, we felt it was a reasonable request. It is not that I didn't believe in a God, I just didn't entertain the thought of Him very much or very seriously. My mom's old-world catholic blind faith with its acceptance that everything divine was unknowable and that we just had to trust the priests was too much for me to accept. My dad, on the other hand, questioned everything, especially religion. He was nobody's fool. I preferred my dad's rather cynical view - God had made the world and then walked away to leave us to our own devices. Ultimately my dad's God didn't give a shit. That made much more sense as I looked out at a crazy irrational world. It especially made sense when trying to reconcile the havoc alcohol played in our family. That all seemed like a million years ago and from a galaxy far far away. The raw fact that I was being forsaken by a missing God rang truer than ever. Even He would not be caught dead here.

As I lay there facing my terror all alone, a strange thing happened. I got pissed off at a God that I preferred to think was not around. Maybe I was hedging my bets in case He was there, or maybe it was just the extremeness of the situation pushing me out of my normal belief patterns. We think we are in control of our own thinking but when it comes right down to it, in times of high stress we tend to default into the underbelly of societal beliefs. All those concepts, thoughts and values were sitting there, right below the surface, waiting for some trauma to push them to the forefront of consciousness – that is, if left unchecked or unchallenged. For me, right then, up from the depths bubbled a conversation with an omnipotent male, sitting on a throne somewhere far above. A God that was prone to inexplicable acts. Sometimes He shined down upon you with a blessing, other times He forsook your very presence and worse yet were the times He sent a curse upon His very own children... as He was doing to me right then. One could never be sure where they stood with that God. Keeping His children off balance was some weird power play – at least I thought so at that moment.

▽

The following conversation is not one I am proud of, even if it was with a God that was clearly in a vengeful mood. I hope anyone who reads my tale will be compassionate for the desperation of my situation and cut me some slack. There is swearing involved but this is how it happened, and I am going to be faithful to my story. That conversation with God started out as a small desperate whisper in my head...

"How could you God?

Why have you done this to me just when my life was finally turning around. It makes no sense... For once I was happy and you just took it all away. Was all my suffering before not worth something? Did I not deserve to finally be happy?

What did I ever do to you that made you want to do this to me?

I may not have paid you homage, but I never cursed you or cast you down! Why me?"

The thought of whether I deserved this fate started to build until it reached a rage of self-righteous indignation. Louder and louder in my mind came the following words.

"How could you!

Seriously! What kind of a God are you? What the fuck! Burying me alive!!!"

That first fuck let down all barriers – as the first time tends to do. I no longer cared if the monsters would hear and come tear me limb from limb. At least that would be more merciful than this God's plan. Letting all boundaries fall and with nothing left to lose, at the top of my lungs I screamed into the void...

"Fuck you God. Why do you get to decide my life? Why this????

Who the fuck made you the boss of me!

Fuck you.

Fuck you.

Fuck you.

And what the fuck!

Burying me alive!

What kind of sick fucking game is this?"

And on and on, until the final crescendo hit and tears unfurled in rage and raced down my face faster than the waters that had carried me to this hell.

"*I HATE YOU!*

I HATE YOU!

I HATE YOU!

YOU ARE NOT MY GODDAMN GOD ANYMORE.

I WILL NEVER FORGIVE YOU!

I WANT NO PART OF YOU!

FROM NOW ON I WILL TAKE CARE OF MYSELF.

GOOD FUCKING BYE"

▽

I am not sure I got that all verbatim, I might have left a few fucks out here and there, but you get the picture. I certainly got the picture. God, if He was really there, got the picture. It was finally over. The door shut permanently on that god. Forever downgraded to the small 'g' category. Whoever he was, he was certainly not the type of god I could love, much less serve. Maybe my dad was right all along. God created us and then left. If that was true, then this whole thing would just be plain old bad luck. I mean REALLY BAD luck. The alternative was that god was one utterly cruel being. A god with an evil streak. Like the one described in the Old Testament. Not meaning to be sacrilegious to his followers, but seriously. Have you not ever wondered how a god of love could slaughter the masses, including women and children for very little reason? Top it off with some good old raping, pillaging and plundering, all in the name of divine justice? I always had a hard time understanding a god with a temperament reflective of the lowest of human behavior. The very thought of being at the mercy of that kind of a god was completely indigestible. It made me wretch. Literally.

A small place inside was rising to fight as that ugliness left my system. When it came right down to it, I could not truly accept that god enjoyed reigning bad shit down on a world he presumably created in love. While it felt right raging away, a quiet little voice inside of me whispered that I had crossed a line. I had inherited my dad's gentle heart that never wanted to see anyone hurt much less be on the receptive end of abuse he may have inadvertently inflicted. He was never mean to another even if they treated him badly. I suddenly felt very ashamed of myself. Ashamed that I had cursed a creator I was not sure even existed or was even around to listen. Having such curses flow across my lips felt like pure poison to my soul, no matter who or what god was. I was in the wrong to hate anyone.

Just like that, my mind was torn asunder and my heart felt like it was being ripped out. God or no god, this made no sense. I was going to have to witness each moment of my life passing, trapped and all alone. Suddenly I was swept away again. This time by a river of tears that threatened to engulf me in the proverbial bottomless pit of despair. I was in a most desperate way.

"I am so sorry. God if you are listening... please do not forsake me.

I do not want to die. I do not want to die this way. I am sorry for everything. I am so sorry. I am so sorry...."

I cried one bitter tear after another as I pled for mercy. My body trembled in grief. Each tear cut through my soul in utter despair. In very short time, my devastation was complete.

Finally, my poor traumatized body heaved one last sigh as a final tear trickled down my cheek. I had cried out every tear of self-pity. There was nothing left within me, I simply gave up and resigned myself to my fate.

The Pearly Gates

It was at this moment that an odd thing happened or, should I say, did not happen. The Pearly Gates did not open. I did not cross over. Instead I was still right there, curled up in a tight ball. Still facing all my existential travail alone. The harsh fact of the cold rocks penetrating my damp body became apparent. The all over pain had faded some but what was left was a dull aching everywhere. It was still pitch black and my only companions were the constant metronome of drips. This was all so very odd. *Why am I still here?* If this experience had not taken me right past the point of no return, then I was at a complete loss for explanations. My mind could not make sense in any of it, and that bothered me immensely.

Across the divide of time and space, the thought finally dawned on me that it must not be my time. While that made no outward sense, my inner knowing prevailed. I slowly sat up. Slowly because my body was quite rigid by now. Finally, some luck. My pack had survived and was still on my back and in one piece. I was overcome with gratitude and then with an intense thirst. First thing I reached for was the water. I could hear Daniel laughing that my first instinct was to drink. Rest assured, I fumbled around for the head lamp next, *because you never know what could happen* - thank you my beloved.

In the beam of light, I could see for the first time that I was being held in a giant cavern, almost the size of a football field. It was magnificent. From the ceiling hung enormous stalactites of every shape and subtle color, all reaching downward like huge columns in a grand basilica. From the ground bold stalagmites thrust their way upward in glorious defiance of gravity. The walls had scattered crystal formations carefully peeking out, half curious and half unsure about revealing themselves fully. Some were clusters that looked like mounds of pure white snowflakes, piled together without losing any of their delicate individuality. Others looked like billowy baby blue clouds piling up before a warm summer shower. And then the granddaddies of them all. Giant perfectly formed crystal spikes that jutted outward. They looked massive from where I sat and were as clear as the water they looked down upon. It was like being inside a giant geode. The cavern had a myriad of stones in a rainbow of colors and textures, all carefully placed for maximum visual pleasure. It felt as if someone, sometime, long long ago, had deliberately planted and cultivated a beautiful garden of rock. *Who or why?* I had no idea. *Maybe just for the sheer delight of it all? Maybe just for me...* A nice thought indeed!

The whole thing would have been simply glorious if it were not for my hideous circumstance. I had always held a fascination for rocks and anything geological. To me, the beauty of nature far outweighed man's creations. Had this not been my tomb, I would have thought I had dropped into heaven. Instead I was going to die in nature's cathedral. The irony of it all did not elude me. I always did appreciate a wicked sense of humor. Maybe there was a god that I had something in common with after all.

In the middle of the cavern was the large body of water that must have broken my fall. It reminded me of a pristine beach on an exotic island where the water looked like clear turquoise. The only difference was that this was no vacation. Not in the least. Still, a big sun overhead to warm my bones and an endless sky to remind me I was free would have been nice. Thankfully the water was warm to the touch, somewhere there must have been geothermal activity happening. No wonder I was not rapidly moving toward hypothermia. The water must also have been quite deep in the center since the last thing I remembered was hurtling through the air and splashing down hard. Had it been shallow, I would not be entertaining you with my tale.

I scanned the entire ceiling looking for the opening, any kind of opening. Surely it had to be there but there was nothing. There was no longer any water flowing in, just the constant little drips that were far too small to have so violently carried me away. I wondered if the rains had ended. Seemed odd since I could not have been down there too terribly long and there was enough water moving through the canyon to last for quite a while. My mind pondered this conundrum for a few short sweet moments. Unfortunately, the probable reality that this would be my tomb was too strong to allow a flight of speculation much air.

With little emotion remaining, I had nothing left to do but to face the fact that I was going to be dead, probably much sooner than later. Somewhere deep inside my inner warrior welled up. The fighter within was stepping into the ring and she was going to go down swinging. You all know that part of yourself. Sometimes I referred to mine as the Dragon-Lady or as Daniel would say, She-Who-Must-Be-Obeyed. When she came calling, watch out. I can understand why she made herself known right then. It certainly was not with the promise of survival. Maybe she was going to help me seize the moment and go out on my own terms. I was ok with that. *Who wants to exit the world as a defeated whimpering mess*? Not me.

After a bit of convincing from that inner voice, I decided to get up and explore my final resting place. My spectacular tomb. Daniel would be so proud. Amazing E finally rallies and picks herself up to bravely face the unwinnable challenge. It was weird, I suddenly felt like I was living my own divine tragedy. *That's right and I won't go down whimpering! Death will not scare me...* at least not today. I could not make any promises for the next day, if I were lucky enough to have one.

The rocks where I sat sloped gently upward to a flat area. Even with my newly found confidence, I still thought it would be best to crawl up instead of trying to walk on trembling legs and risk twisting an ankle and falling back into the water. *Facing certain death and I was afraid of twisting my ankle?* The mind does work in mysterious ways. I was also afraid of losing power in the headlamp and not being able to see. Me, the living dead, afraid of not seeing. More irony. But I wanted to see, period. Since there was no one to argue with me, I won. There would be about 12 hours of light on high beam and 24 hours on low beam or so I rationalized, trying to recall what Daniel had told me many times before but it never seemed important enough to remember until now. It sounds like a lot of time to have light, but my body was in relatively good shape and certainly was not going to die of malnutrition or succumb to any life-threatening injury before the batteries would fail. No, it would take a while to die a natural death and I did not want to do that alone AND in total darkness. Those were my terms. Period.

Inside the pack I also found my cell phone, carefully packed in a sealed zip lock bag – *you know, just in case*. The *'just in case'* syndrome was proving to be incredibly accurate. If I ever got out of this mess, I promised myself that I would adopt it full time. Looking at my phone there was no service, no surprise. With all the pictures and videos I had taken earlier in the day, I knew there would not be much battery life left either. I gathered up the courage to take a quick peek. Maybe it was the fear of seeing the images of us having fun exploring the beautiful canyon on that bright sunny day that would anchor the horror of where I found myself right then. Maybe if I did not see the truth of who I was a short time ago, then maybe I could pretend that this was not really happening. Shortly I would wake up and be back home - that was the fantasy I wanted to hold on to for as long as I could. But I looked anyway. The last thing taken was a video of Daniel jumping around, taunting me with a game of tag as I giggled like a schoolgirl having the time of her life with the boy of her crush. How silly and carefree we were together. It was right then that a laser beam of love, all the way from the surface, traveled down at the speed of light and pierced my heart. *My Daniel... my Daniel... where are you?* In that flash I felt the depth of sadness that he was experiencing. It perfectly mirrored mine. The only difference was that he was on the surface, alive, and I was far within the Earth... buried alive. We were both in the same emotional hell, only his would go on and mine would end shortly. Maybe I was not the unlucky one after all.

Along with various snacks that I had no appetite for at that moment, there was a small pocketknife I always liked to carry. Daniel laughed at its size and teased me that I would tire out trying to protect myself before anything succumbed to the one-inch blade. We all saw that movie though. The one where a man was running through the desert and fell into a crevasse. In the end, he had to amputate his own arm with a tiny rusty switchblade to set himself free. While my situation was more than an arm stuck between rocks, a simple cut or two to the wrists would be all it would take to get me out of my mess. I paused to take a deep breath. That decision could be saved for later. I wasn't quite ready to take my own life. For the moment, I put everything back in the pack, turned the beam off and started carefully picking my way up the embankment by braille. One stone, one hand, one knee at a time.

The flat surface at the top was entirely covered with moss. As I set my hand down something amazing happened. The moss lit up with a soft green glow. Making sure this was really happening, I quickly started touching all around. Light emanated outward from each touch like a softly exploding web of radiance. Some weird phosphorescent process was being ignited by my touch. I did not understand, nor did I care to understand. It was just plain magical. I would have broken down into tears had I any left. I was not alone. *I WAS NOT ALONE!!!* My inner voice finally had something positive to shout about. It was just moss, but it was alive, and it responded to me. For some reason that lifted my heart immensely. Finally, someone, something, I could talk to. And I had a lot to say. The craziest part was that I was sure it was listening… and that maybe it even cared. Some people would call that anthropomorphizing, attaching human-like feelings and emotions to something that is not human. For me it didn't matter, it was cathartic. I had another life form with me, and we were interacting. At least that is what I really wanted and needed to believe at that point. I had a friend.

▽

In all fairness, maybe I had done something redeeming after all. I am not sure if anyone has ever had such a fantastic burial place. Even the most magnificent of man's creations, the towering cathedrals built at a time where all art pointed toward the God of Creation, paled in comparison to where I was. Then it dawned on me. Maybe this wasn't random. Maybe someone, somewhere, knew me well enough to have picked this as my final resting place. A fragment of awe and possible gratitude started to form but did not get very far.

Dawning of Hope

Eventually the thrill of watching the moss light up with my touch wore off and I decided to turn the headlamp back on to take another survey of my surroundings. *Was there anything I missed?* I carefully started tracking the beam, beginning from where I was standing and then shining outward in an ever-growing spiral. There was a series of rocks right under my feet that had a faint tracing of alignment. *Maybe a path or maybe just my imagination needing something, anything to hold on to. But maybe...* Flashing the light to the outer walls revealed a few dark indentations that might be passageways. *Maybe a way out?* It was hard to tell at a distance and the strangeness of the terrain was not something I had any experience with. Whether or not they were shallow cavities or openings that actually went somewhere was impossible to tell from where I stood. Of course, I had to go explore. Even though death seemed the only game in town, I was not going to take it lying down when there might be a glimmer of hope.

First, I needed a plan on how to manage my limited resources - *just in case*. I wished Daniel could have seen me right then. He would have known that I secretly listened to every word he said about surviving in a hostile terrain. I did find his adventures fascinating, just not something I would choose to do. My meager portion of food would be enough to allow me plenty of time to explore. I was never a big eater and felt perfectly comfortable being on the hungry side.

I still had water left and worst case, I could go back to the lake and drink to my traumatized heart's content. The thing I feared the most was being without light, so managing battery usage took precedence. I knew about how much time I had left so if possible, I would turn them off and manage without light.

There was something about planning that made it seem like I had a chance of making it out alive. That gave my mind something to cling to. Instead of succumbing to the absurdity and terror of it all, I single-mindedly focused on a strategy. Off went the lamp as I made a step forward hoping the generosity of my new green friends would be sufficient to light the way to the outer edges of the cavern. Nothing happened. I took another step and still nothing happened. *What was going on? Had I just been hallucinating?* Nothing at that point would have surprised me. I bent down and touched the moss with my bare hands to double-check reality and sure enough, it lit up. *Maybe it needed contact with a living organism?* I certainly could appreciate that need more than ever. It was easy to test the theory and sure enough, my bare feet brought it back to life. Relief warmed its way through my cold body. My one and only friend was still there. I was truly thankful for this small gesture from a seemingly indifferent universe.

It took a while getting used to navigating with a soft light that barely glowed to a foot above the ground. At least I knew there were no imminent overhangs to clobber my head on. That would be all I needed – wandering around in circles with an addled mind until I dropped to my knees in the final moments of death. The thought sent a shiver through my body making sure it didn't get too hopeful. It was about 75 yards to the far wall, at least I thought. I was never good at estimating distances. *It's just over there a bit* - would be my typical response. Daniel never quite got used to my lack of precision. He always seemed to forget and would ask me how big something was or how far away something else was. My answer was always the same, *I don't know.* Once again, he would give me tips and, once again, I would quickly forget. But at least I was good at following paths... speaking of which, it really did look like a very old and crude line of rocks heading off to the back wall. *How could that be? Had someone been there before?* I could not imagine, especially since I had to be hundreds and hundreds of feet underground. Who knows, according to my calculating ability, I could be buried with miles of dirt above my head.

▽

After some time of carefully picking my way along, I felt the moss growing thinner and the surface of rocks poking through to the soles of my feet. It was time to put on shoes and time to part ways with my only friend. Turning on the headlamp, I looked around to say one last goodbye. It was odd that I felt an attachment to a place that I desperately wanted out of. At least I knew where I was. Where I was going was a complete mystery. Ahead were the dark areas that could possibly be a way out or maybe just false hopes of freedom. I decided to trust chance and the first opening I would be lucky enough to find, I would unquestioningly follow it - no matter where it led. Not that I was feeling lucky in the slightest, maybe it was more that I had nothing left to lose so I had no real preference.

Call it fate, call it luck, call it whatever you want but my first try ended up being a real opening in the rocks. The tunnel looked natural, not like someone had carved it out, but I was not certain. *What did I know of tunnels? Nothing!* The only thing I cared about was it leading me somewhere. Anywhere. I just wanted and needed to move. *How cruel would it be if it trailed off to a dead end?* Clearly, I was never the optimist, thank you dad. Expecting another level of cruelty from the universe was my habitual inclination. My adventure man would have loved this. Even with death on the line, Daniel would have been completely focused and absorbed in the mission. One track mind. How nice for him. Mine, however, was a bit harder to control and liked to wander freely. He said meditating helped his mind stay still and focused. So far in life, I had not had much patience for quietly sitting with myself, but that was all about to change, like everything else.

Daniel had explored caves and said it was always best to mark your way. Use string if you have it and if not, make arrows out of rocks to point the way you are going. I did neither. I had no intention of ever going back. I did not care what lay ahead, I was going there no matter how nervous I felt about the unknown. It was a bit concerning that I would have to keep my headlamp on now since there was nothing else to rely on to light the way and I certainly could not manage in the pitch blackness. Too much could go wrong, and I was still feeling protective of a body that I was not sure I would be occupying much longer. While I was alive my biology demanded it be looked after. And there was that little glimmer of hope starting to kindle despite the bluff and bluster of my cynical side. If surrounded by complete darkness, my claustrophobia would kick in and I would most assuredly go mad. That biology I would never be able to control.

The tunnel looked natural and safe enough, so I started walking. It kept winding its way through the darkness, intent on some unnamed destination. You know how it is at the end of a long hike, when your body is on autopilot and your legs just keep moving, one at a time, all on their own. That was me. Mindlessly walking and not knowing how much distance I covered or how much time I spent rambling forward. Occasionally there would be a choice to go left or right, I always chose right, like a good miner marking his way. Daniel would have been counting his steps and calculating all the details. Things like that never mattered to me before and certainly did not now. I walked and walked until I could not go any farther. I stopped from time to time to rest, sip some water and nibble on a couple of nuts. Just enough to keep going. I wanted to ration my food supply just in case I needed it later. If I reached death's door and there was any food left, I would eat it all in one final orgy of oral satisfaction. A last supper of sorts.

At some point the air started changing. The temperature was dropping as I began to feel a subtle movement across my face. At first, I thought it might be my imagination but soon it was clear, something was changing. Finally, around one last corner there was a giant gust of air as I stepped into another cavern. This time instead of water to greet me, there were piles and piles of rocks.

Out of the Rubble

Something wasn't right. As I gradually took in the site, it became apparent that these were not natural piles of rocks. These were the leftovers of structures that looked like they had been violently toppled or even blown apart. The cavern looked like it came right out of the typical war scene from the movies or the evening news. You know, the ones where the city is completely bombed out and nothing is left intact except for a few jagged walls holding on by sheer will. Not even color remained. The images are always a pale, sad grey. What I saw in front of me looked very much the same. Poking out of the rubble were remnants of walls with glimpses of pathways winding in and out of the chaos. It looked like a city had once thrived there. The cavern was quite large. Probably twice as big as the one I had landed in. If all of that was not strange enough, there was a very dim light emanating from the high ceiling. I turned off my head lamp to be sure what I was seeing was real. It was true. There was some light. It reminded me of an old worn out sun in its final days of duty. Only enough energy left to produce a small sliver of what it was once capable of creating. The fragment of light was only sufficient to cast eerie shadows that looked ready at any moment to morph into otherworldly creatures. The whole thing sent shivers up my spine.

With the weirdly homogenous color and odd shapes, it looked like some alien planet slowly being absorbed back into the natural elements. Even stalactites had penetrated down and through some of the ruins. This had to be extremely old since it takes a long time for them to grow. No matter, if people had once lived there, which they clearly had, then they would have had to come from somewhere and presumably have gone somewhere. Right then I did not care much about their story, I cared about mine. This meant that there had to be a way out. My heart started racing at the thought and my knees suddenly started collapsing.

It was probably a combination of my blood sugar dropping and the adrenaline of the fall finally starting to wear off that started me spinning. I had no idea how much time had passed since this whole nightmare started. It could have been several days by then, but without any of the familiar demarcations from the surface, there was no way to tell for sure. I was clearly in shock and exhausted. After steadying myself, I knew I needed to find a place to rest. Single-mindedly I entered the ruins in hopes of finding a small nook or place to crawl into and collapse. Maybe then I could retreat into a deep sleep and maybe then I could wake up and life would be back to normal. Maybe then I would find that this had all been a very bad dream. Yes, that was all I needed. Sleep.

Snapping me back to reality was a small clicking noise coming from somewhere in the cavern. I spun around but there was nothing to see. Whatever it was, it sounded like it was slowly making its way towards me and it appeared to be coming from many directions all at once. There was nothing and everything horrifying to conjure up in my mind's eye. Since I had no idea what could live so far underground, it could be anything.

As the noise grew closer, it started taking the shape of a chattering more than a clicking. Raw instinct dictated that I start moving and find safety quickly. Without question, I hugged the wall of the cave to my right and started running. No sooner had I rounded the first pile of rocks than I came upon large steps leading up to a platform set against the side of the cave. The wall was unnaturally smooth compared to the rest of the cavern. It must have been man made even though there were no visible bricks or marks except in the center. Right at the midpoint was a giant rectangle shape. I would venture to say that it looked like a door except for the fact that there was no handle nor any hinges. Maybe it was just a line drawn or carved into the surface for some decorative reason and not for someone's salvation. Like mine. My mind started racing again trying to make sense of it all. *Stop it! No time to think, just get to higher ground!*

The sounds were getting louder as I managed to get up the first stair. These were not the typical height we are used to but rather almost three times the normal size. After I lugged myself up the first step, I quickly spun around to catch a closer look at what was coming towards me. They were hard to see at first since they were still scurrying in and out of all the nooks and crannies. By the time I made it to the top level, they made themselves known. A herd of tiny four-legged creatures were converging on my coordinates. A lot of them. The dim light made it hard to see what they were exactly, so I turned on my headlamp. I had to do several double takes, back and forth, shining the light, taking away the light, all in an attempt to make sure I wasn't hallucinating. Nope, nothing changed. Yup, it was a sea of bright little eyes and small chattering teeth approaching.

These creatures were the size of a typical feline but with features that were a weird hybrid of animals that made little sense all put together. Mostly they looked like the cats you picture in the Egyptian courts. The exotic long slinky ones that perched themselves above the throne to keep an eye on the comings and goings of the inner court. They were considered sacred and would be buried with the Kings to help guide them through to the other side. How appropriate, except for my companions might be forcibly taking me over to the other side! Their slender little bodies were a light sandy color, close to the color of the dirt in the cave. The tails were black and white striped like those on a lemur but bushy like that of a raccoon. They had large black pointy ears framing small white fox-like faces. They also had huge golden eyes in the shape of almonds, rather large considering the size of their heads, and understandably so, as they had obviously evolved to adjust to the lack of light. But it was the shiny white teeth that would have made them almost comical, if the whole thing had not been so scary. My light reflected off their tiny teeth making them look like they were glowing. They reminded me of a small army of Cheshire cats. The only difference, and it was a big difference, I didn't think for a moment that they were smiling at me. It was more like the pre-wired response of a cat preparing for the kill. The odd little chattering that happens as they track a poor fly minding its own business, unaware of the lurking predator voicing its primal anticipation of the catch and quite possibly a little snack.

My back was up against the proverbial and literal wall. Back then my response to a challenging situation was quite different from Daniel's. Instead of preparing for a positive outcome like he would, I always prepared for the worst-case scenario. If I had a plan in place for the worst, then nothing short of that would throw me off. Unfortunately, I could not come up with any such plan in this situation. Getting eaten alive seemed imminent. I knew that my pocketknife would not be sufficient against so many. Daniel was right. It was a bit of a joke. In that moment size did matter. With nowhere to go and no plan in place but to survive, I stood there looking down at all the creatures as they sat there looking up at me, teeth chattering away. By now dozens and dozens had congregated around the bottom step waiting in anticipation of something. *A meal? A soliloquy? A complete mental breakdown?* Anything was possible. After all, the platform was rather stage-like. The waiting for someone to do something game got old fast. Making the first move, I turned and ran to the wall. Maybe, just maybe, there was a special switch, handle, something, ANYTHING to open this thing, if it was even meant to open! I had watched too many horror movies to really trust the benevolence of fate. Up close the wall remained smooth. There was nothing to grab onto, no handle to turn, no secret button to push. In desperation I yelled out a reflexive explicative while placing both hands on the wall just hoping that...

No sooner had I gotten out the first three letters of *"Shi_"* than the door swiveled on hidden hinges and effortlessly swung open. It was as if I had uttered the correct ancient magical code. I was being let in. A stroke of luck... or not. Caught completely off guard, I tumbled headlong into the darkness. Before I could get my feet underneath me the giant door closed as fast as it had opened.

"Noooooo........." I screamed out loud but there was nothing I could do. The door had closed tightly as I was falling headlong into darkness once again. Then everything went black as I hit my head on something hard. That was the last thing I remembered for a time.

CHAPTER II

A New Ending

I had another rude awakening but this time there was nothing but a sharp pain coming from the side of my head. My headlamp must have gotten completely knocked off and in its place was a large bump the size of an Easter egg. My head was sticky to the touch as something had dripped down and covered the entire side of my face. I assumed it was blood, my blood. *How long had I been out? Where was I?* Pointless questions. Trying to put a time frame on anything anymore had absolutely no relevance, and how was I to know where I was? There were no earthly markers that I could relate to. Finally, I decided to try and open my eyes while lying very still. By now you understand the drill. Do not make any waves or call any attention to myself. Survive at all costs.

I expected more blackness when I woke up but instead in front of me was one of the little creatures sitting there like a squirrel, enjoying a granola bar – *my granola bar!* The little stinker was munching away and looking at me with mild curiosity. Clearly not afraid and not intent on eating me, at least not for now because strewn about were the remnants of ALL my food. Bits of orange peels, apple core, wrappers from the remaining two granola bars and an empty bag of nuts. All my food was gone. It had even gotten into my Chapsticks, as they were both laid to waste. My last supper, my final orgy of oral satisfaction, had been devoured by another. The look of contentment on its little face was something else. It was quite happy with itself to say the least. Like a pig on a rainy day, wallowing in the deliciousness of mud after a long drought. There may even have been some adoration in its eyes as it looked at me thinking I was a god of plenty bequeathing it magic manna from some alien heaven.

I shook my head - I could not believe this had happened. The little shit ate it all. It must have snuck into my pack while I was knocked out. All I could think of was the expression - *just when you think things can't get any worse...* Right then I fully understood why someone came up with that saying and why it has resonated with sufferers across time. Never count on the current bad being the worst, there is always the potential for more to come. I thought this train to nowhere had but one track and now it just skipped over to a new one that was heading downhill even faster than before. At least before I had room to explore and entertain a shred of hope. Now I was sealed in some strange ancient edifice with no food, a shred of water and what? Nothing but super bad luck. On the other hand, this could be a humane gesture from a god that did not appear to like me so much. The end would simply come sooner than later. *Maybe I should just lay down and wait it out...* Oddly this time I was not overcome with the same fear or anger as when I first landed in this no-man's zone. Instead I felt strangely empty and quiet.

Then it dawned on me - *why was I seeing all of this?* My headlamp was not on, in fact I had no idea where my headlamp had gone. But the point was that I was seeing. The light was dimmer inside than the faint sun outside but because the light was contained in a smaller space, I could see better. The light cast a beautiful blue hue that made the room look soft and dreamy. As I pulled myself and my achy head up, I noticed a round fountain of sorts with a tall white pedestal, like a stone birdbath or baptismal font, right in the middle of the room. Around the periphery was a small border. In the center of the bowl was a smooth orb the size of a basketball. It was made of an exotic crystalline material. It reminded me of an opal – a soft milky white that had an inner opalescent quality that shifted ever so subtly. It was of a quality and size I had never seen before.

Clearly whomever had inhabited this space had been very large beings. Everything was oversized, just like the steps that led up to the platform. The basin reached almost up to my neck. If I carefully stood on the outer ledge, I could look inside. Finally, my curiosity was stronger than my fear and I stepped up. The sphere was sitting in a pool of liquid, I assumed to be water because it was crystal clear. At the bottom were small carefully scattered stones of different colors and shapes. My heart leapt for a moment at this secret treasure, utterly forgetting my worsened predicament.

As a little girl I would spend hours sifting through rocks trying to find special ones. The 'special' designation could simply be a color vein running through an ordinary rock, or maybe just an unusual shape. If I got lucky it would contain a little fossil or crystalline formation. My appreciation was higher than my standards. I was easily impressed when it came to nature's handiwork. Anywhere and everywhere I went, I was always on the lookout for a special prize under foot. Whether it be flower beds, the park, up at our cabin or even in the street, everywhere was fair hunting ground. The uniqueness of each stone was simply mesmerizing to my heart. I would wonder how they came to be. There was no way in my mind they were random acts of creation, despite what geologists had to say. I knew that they represented something more even though I wasn't sure what that could be. Even in college when I studied art history, it was never the magnificent cathedrals that dazzled the masses or the opulent works of art they contained that spoke to me. No, my heart was still enamored from when I was a little girl and would pick up little pieces of the earth and put them into my pocket. Now I was surrounded by that very same earth. Buried within just like all its extraordinary treasures. Except I was not going to be discovered and put into anyone's pocket to be carried home and adored in a glass jar. It may seem odd to you but upon seeing those stones, a small crack in my heart opened and through it the faintest feeling of love began peeking in. Finally, I remembered that as a small child I knew and loved a god. He quite simply was the One that created all the things I held in my little hands. My sacred pieces of earth. Eventually time and life destroyed that connection. But now, in the darkest of places, that god had gifts that I loved waiting just for me. Maybe he was even there with me. A big maybe, but possible.

The sharp throbbing of my head yanked me back into reality. Just then my new 'friend', loosely termed, jumped onto the edge of the basin and started lapping up the water. It had worked up quite a thirst at my expense. Clearly it knew what it was doing, and I assumed it would not be drinking from a fouled source. Monkey see, monkey do and in went my shaking hands so I too could lap up as much as my stomach could tolerate. When finally sated, I took out my bandana to clean the wound and wipe off the dried blood that caked the side of my face. In real life, not this bizarre reality, it would have required a visit to the doctor and most likely more than a few stitches. But so what if I would end up with a big gaping scar on my soon to be dead head. I did not really care, certainly not at that point. But tending this body was another thing I was learning was part of the prewired matrix. If there was anything I could do to make any of this slightly better, I would. If tending my wound counted for something, somehow, somewhere, I had to do it.

For some reason, gone was the panic that first overwhelmed me in this journey. While I certainly was not happy with the new situation, I was not entirely unhappy, even though I was now confined to an even smaller space. It was rather calming to be safely contained and the room had something quite special about it. There was a certain ambiance I could not quite articulate in my somewhat befuddled mind. It was difficult taking in the rest of my surroundings for the light from the orb was so subtle that it did not reach all the way to the walls. I could feel they were close by even though I could not see them. I had no intellectual idea what this place was used for, except that its dwellers were of large stature and it was carefully hidden away. Protected from whatever devastation took place outside its walls. The atmosphere told me it was used for peaceful purposes - I was sure to my very core. The air was not only fresh, it also hung with a solemn sacredness, like that in a revered sanctuary. All in all, there were worse places from which to leave this planet. Maybe it was my exhaustion speaking or the lack of any fight left inside. Either way, reassurance was trying to work its way in through the cracks but not too quickly or too overwhelmingly. I still had a way to go to reconcile this turn of events and let any real hope take root.

There was nothing in my immediate vision except for a large elaborately designed stone bench placed right behind the basin and opposite the secret door that had allowed me to enter. The bench was quite extraordinary, almost breathtaking. Clearly it was made for someone very special to sit on. It reminded me of the Ark of the Covenant. Whatever that conjures up in your mind is probably close to what I was seeing. Resting on either end were two masterfully carved angels of stone. Their wings stretched to wrap around the special one seated in its protective embrace. Each feather was lovingly carved to perfection. The expression on their faces was a fierce kind of joy. Call me sacrilegious, but it looked like the perfect place to rest an aching head and utterly exhausted body. At that moment in time, I was that chosen person because I was the only one present and I decided it to be so. It felt good declaring some authority in a situation that was completely out of my control. I had nothing but time to consider whatever needed to be considered, and at that point it could wait. So up I went, wrapping myself in the space blanket - *another warm tribute to my beloved's preparedness*, placed the now almost empty backpack under my head and without any hesitation, shut my eyes. It was as if I had crawled into a cocoon, resting in a crypt, encased in a sarcophagus and buried far beneath the ground. A rather macabre Russian doll experience of sorts. As the last tiny figurine, one could not be more tucked away than me. With no energy left to carry any cares, juggle any fears or entertain any worries, I was able to fall into a deep state of unconsciousness. It was way beyond the normal state of sleep. I had completely left my pain and this plain behind.

Another Reckoning

When I woke the room had the fresh feel of a new morning. The cool light from the night before had transmuted into the dimmest of warm glows. Perched on one of the angel's heads, like it was a special platform designed specifically for its fuzzy little bottom, sat my furry four-legged friend, staring right at me. For all I knew, it could have been created just for him. He looked rather fitting and regal. Oddly, I felt physically refreshed considering all I had been through. Then I remembered my head. It wasn't aching any more. I reached up to feel the giant knot and gash, but they were not there. I don't mean that the swelling had greatly reduced and the wound was closed, I mean the bump was completely gone and the cut no longer existed. The only thing I felt was smooth healthy skin. It was as if the wound had never happened. In case I had dreamed it all up, which at that point was quite possible, I reached for my bandana to see its condition. And there it was, confirmation. Not sure whether what I saw was good news or bad news, but the cloth was baked to a crackling crunch with my old dried blood.

I jumped down and ran to the basin to make sure that it too was real. It was still there, hard and cool to the touch. The giant luminescent orb was there. The collection of stones were all there exactly as I remembered. Throwing all caution to the wind I stuck my hands in again and drank to my heart's content. That took a while since my heart was parched to a delicate crisp. My new friend followed and joined me in the liquid feast. Finally, we both sighed a big breath of satisfaction. There was a warm tingling as the cool water went swirling down my throat. As if it were alive, it reached deep into the well of my being, all the way in to soothe my devastated soul. Who knows, maybe it could heal that too. My ravaged state was not just the end result of this unfortunate adventure, to be completely honest, I had carried it for a very long time. The cross I bore predated this by many moons. I would have loved to have broken down in tears right about then, but my tear reservoirs were still rather empty since the great outpouring a short time ago. When I said that I had cried the very last tear I would shed for myself, I meant it. There really were none left for self-pity - maybe a few for other things though. As for aches in my heart, panic in my mind and fear in my body, there was still plenty of that to go around. It would be nice if I could calmly die in a place of acceptance. Acceptance of my situation and more importantly, acceptance of myself. It would be a relief to let it happen gracefully and quickly.

The only thing I had left to do was to crawl back onto my stone throne and let the final process begin. Yes, I said 'throne' and 'mine.' While I was certainly not the first to sit upon it, I was the only person in line, so I staked the claim. *If this is my tomb then this is my room, thus my throne.* Period. The condemned Queen of Nowhere assumed the lotus position and decided it was time to have a deep talk with a creator she knew little about. And just maybe she could find a place of understanding about this life that was about to end. There I sat, staring into the very still room. I was not going to fight my circumstance anymore or the god that many people worshipped. I was going to open my heart and see if a process of reconciliation would happen. If it were possible, this surely would be the place for it to happen. I really wanted to come to know the real God – the one with the big "G."

We are all familiar with parts of the death process as reported by those who were either involved in a slow march or a sudden turn of events, but didn't stay on the other side. For whatever reason, they returned and were able to recount a near death experience. Most everyone speaks about a 'life review' process. This is where a person's entire life flashes before their eyes to be examined and evaluated in exacting detail. Not to be condemned but rather to learn. It is not the sort of flash that we associate with living in time because how could one see an entire life in one flash. No, the flash they are referring to is one of light. Light that exists outside of time, where a million years can happen in an instant or an instant can last a million years. In that arena, quantity of information is not bound to an amount of time nor is time forced to progress step-by-step. The fullness of a single life and all of its intricacies can come to one in the mere twinkling of an eye. Since death was not yet on the line, my review was going to be a slower process of reliving the moments in time, in actual time, laid out before my heartbroken eyes.

The challenge started when I was a young girl. I never truly felt like I fit in anywhere and that certainly held true right up to the day I fell into the earth. In my youth, there were never any cliques that resonated with me or that I hung out with for more than a short period of time. It always felt like I had to pretend to be someone I was not in order to be accepted. I could only do that for so long and the jig would be up – at least for me since I am sure no one had a clue or a care that I wasn't fully present. Everyone seemed excited to be caught up in their own experience, I simply got bored with theirs. Everything felt one step removed, even in the throes of passion that I eventually enjoyed with my male companions. I often wondered what was wrong with me... then I met Daniel. Until then the world never felt quite right. It felt hollow - *no pun intended given my new circumstance in the hollows of Earth.* In the depths of my heart not much rang true, not even my existence. If I had to classify myself, I would have said that I was just a visitor who was here to observe but never to fully inhabit. That is what my life felt like – being a witness, not a participant.

Tucked back in the recesses of my mind, there was one single experience, many years before, where it all came to point in a profound way. From that time on, the world was forever changed and my trajectory in it would never be the same. I learned early on not to talk about what happened. It made people uncomfortable so they pretended not to hear what they just heard, or they would offer me some banal platitude in response. Either way, it left me feeling that a sacred part of myself had been trivialized and violated. I vowed to keep the sacred things protected, close to my heart and secret. Daniel was the exception. In him I knew that I was accepted and could be honest. He may not have always understood but he always listened. That meant the world to me. Only a few times did I let him into those protected inner areas but quite honestly, I rarely entered them myself. This moment was different. I had nothing to lose by going there. In fact, it felt like those realms were my last bastion of sanity, the final hold on life as I once knew it.

Caught Between Earth and Sky

My first out of body experience happened when I was just 7 years old. I was not suffering from a life-threatening childhood disease nor was I hit by a car with my life hanging in the balance. Rather I was at our summer cabin in the northern woods of the congenial Midwest.

It was well past dark when I decided to go for a walk along the wild riverbanks. As a child I loved being alone and absolutely relished being up at our remote cabin. Throughout the year I longed for the summer months where I would be out of the city and far away from people and all the busyness of school and routines. On that fateful night, something inspired me to go out for a walk. Typically, that time of night was all about 'winding down', as my mother would say, and getting ready to go to bed. There was nothing dangerous in the area and my parents were probably too caught up in some drama of their own to pay much attention to me, so off I went without a care in the world.

It was a warm night with skies so incredibly clear that the heavens seemed brighter and more alive than usual. If you have ever been to an area far away from any city lights, you will know what I mean by how intense the night sky can be when the presence of man is outweighed by the power of the heavens. The nights at the cabin were typically so dark that even satellites were easy to spot if you were patient and knew what to look for. They were the lights that moved across the sky in a steady trajectory. Occasionally the northern lights were even visible. Now that was quite the treat for urban eyes! But on that special night, something inspired me to leave the warmth of the cabin and to venture out alone. I am not sure what it was that called me, I just remember feeling compelled and excited to be by myself.

I walked up the river until I came to a clearing at the beginning of what was called the Conservation Land. Most of the land along the river was owned by the local power plant so that they could adjust the flow by increasing the amount of water let out of the dam further upstream. That meant that nothing could be built along the edges of its banks so they could fluctuate the depth. The only buildings that managed to be there were a small string of cabins on the tall banks of the river in the thick of the trees. The old farmer who owned the land probably had it grandfathered in. We were lucky to have our little spot surrounded by all the open land. This meant that summers were spent with lots of room to explore and run wild. I loved it.

Eventually I found a soft grassy area at the edge of the river bank to lay down. Being out by myself when it was so dark was exciting but being able to quietly gaze up at the stars was absolutely thrilling. Encircled by nothing but tall ponderosa pines, I felt completely tucked in and safe. Below me were the sandy banks leading to the water's edge. It was a rather unusual night in that the heavens were extra magnificent. The Milky Way was brighter than I ever remembered, full of shooting stars and even the satellites were flaunting their presence as they danced along their predetermined celestial paths. And then out of nowhere it happened. It just happened. It was nothing I intended, expected or could even have conjured in a dream.

As I innocently lay there staring up at the heavens, there was a sudden *whoosh* and out I went, heading right up towards the stars. I left my body behind as easily as I could take off a jacket. There was no pain, no discomfort, just a *whoosh* and it was done. I zoomed upward, high above the riverbank and then hung there as if I were a new star waiting to be born into the heavens. As you can imagine, it was a bit disconcerting. Not scary in any way, just completely out of my experience or knowledge base. My seven-year-old world was rocked on its very foundation.

I marveled that this could be happening. It wasn't good nor bad, it was just amazing. Curious, I turned around and looked down at the riverbank where my tiny body still lay. I could see it as clear as if it were a bright sunny day. Then the most staggering of realizations grabbed a hold of my entire being.

"If I am way up here and my body is all the way down there… clearly, I am not that body." It was absolutely astounding. The discovery, *"I*

am not that body," burst through it all. *"I AM NOT LINA!"*

I wasn't who I thought I was, period. There was nothing to dispute what I was experiencing. I saw my body lying right where I left it. I was no longer in it and yet I was still fully me. I was fully aware, fully awake and fully able to think. I was alive yet I didn't even have to breathe. I could think yet I did not have a brain. Life was pulsating through me, yet I did not have a heart. I simply no longer had a body to contend with. Living was not dependent on having a body. I did not need my body to be me!

The next question was completely obvious, as I am sure anyone would have asked if they found themselves in that situation. Who knows, maybe you have been there and maybe you already have asked this of the universe. If so, then you would understand what came next. It was then that I turned my attention to face the heavens and with my whole innocent heart I implored…

"Well then who am I?

If I am not Lina…. who am I?!"

No answer, just the small echoing of my thoughts reaching out into the great unknown.

This time in my mind I shouted more loudly.

"Who am I?"

This time the question felt as if it were resonating into the ethers, through the solar system and out into the galaxy. It was a very big question. Surely someone was listening.

No one had ever spoken to me about such things. We did not read about out of body experiences in grade school, at least not in those days and where I came from. At home these things were not discussed. At church we learned about the miracles Jesus performed but never anything about a mere human doing something extraordinary like leaving their body behind... *while still alive!* At that age I had never heard of a near death experience. I was only a kid growing up with conservative parents in the conservative midwest. Things like that were just not in the public domain, much less in mine. Maybe it was because I was a child and not as firmly rooted in beliefs or a perspective of self-identity that made it so easy to accept.

As I hovered there in the heavens, caught between the Earth and the sky, my question kept echoing outward...

"Who am I.... Who am I.... Who am I...."

Finally, I received an answer. Yes, I was answered. I was right, someone was listening to me and cared enough to answer. It was a simple response that consisted of only two small words. Each was repeated three times.

I AM..... I AM..... I AM

While the message was clear and easy enough for a seven-year-old to remember for the rest of her life, understanding the meaning was an entirely different matter. You may think this was a tremendous blessing that would set me on some extraordinary path of enlightenment... *Why if only I had known the secret of my existence, who I really was, my life would be utterly different. It would be amazing.* But for me it was not a blessing. As the years went by, it turned instead to be a curse.

When I got back to the cabin, I remember attempting to tell my parents about what had just happened, but they showed no interest except for wanting me to quickly get to bed. So, like a good little girl I went to bed and tucked the experience securely away. Thinking, maybe even hoping, what was hidden could be forgotten. Except for one problem, it permanently colored my entire existence. From that time forth I could no longer fully accept life as it presented itself nor could I reside up in the heavens. The older I got the less sense anything made. I did not fit in anywhere and I did not understand why. It was as if Lina was left to float around between two realities and to endure this secret all by herself.

I truly believe that experience fueled one emotion that reigned supreme. From that day forth I suffered from a devastating sense of aloneness. You may know her stepsister, loneliness. The difference is that when you are lonely you are in a state of longing for that which you can see but cannot have. You see the people around you and desperately want to connect and belong but do not know how or you do not feel worthy. When you suffer from aloneness, you have a deep sense of being all by yourself. You see the world of people all around, yet you know that you do not fit in. And you do not want to fit in to what you see. You would rather be alone. To you I may just be parsing words, and in some senses it does not really matter, we all know that both sisters will mercilessly tear down the fabric of your being until you get to the point of questioning the amount of energy it takes to live and if it is really worth it. For me, living in a world where nothing made sense and where I did not belong was like living in hell. Allowing this memory to come forth, I could not help but notice the giant irony staring me straight in the face.

You thought you were all alone before? You thought that you had plumbed the depths of aloneness? HA! Was that the voice of the cruel god mocking me or just my own mind pointing out another satirical aspect of my absurd situation? There had to be a reason that my greatest fear had manifested and been accentuated to the extreme. *Maybe this was not a random event?* It all started to make some sense and I like to make sense out of things. I suffered from aloneness and now I was experiencing the great grandmother of them all. The realization of my dire situation felt like I was falling into a bottomless pit of despair.

Maybe my mom was right after all. The god of the old testament was a rather fickle one that was prone to settling grievances in catastrophic ways. Rather a sad thought if he was in control. *But what had I ever done so bad to another person or creature to deserve this level of retribution?* The only person I ever treated unkindly and unforgivingly was me. Maybe I was at the hands of my dad's absent god, the one that set the wheels in motion and then took a quick exit. He had set up the laws of the universe and then left us to our own devices. But that too had a cruelty about it. *How could an entity capable of creating such an amazing world full of beauty and splendor not care enough to be present and have an ongoing hand in its endeavors? Why didn't it care about what was happening to me?* Finally, I had to admit, maybe my quiver of explanations was simply insufficient. Maybe shit really just happens or maybe I just didn't know who the real 'God' is.

There were plenty of flaws in all my lines of thinking and plenty of time to dig through them if I wished. I surely was not going anywhere. For now, this turn down memory lane left me feeling uneasy and tired, and very thirsty. There was something soothing about the waters that my friend and I were enjoying. I felt no fear about their potential adverse effects. *What did I care?* If drinking them meant that I died more quickly, at least I would die with one longing quenched.

Growing up

After a nice long nap or maybe it was a full night sleep, it did not really matter, I felt quite refreshed. The only thing that changed in the room was the lighting. When I woke this time, the orb was back to glowing blue. My companion was still there on his perch, keeping track of me. On the second day in my new domain, I decided to scavenge around and attempt to find my headlamp. It would be nice if I could come to see and know my final resting place. This decision came without a lot of feeling attached. There was not much to feel at that point. I just needed to move and do something.

Down on hands and knees, and with the help of my friend, I began searching. To him it was a typical feline game of trying to catch the moving object, i.e. my hands. I had always had a special penchant for felines, so this ritual was familiar. Not knowing exactly what species he was, or anything of his true nature, I decided to throw caution to the wind and pretend his domestic instincts would prevail – in other words he would not take a chunk out of my moving hand. He did not. In fact, he played very gently and respectfully. It didn't take long to find my only source of bright light. It had landed a few feet away from the basin but lay hidden in its shadow. Unfortunately, when it hit the stone floor something inside had broken. I was not really all that surprised and while disappointed, by then I cared less and less about these small dashes of hope.

Throughout life I was used to not letting them get too high, my hopes that is. Home life was a battle between the sober parent who was trying to deal with life and the one who wanted to escape the world through the bottle. My sibling and I were stuck between two warring parties who wanted to be in love but were not able to find a place of connection much less harmony. Some people are not a good fit. My parents were a prime example. The house was filled with ongoing tension even though my mother tried desperately to keep up a smiling face. She had a lot of fortitude and was able to do so for many years. But the reality of home life was not something I could pretend away. Getting my hopes up after each binge and the promise of change only lasted so long. At some point I became jaded and because I was a child, the ability to separate out feelings from traumatic experiences was just not possible. What happened at home defined all aspects of my life. It went to the core of my being, a rocky foundation from which all else would be built. No wonder I could never muster up the courage to dream of wonderful things. No wonder when I thought back on my life, it was never the good things that my mind gravitated towards. My world growing up told me that good just does not happen. Not even for one allowed to venture to the stars.

The out-of-the-ordinary experience was not something totally foreign to me before that fateful night when I left my body for the first time. My childhood had been riddled with profound night terrors. I would wake up and feel people in my room, I could not see or hear them, but I knew they were there, walking around and talking about me. Sometimes I could feel the pressure of them sitting on my bed and staring right at me. It is that same sense when you know someone is staring at your back. You do not have to see them to feel their burrowing eyes. Other times I could hear their breath as they waited just outside my room. I was completely and utterly paralyzed with fear. It felt as if my body was a mere shell and I was stuck inside, unable to do anything but look out through the two little peep holes of my eye sockets. I would fight and fight to try and get back into my body, to fully inhabit it and take control of the muscles and bones. It felt like a struggle of life and death. Eventually I would prevail and regain full control of my body. Immediately I would use my lungs to their fullest, screaming in terror for mom and dad to let me into their room. Upon approval, I was an obedient girl at that point, I would throw all caution to the wind, race into their room and dive in bed between them. Then and only then would I feel safe and be able to surrender into the sweet arms of sleep.

Obviously, this was not ideal for the young couple, especially since it happened on most nights. At some point a well-meaning physician told them to draw the line and not allow me to come in anymore, that it was not good for my development. I now understand why they made that choice but at the time it felt utterly heartless. There was something deeper happening that the medical profession had no idea how to approach. From that day on, it was the ring of stuffed animals that surrounded my body at night, that kept me safe. Slowly I turned off the spigot and the nightly visitors eventually disappeared, only to be replaced later by a different kind of terror.

A Slice of Solace

Without my headlamp, the glow from the orb was not enough to see all the way to the far walls. I had to go by feel. I am not sure why I had not tried to find the door that I had tumbled through earlier. I had unquestionably accepted my fate, as most of us learn to do. My hands searched the entire area but there wasn't even a hint of a door much less a handle or knob. The wall was as smooth inside as it was outside. Exasperated and resigned, I slid down, propped myself up against the wall and sat there. Blank as the darn wall.

Eventually the wheels in my mind started to grind. I was not going to wake up from a bad dream and this was not going to go away. Somewhere in all of this, I had been clinging to the hope of that happy ending we all love to see in the movies. I had experienced lucid dreams in the past, but they never lasted this long or existed at quite this level of tactile acuity. This was really happening to me. Finally, I had to fully accept where I was. As if on cue, my friend came over and rubbed his pointy little face on my thigh, and then curled up next to me. This small act of compassion touched my heart deeply and brought tears to my eyes. Animals have a certain way of cutting right to the truth of the matter and capturing our hearts. Some may think they are not as smart as people. I think they are as smart and since they are not burdened with all our complexities, they act more intelligently and more authentically than us two-legged types. No wonder I liked animals better. I could know them and trust them. In response, I reached down and caressed his bunny-like fur. He responded with a mighty purr. We both sat there for a long time. Him purring and me enjoying a slice of solace.

If you are familiar with the disease of alcoholism, you know that one of the coping methods of the enabler is to put up a false front that everything is ok. But something happens when you try hard to convince the world that something is not really happening. You begin to lose touch with what *is* really happening. The line between what you wish was happening and reality begins to blur. This was my family. My childhood set the precedent for an uneasy relationship with reality... even before the heavens told me that nothing was how it seemed. As I sat there leaning against the cold hard wall, I vowed to myself that I would accept the truth of my situation, no matter what. That I would no longer play dead or pretend to be alive. From that moment forth, I would be fully where I was and accept whatever reality I found myself in. I would be authentic, no matter what.

The truth, right then, was that I was buried alive. No need for any hopes to be dashed any more. There would be no way out for this body – and that was the truth. Early on in life I was made keenly aware that I was not this body. This I knew to the depth of my soul. Then it struck me, if I was not really this body, I was not really a prisoner held here against my will. Just maybe I could go places, do things and have experiences in that other reality. You know, the one where all the stars lived. The one I looked at from high above that riverbank many years ago. I had no idea what kind of a god existed in that reality, but the experience was one of complete peace and tranquility. And it was real. I was ready and determined to try and find my way back there.

My mind started buzzing with a gentle anticipation. It felt as if I was standing at a new door, one that led to the truth. It had been there all along, but I had never really wanted to see. Like the door I just searched for, it was there in one moment but in another, it was not. Hiding in plain sight. But this door was my very own door. It was within me so surely it could not hide indefinitely. Somehow, I knew that it had something to do with a way out. Maybe not literally, but figuratively it was going to unlock the only freedom available to me, the one inside. It is that very same opening that most people have forgotten even exists. I once knew but I too had forgotten. It was there, I simply needed to figure out how to find it and then how to open it.

I strongly believe that everyone gets an invitation to walk through that door at least once in their life. An invitation to step into the truth of who they are. For me it felt like someone had sent mine a long time ago and was just patiently waiting until I was ready. Unfortunately for some it comes at the very end of their lives, like with me. Finally, it all started to make some sense. Sometimes we need that extra push to see. I must have missed many opportunities on the surface for my call to become as loud as it was right then. *What would it have taken me to look for this door in the midst of living? What had I ignored in life to have missed the summons for it now to become so loud?*

Maybe life really had this trip planned for me all along. Maybe the ticket was purchased eons ago. Heck, maybe I was the one that bought the bloody ticket.

Good Vibrations

I do not know when the vibrating started or when it ended. It just began one day and then eventually stopped, but not until it had tormented me for many years. The experience was very similar to the ones where I could feel the disembodied beings around my childhood bed. As I got older that shifted in a significant way. It would happen right in that delicate time between slipping out of wakefulness and beginning the journey into the darkness of sleep. It felt like I would fall into a micro-increment of time, in between the two states and get stuck. During those drawn out moments, I was trapped within the shell of a body that I was in the process of exiting but had not fully cleared. The difference was that instead of sensing beings all around me, a weird trembling started from deep within my being. My whole being would begin to vibrate at an increasing rate of speed as if something were trying to shake me loose and take me away. To where, I did not know. It was a total mystery and I was terrified. Surely, I thought, it was some unseen evil trying to take possession and draw me down into its reign of torment.

Maybe the heaven and hell of my Mom's religion did have an impact on my youth or maybe it was those niggling beliefs of the mass consciousness that were dictating that interpretation. Whichever it was did not really matter. What was happening at the time was very real, and it was terrifying. I would fight as hard as I could to cling to my physicality. Eventually the vibrating would stop, as if it finally gave up and released its hold. Then and only then, was I allowed to slip into deep sleep. The next morning, I would always remember what happened, in exacting detail. The full horror of it all was indelibly imprinted.

The vibrating stopped in my early twenties. It was at that point that I started pursuing my own health – physically and mentally. I started taking exercise seriously and force fed myself health food until I actually enjoyed it. My father went into recovery while my mom was still putting on the brave face of denial. While I was out on my own trying to resurrect the ashes of an incinerated youth, my sibling had long since left the scene. What I remember about him was that he was fighting his own demons, in his own unique way. We never took the time to get to know each other as adults. Right then I felt bad about that lost opportunity.

Maybe the whole vibrating experience was there because of my mental state. That meant one of two things. The devils' workers found an easy victim to drag into their dominion or it was the grace of some angels trying to pull me out of damnation. Back in those days I thought those were the only real choices. At that time, the former was all I could think of, I never considered the latter. But maybe there was a third choice after all - I could have just been plain crazy!

At this point in my abominable journey there was literally nothing to lose. I was willing to take my chances and walk through that invisible door, no matter where it would lead. I was literally cast into a hell of solitude, sitting in this sacred building and buried in the godforsaken depths of the Earth. *How could it get worse?* Not meaning to tempt the fates, but I was willing to take my chances. Looking over at my throne of stone, I promised myself that I would climb back up and sit there until it happened. Whatever that magical mystical 'it' was. I was going to find my way out one way or another. I would find that darn door. In body or in spirit. I would still be breathing, or I would not. It really mattered not to me, I just wanted it all to end and to be free one way or another.

Tinky and Me

My friend really needed a name and since it was obvious that we were going to be companions for the rest of my short life, I was going to find a fitting one. My death was not going to happen quickly, so I sat down and prepared to take a flight of fancy. Like naming some odd creature that decided it was his job to keep vigil as I slowly perished. Right now, my friend, my only friend, was providing the only comfort I had. Purrs are potent tools from the feline's quiver of magic. He deserved a name and that is what I was going to find. It was clear that he was not going to leave my side and I certainly was not going to leave his. I slid all the way down the wall until I laid horizontally and could stare upwards, imagining a sky full of stars smiling back at us. It is weird because it did look like some were just beginning to appear in the darkness above. Out of nowhere an old childhood song came forth, with some minor updates…

> Twinkle, twinkle, little friend
> How I wonder where you been.
> Down and under the world so deep,
> Why would you my counsel keep.
>
> Twinkle, twinkle, little friend
> Why with me until the end.
> When you show your little light
> Gone away is all my fright.
>
> Twinkle, twinkle throughout the night.
> I pray to some god with all my might.

Twinkle, twinky, winkle, winky, inky, tinky……. Tinky. That's it, I shall call you Tinky! I knew a name was in there somewhere. The twinkling star of my heart. The one that keeps watch over me and maybe someday will light my way out and we can both sit under the stars together. With that I grabbed him in a big exuberant embrace. Apparently, he did not quite share the same thrill of a hug and quickly squirmed out of my arms and proceeded to climb up onto my shoulder and perch there, just like he did on the angel's head. This will work for me too. Thank you. So there we were, two peas locked in the same damned pod. Tinky and me.

Slowly I got back up, making sure not to disturb the new accoutrement from his perch on my shoulder. We made our way back to my throne to fulfill my promise of finding that door. The vigil began and would not end until it was found.

The Vigil

Sitting and meditating was not my thing. I tried from time to time but it never evolved into a real practice. Not like it had been for Daniel. The truth was that I never really wanted to take the time to let it grow and develop. It felt like I spent enough time in deep contemplation and quietly being alone. For Daniel, sitting in the lotus position, eyes closed, hands held just so, was exactly what he needed to balance the rest of his busy life. It amazed me to watch him go through the process from when he first started to where he eventually arrived. Initially he could sit still for no more than ten minutes. I used to press him to try for longer periods of time. Not willing to do it myself, I was judging him on what I thought was the enlightenment threshold. Surely it would take more than a measly ten minutes a day, as I would gently enlighten him on that fact every chance I got. Eventually he was able to sit for significant periods of time, while I did not sit for any. I can only imagine what turn his practice had taken since this tragedy. Trauma has a way of either driving one deeper into the self or away from any reflection. Sadly, I thought I would never know what happened to him. What I did know was that it was driving me in deeper.

I assumed the position and took in a long deep breath. Tinky, perched on the angel's head now, was holding vigil with me. We were ready.

Still ready...

All is good...

Breathe a little more deeply... more slowly.. another breath

Follow the breath...

Keep following...

I sat and sat and sat some more. Nothing and nothing followed by more nothing. Except that my mind was in agony. It is one thing choosing silence amid the loudness of living. It is an entirely different matter when you are stuck in permanent silence, all by yourself. Granted I probably did not give it that much time but facing my death with a blank mind was not feeling at all in line with what I really needed. I promised myself to be authentic and so I was going to follow my real needs. I wanted to think. I needed to think. Relaxing back, I laid down with my arms under my head, one leg crossed over the other. Tinky sensed the shift and jumped down to assume the appropriate side snuggle pose and proceeded to give me his belly to rub. I assumed we were entering a new level of trust and so I began. Much to my surprise, my little Tinky boy was not a boy at all…. Tinky was a little girl. My little medicine woman!

I smiled deeply. For some reason, being with another female, even though not of the human persuasion, was a special gift. There is a bond between women of any species, as there is with men. When a guy sees a dog that has all his business still intact, their response is always a nod of acknowledgement and solidarity, 'yeah bro'- they still belong to the club. Women are like that, but it is not just about physiology. It's more about a different way of looking at the world – looking at it as protectors of the deeper realms, the ones that understand. I understood Tinky much better from that point forth.

Somewhere between the rubs, Tinky and I both drifted off into sleep. During this ordeal, sleep, so far, was deep unconsciousness. Not this time. The night, loosely termed, was full of struggle and nightmares. I remember monsters about to overcome me but not being able to move, people driving me into a frenzy of anger, yelling and screaming, demons laughing.... And so it went until I finally pulled back into reality with a shiver and cold sweat. I cried and cried. My eyes had finally filled back up with tears and even though I could not, they ran free.

I kept being pulled back into the quandary of which god to appeal to, which god to plead to, which god should I tell my final sorrows and fears. I had lashed out at a god and in return was gifted with even more constrictions. That god clearly thought that being buried alive was not penance enough, that my agony needed to be even more tightly contained.

It is hard to give up on life and to accept one's destiny, especially one such as this. I felt like an emotional yoyo, up and down, spinning all around at the mercy of another's controlling hand. One moment I had hope, then I was angry, then I would forget where I was and smile, then in another moment be back to swimming in a flood of tears and on it went. All the tightly held emotions of this all too short a life wanted their time in expression before it was gone. So out of compassion for all that they endured, I decided to let them all have their moment. Each feeling would be allowed to have its say, to tell its unvarnished truth. No feeling was left to protect, no dark recesses left to hide in and absolutely nothing held too sacred to come into the light. In return I would listen without judgment as an homage to my promise of authenticity and a need for closure.

Homage to Authenticity

As I lay there in deep reflection, the first memories to come forth were presented by a small innocent voice from within. My inner child had come not to receive comfort but rather to give. She had many things to say, all of which caught me off guard. Her message was simple. She wanted me to know that everything, absolutely everything that happened in my life was perfect. Even in the troubled world of my youth, where it felt completely out of control, fraught with unpredictability, full of tension and seemingly bad decisions being made by myself and my family, that all was just as it should have been. Her reassuring kindness met a skeptical heart. She went on to tell me that everything right then was also perfect, just as it was in the past. I had always been carefully looked after and was still up to that very moment.

"How could everything be ok, especially where I am. Perfect? How can this be ok? It makes no sense! How could this all be perfect and WHO is watching over me!" I responded to my inner dialogue with much consternation. Even though her words simultaneously agitated and dumbfounded me to no end, I asked with an open and

pleading heart. Even though I was immensely irritated, I really did want to know.

Before my eyes, she carefully laid out all my long-lost memories, starting with my youth. Staying up all night giggling with my girlfriends, roughhousing with my brother, mom's pure loving embraces, my dad's silly bedtime tales, playing house with my beloved dolls, running around like a wild banshee, playing games with the neighborhood posse, spending joyous hours alone working on puzzles and on and on. I saw it all. The surprising part was because I had only ever focused on the dissonant strands in the weaving of my life, forgotten were the wefts of joy. As she unrolled more and more of the tapestry, I wondered how I could have turned my back on and walked away from all those precious times. They far outnumbered and outweighed the painful memories. *Why is it that I let pain color my world instead of joy?* Somewhere there was a lesson... I was not so sure learning it mattered much at that point. All I knew was that I had hidden the past very well, even from myself. Long lost memories started pouring forth without any judgement.

Never did my parents know that for a time I was bullied in grade school and was terrified of being beaten up on my way home or the dread I felt when mom chaperoned on school field trips. The kids would surely call me names and then she would know the truth about who I really was and would not love me anymore. I was deeply ashamed of that truth – the one that said I was unlovable. Please do not get me wrong, this is not a sob story, and I was not an angel by any means. Often, I used kids in desperate fear of having no friends and then would unceremoniously dump them when a better set came along. I was sometimes mean, as only children can be. And so, it went. But the biggest pain of all was not having a sense of belonging. From the very beginning I was truly a loner, cast up towards the stars to hang all by myself... *Who would understand?* I did not belong no matter how much I tried, there was nowhere I honestly could fit in. Not even with my family. I did not even belong with them. Eventually I stopped caring. I was truly alone in a world that did not seem to care much what happened to me.

With each passing decade that came before my inner eyes, the voice inside matured but never lost its purity or clarity. Intertwined were not just the outward experiences of my life, but also all the thoughts and feelings, dreams and fears. It was all there. My teenage years, just like my youth, came without judgment or hesitation. I remembered everything. The excitement of getting older, discovering boys, gaining more freedoms and all the pain that came with those new territories. While it was easy to blame my parents for the distress of not providing stability and consistency, I used it all as an excuse to behave rather badly at times. I chose not to be respectful. I chose to lie to get my way. I skipped school to get high with friends, I chose to have sex at a very young age and all under the guise that I could do whatever I wanted, and no one could stop me. And no one could stop me, not even myself. In fact, that could have been a motto for my entire life. *I will do what I want!* A belligerent stance that did not care if I cut off my nose to spite my face. Which I seemed to do on a semi regular basis.

My parents and I could pretend things between us were fine but that did not change the truth. Home life was a constant battle ground. Every day I witnessed unhappy people ill-equipped to handle life and take responsibility for their own reality. At the end of high school my anger towards them had reached a breaking point. Especially toward my mother. My deep hurt from the duplicity of her pretending to the world that all was perfect while our family was being torn to shreds, turned to unvarnished rage. One day I could no longer hold it back. It all came pouring out in a vengeful torrent. I wielded the sword of truth in anger and retribution. Nothing good will ever come out of that combo. The wound I inflicted on that day drove a wedge between us that we would never fully recover from, not before she passed. She still loved me as only a mother can - unconditionally. I loved her too as only a daughter can, but the fragile chords of trust between us were strained. Of all my regrets, that is one that I will have to live with the rest of my life and now will have to die with shortly. I wish we could have been deeper friends.

I am sure my parents would have been there if I had honestly shared my struggles. Had they known that as a young adult I often considered devising an early departure from the world, they would have been appalled and frightened. The trauma my father experienced at a young age when he lost his father to suicide, would be something that cut too close to his hidden wounds. They were not mean people, just lost and traumatized by their own stories. They wanted the best for me just as I did for them. None of us knew how to do that – to give or receive the best. If I had asked, they would have responded. Maybe not in the way I wanted, but they would have tried, surely. But I never asked, nor did I share my deep struggles with them – or anyone. While their battles were painted right out in the open, slashing through our lives in vivid colors, mine were hidden away in muted tones. I buried them deep – just like I was buried now.

My twenties were filled with the same pains, only by now they were taking a bigger toll. I tried to rein in the downward spiral by controlling everything, from exercise to what went in my mouth. Starve, binge, starve, binge, rinse and repeat. Eating and everything else in life, had become something that I had to intellectually confabulate instead of naturally live. I lost the feeling of natural. The feeling of just being. I thought I should be a certain way, so I tried to stuff myself into that mold all the while smiling and pretending that I had it all together. My mother and I were not so different after all.

My anger toward my father came in a slow steady drip. We tried to spend time together as I got older, because that is what fathers and daughters do. But it never ended well despite our best intentions. We just pushed each other's buttons too much. There would still have been a chance for amends if I were there, as he still walked the surface but alas, I did not. The saddest part for me was knowing that he was left living with what could have been and with no chance to change the hands of fate. I knew that would torment him until his final days. By this point, my father would have been sober for over seven years. He had tried to make amends but was never able to fully open his wounded heart to heal, for our relationship to heal. I think his inner child, the voice of reassurance, was no longer available, just like his god.

The rest of my twenties were focused on picking myself up and trying to mend the broken threads. I read self-help book after self-help book. I partook in women's retreats, even exploring things like sweat lodges and various alternative therapies, all in an attempt to turn the momentum of life in another direction. Eventually it did but very slowly. Then one day all the imperceptible changes added up to the point where I could meet Daniel. For once, I attracted someone who was truly harmonious with me. I had broken the cycle of my parents, the cycle of conflict. That marked a significant turning point. I could then start manifesting things that were good for me. It was right at the point of really living that it was all cruelly snatched away. Right at that point where my story really began.

Throughout life I had just two prayers, they never changed. The first was to be like everyone else, fully buying into life and then just living it happily oblivious to its meaning. Second was that I just wanted to be me. I just wanted to be who I was created to be. That was all. Whatever that was, it was fine with me.

Having gotten all the pain and shame out into the open, a new space deep within was opening. All the buried grief needed to come forth and it needed the right time and surrounding to do so. It was funny that there on death's doorstep, I felt more alive than ever. The irony of the situation was not lost on me, nor were the rest of the ironies that had been spilling over into my new reality. Feeling more alive than I had ever felt, while poised at death's door, was the ultimate one. It was liberating and funny, with that special sense of humor that only death provides. At that point, any kind of deliverance was welcomed. To be able to heal old wounds was truly appreciated no matter what. I just wished liberation included my physical body, but my story was far from over.

My life was being revealed in a magnificent tapestry. Each moment was carefully woven in forming a living pattern. You would think that all the painful memories would have left breaches in the cloth or at least worn and unsightly areas. It was nothing like that. There was no ugly. For the first time ever, I looked at my life with wonder and awe. It was not only remarkable, it was beautiful. The colors of sorrow were indiscernible from the colors of joy. Separate but blended in absolute harmony. Gone were the shadows of self-criticism and the personal loathing that had tinted my time on Earth. I knew without a doubt that I was only being me, having experiences and learning things on a much grander scale of importance. The challenges no longer appeared as problems. They were all perfectly woven into the magical matrix of this life. I realized that my spirit delighted in it all. It had no judgement towards me and my decisions. It just loved me totally and completely and it loved exploring all of life through me.

As I continued to look, each thread began pulsating in absolute accord with every other thread like it was breathing. I had never seen anything like that before. It was alive. But of course, it was my life! As I watched this miracle, all my memories began to leave. One-by-one they gracefully flowed out of this body and merged back into the weaving. Simply reabsorbed as if they were returning home. Soon they were all gone but I was far from feeling empty. I knew, without a doubt, that this life simply rested in me for a time. In reality, it was a separate entity, in and of itself. I did not own my life, that was clear. Just like I knew that I did not own this body. And like the body that was not really me, my life in some strange way was not really me either. I was allowed to live it, as a courtesy. As a courtesy to myself and as a courtesy to everyone else. Somehow all the variant parts mattered, and they mattered deeply. Living this life, in all its glory and challenges, was uplifting to all. I let that sink deeply into my soul as the boundaries of where I ended and life began started to fade. My life was not just connected to all life, it was all life. It wound through me and I through it, dancing and flowing together in nothing other than absolute joy. Life was complete magic and I was part of it. There was nothing I had to do or not do. It just was and it was perfection.

My inner child was right. While I did not understand it all quite yet, I knew it was all perfect. Everything about my life was spectacularly beautiful. Even the horrific situation I found myself in took on a different hue.

You never know when the grace of God will come to you but when it does there is no doubt what it is and where it came from. Moving down and through my entire being it came. No part was left untouched or unloved. In a twinkling of an eye, my final despair was transformed into the pure gold of peace and understanding. I had nothing to do but to receive it. And that I did. I opened the whole of my heart to my creator and relinquished my life. Finally, this was the kind of God that I could love. A God with a capital "G."

Before that thought was complete, there was a flash of light and I was yanked back into my surroundings with a thud.

The Flow

As I adjusted to being fully back into my conscious mind, the idea that my life was not something I owned, was shifting my very foundation. That idea flew in the face of everything I was taught. The foundation of our world is that your life is yours. If I was not my body, which I knew I was not, then why should I lay claim to ownership of this life? Strange chills began to run throughout, as if I was being adjusted at a subatomic level. Hard to explain but it felt like every cell started moving and coming apart. I was in a state of flux. Not a scary feeling in any way. I was just changing. Instinctively Tinky jumped up and went to her perch. I sat up, crossed my legs and assumed the position as if it was the most natural thing in the world.

My body instantly felt very heavy. And it got heavier and heavier... and heavier. All the molecules that made me no longer connected in the old pattern. They were recombining and becoming like the stone that was surrounding me, immovable, dense and timeless. It was oddly comfortable and not at all surprising to blend with something that I had always loved and treasured. The feeling was not only natural, it also provided a bit of mercy as I was allowed a break from the fluidity of flesh and the trauma I had been experiencing. I could finally take rest in something solid. *Was this how I was going to exit life? To be found a millennium from now as a strange statue sitting on a strange bench in a strange building in a strange land.* I kind of relished the thought of becoming THE actual monument to myself.

I am not sure how long I rested in that state. It might have been days or it could have been minutes. It just was and it was perfect. I was finally at rest, and still alive.

At some point my stone state started to slowly dissolve. I became aware of my breath again. With each inhale, memory of my body was drawn in and with each exhale I expanded and grew lighter... and lighter. Soon my entire body expanded to fill the room. Just as it was pressed up against the walls, I felt a familiar *whoosh*. Yes, the same *whoosh* as in my youth. I left this body with absolute ease and found myself sitting in a very old study, lit only by candles and surrounded by well-worn leather chairs and important looking books - books and books and more books. It was the kind of study I had always fantasized belonging to a wise sage who is dedicated to unraveling the mysteries of life. The mystic. The scholar. The one-who-knows. You can imagine my surprise when who other than my inner child walked in and sat right in front of me.

"Oh my, did I startle you? So sorry, maybe this is better..." She, the little rascal from within, suddenly took the shape of a wise old man replete with long flowing hair and white beard, holding an elaborately carved pipe.

"How is this?" He kindly asked.

I was so caught off guard that I was left speechless and a bit troubled. I had just been a stone, at one and at peace with all that is and then as light as air with no boundaries. And now I was confronting an inner shape shifter! But she was right, the new image was more in line with who I pictured would be living in my library.

"That is fine. Yes, that will do, I guess but what is going on? Am I finally dead?" I replied in earnest.

"Ahhhha!" Laughed the old one. *"You have many questions and more important ones than that, I am sure, and luckily we have no time!"*

"No time?" I replied, *"I am on death's door! Is this what dying is? Are you here to show me the way?"* Yes, I did have a lot more questions but whether I was going to die shortly seemed pretty important to me. As much as I wanted this life to end, when it came right down to it, I really was not sure I was ready.

The old man paused and said, *"To put you at ease, I am the part of you called forth to assist at this time in your journey. We are in a place that you have created. It is where your imagination has taken you, a place that represents learning and wisdom. It is all you my darling. Me, the chairs, the books, it's all from within you."* It must have been the incredulous stare that kept him going.

"You will eventually die, but not today. I promise. You still have much to do, in time. Let me clarify. You have much still to do in the 'realm of time.' You see right now we are not in time; hence you have 'no' time. Beyond the world that you know, there lie infinite realms that are not governed by that which you think to be absolutes. Time is one of those seemingly fundamental laws that is not true everywhere." He made it all sound so easy and breezy, like I should say, *'But of course!'* But I did not.

"I am not so sure about that, but it is good to know that I still have something to do in the world that I know – in time, as you put it." I was genuinely relieved, and he was right, I had more pressing questions than trying to wrap my head around time and no time. I had heard of space/time vs time/space but it was always a bit baffling and its relevance to my situation was not so pressing. Eventually it would be, but not on that day.

Feeling more at ease, I went on, *"The most amazing thing just happened. I experienced the interconnectedness of all there is. A universe without boundaries and full of beauty and love. I now understand what it must look like from the perspective of angels, people like you."* I was still not quite convinced that he was just a figment of my imagination. *"But I am still very much from Earth and really want to know who is orchestrating this whole thing? Who put me in this place? I want to know what kind of a God exists who would do this? If everything is so wonderful and perfect, then why doesn't this feel so darn fabulous. It certainly would not be my choice. What is going on?!"* My blissful, all knowing, all accepting state had taken a quick U-turn back into a state of agitation.

"I am sorry if I appear to be so angry, I am trying to accept this all, I am seeing the wonder of being me, I am letting go of my attachment to this life as mine but I am struggling with, well... I am struggling with being buried alive, quite frankly." A few stray tears were welling up from my human heart since my other one was firmly at peace.

He sat there intently looking in and through me all the while stroking his long beard – exactly what I would expect one like this would do. Quietly pondering and waiting, waiting for the right question. So, I tried again…

"But who creates each of the tapestries, each life I mean? Mine was clearly in a carefully constructed design, the way it all fit together and moved and flowed. It all seemed so seamless and perfect – except for being here."

Finally, the reply I had been seeking. His answer was simple, *"Why it is you who creates your own life. You are the designer and implementer. You have help from your guides, of course. They work with you and make suggestions on what would work best given the myriad of factors involved and your soul's intent. Ultimately it is you who approves the design and agrees to the terms."*

"You mean to say that it is all pre-designed in advance? How can all the details be pre-set before we are born? That would fly in the face of free will and I want to, need to, believe in free will!" My question revealed an old paradigm that was still trying to hold on for its dear life. Everything being predestined, even though it appeared to be from my own hands, still flew in the face of my one cardinal rule. As master of my domain, *I did as I pleased.* This would be something hard to reconcile, not just for me but for anyone, I would imagine.

My inner old man looked at me with kind eyes, *"The fabric of your life is not static, not by any sense of that word. Just look at the tapestry. It is always growing and adjusting to the decisions you make. It is not the details that you, or your guides, are concerned with. It is the overall experiences and lessons that need to be learned and how they can be delivered in the most effective way. That is the goal. The only goal. To grow and learn specific things. Those are the things predetermined – what needs to be accomplished. If it makes you feel any better, there are no absolute guarantees that the soul will adhere to the plan. But even then, even when things seem to go awry, there is time... or should I say, thankfully there is no time. The lessons will be learned in another way, maybe another life lived or a life transfer. The lessons will be learned one way or another no matter what. That is the flow of the Universe. Incessant movement of experience constantly working their way back to harmony and oneness."*

Well that did not leave me feeling so great about what I once held as my sacred right – doing as I pleased. It now felt like a rather foolish and childish attitude. *"That makes sense, kind of sad though. I wonder how many people actually stick with their plans."*

"Many more than you think. The plans have a lot of flexibility inherent

in them and an ability to change direction if needed. Take you for instance..." he ventured to say.

"No, let's not take me quite yet. I am not sure I am ready to hear. Even though I saw my life without judgment, I still can't shake the feeling that I must have screwed up badly somewhere to end up down here."

In the most reassuring baritone he could muster, the wise old man continued as if I had not said a thing, *"You saw your life as a whole. You saw it move and bend with ease. You saw its perfection. You saw its beauty. Why are you doubting where you find yourself?"*

This was a bit too Zen for my newly expanded mind. *"I don't know."* That was all I could come up with. I just did not know.

"Can I ask another question?"

"Of course," he replied.

"You said that if we don't fulfill the plan for a given life that we may have another one in which to try again. That is most reassuring. I had always wondered about reincarnation and hoped that it was true. But you also said something about a life transfer. What is that?"

He paused for just a minute as if to gather the exact right words out of the air, *"For now, just know that each life lived is not lived for just that person. Each life is truly a courtesy to the whole and a part of the agenda of the whole. You don't have to live the actual life to learn from it."* With that he leaned over and gently placed his index finger right between my eyebrows and POOF... he was gone, the study was gone, and I was sitting alone in a pure white space.

Suddenly the whole of my vision was opened to see an infinite amount of lives. Each was made up of all their inherent complexities and woven masterfully together, without ever losing any of their uniqueness. Always changing and yet maintaining individuality.

The range of colors was indescribable, each life had a combination of hues that made it unique and identifiable. I apologize for the lack of words to describe this fantastic vision. In our reality we perceive just a small slice of the full spectrum of color that is available, here I saw it all. I did not know if these were all my lives or included all the lives of everyone else. It really did not matter because I was in all of them and all of them were in me. This must be the oneness that the sages have been trying to tell us about since time immemorial.

Suffice to say that I knew I would never see another person in the same way again. I would never look at another's choices with the same judgmental eyes. That is if I ever had the privilege of seeing another again. More was coming, that I knew to my very bones, but what that would be or if it would include the company of others, I was not sure. My world had just expanded exponentially without me moving a muscle. *Would the rest of my life be one lived solely within, a wanderer of the invisible realms, living in the inner realms of the world? Or would the adventure continue with my body in tow?* I can honestly say that I did have a preference. As much as the invisible realms were amazing, I just hoped that the plan for this life would include using this body. My longing would soon be revealed, one way or another.

CHAPTER III

BURIED

The Temple's Secrets

As I spent more time in contemplation and meditation, the lights in my consciousness continued to turn on. The room reacted to the changes within me and responded in kind. The milky orb reflected the state of my heart perfectly as it was now pulsating brighter and brighter. At regular intervals it shifted in its opalescence to cover the pale shades of the rainbow and beyond. The walls also responded and began to come alive with a glow welling up from deep within. It is hard to describe because I had never seen anything like that before. They simply emanated the most beautiful soft ivory light. The light was not focused like our fluorescence, it came from everywhere and imbued everything with its glow. And at last, I could see where I was contained.

The room was not square at all. The walls swept around in a beautifully curved arch. They were made with seamless sheets of an infinitely deep alabaster that had veins of silver woven through and a splattering of gold glittering here and there. The ceiling was domed and made from a dark blue stone that reminded me of lapis. The walls were tall, around 30 feet high. About eight feet up from the floor were carefully carved niches that looked like they once contained something very important or very beautiful, or maybe both. Between the niches were magnificent staffs of metal. They reminded me of sand-casted roots, weaving their way up to hold perfectly shaped crystals on top. As beautiful as they were, I was sure that they were utilitarian. Maybe torches that were ready to be lit by some unknown switch. *But how to trigger them to come on?* I was not sure, but maybe like the room, they would respond to some hidden cue at some hidden time.

The font in the center held no surprises. Its clean simple lines retained their elegance and power even in the light. My throne was as spectacular as I had believed it was, maybe even more so now that I could really see its fine details. Facing the bench and to the left was a rather large staircase. I am not sure how I missed that before, but it was certainly there right then. It was not a wide staircase, but a grand one indeed. With a curve that gracefully swept up and to the right, it eventually disappeared into a mysterious darkness. The floor appeared monochromatic at first, but with the light I could see a giant checkerboard tiling in shades of ivory. It too had a soft burnished glow, albeit very subtle.

I viewed my surroundings with different eyes. Something forever had changed within me. I felt more like me than ever before. One of my prayers was finally coming true. I was home in my body, in my mind and in my heart. My whole life I had yearned for this. Right then I was, finally, able to be me. It felt so incredible to be alive. It mattered not that I was trapped or going to die soon. What mattered was that I was alive, like I had never been before. The funny thing was that I no longer felt trapped. I finally felt free. Tinky stood, arched her back and nonchalantly shook, as cats do, and then sat right back down. She took everything in an effortless stride. I finally understood what that felt like. From the depths of my being came a primal scream of joy.

△

This was truly a magnificent place to be, both inside and out. As I let that sink in, I wondered if this building could in fact be a Temple. It made much sense. The devastation that took place outside did not occur inside. The place was untouched. I could see why no one had ravaged it. For one thing entering was a real trick and I was still not quite sure how I managed that feat. It also appeared that exiting might be tricky as well since no sign of a door had appeared, even in the light. The peaceful atmosphere was otherworldly – well at least nothing I had experienced in the world I knew. No doubt it held many secrets it was intent on keeping. Secrets of long-lost magic, lots of magic, and not just what was happening to me. Clearly it had been emptied of its content. They might have been taken out or hidden just in case the building fell into the wrong hands. At least I imagined they had been removed since there was nothing of comfort, no fabric, no cushions, no furniture, not even a sacred text to be found.

I sat there for a time just letting it all sink in. Where I was, who I was and even touching on what I was. All very big subjects in an average life but often not getting their due because of busyness. Lots of busyness. Busy. Busy. Busy. For me, life had now conspired to create a space devoid of any distractions so that time was all I had. Time to be and time to contemplate. I was no longer convinced that this ordeal was a curse of some Almighty, even though my circumstances were still hard to reconcile. As the wise old man from within said, this could simply reflect a plan between myself and the ones in charge of my well-being and growth. That idea made more sense and was immensely more palatable than my old conundrums. Still, it would take a while longer to fully inhabit this or any other understanding.

△

With nothing else in my physical space to do, exploring the stairs would have to happen. They looked immensely fun to climb and, at the same time, a bit scary. But I was ready for anything, or so I thought. As with everything else in this strange place, the stairs were on a very large scale. Climbing the huge steps would take some energy, but I had plenty of that available. In fact, I was feeling remarkably strong considering the lack of any sustenance, except for drinking the water from the font. The waters were doing something. What alchemical process was going on, I was not quite sure, but no matter. It was happening. I wasn't hungry anymore, I was healing at lightning speed and all my thirsts were being quenched - both inner and outer. The only reservation I had about exploring the stairs was that they led up to darkness. I had enough darkness to last the rest of my days but then again, what did I have to lose?

Carefully I approached the staircase. While feeling at ease with myself, I still didn't know much about the place I was beginning to call home – the Temple. Taking one large step at a time, I bravely began ascending into the unknown. Magically, the darkness gave way with each step I took as the wall right in front burst into light from one of the magnificent torches. Not all of them at once but one at a time, just enough for me to see the next step. I was being led one step at a time, trusting that the Temple would take care of me. The whole thing reminded me of a corporate retreat for team building where you fall backwards while blindfolded and trust that you are going to be caught. That your team had your back, so to speak. Right then, I had to fall forward into darkness and hope that there would be light. And it happened, it kept responding to my presence. Light would be provided as far as I needed, nothing more and nothing less. I had a team somewhere that had my 'front.'

Slowly I wound my way up until I came to a platform with an opening to the right. It was a doorway that led into a room. I took one step into the room hoping for a response, but there wasn't one. The room remained dark. With newfound confidence still intact, I closed my eyes to feel the connectedness, to being one with the room. From a humble heart, I asked for there to be light. The room immediately responded and started to emanate a gentle green hue. Tinky would have clapped in delight if she knew how, so I did for her! What had once been a bedroom or room of repose, came alive with light. There were benches of different sizes and maybe some tables, but it was hard to tell because of the different scale of everything. The room was surprisingly opulent compared to the simplicity of the lower level. Each object was beautifully carved with reliefs of vines, fruits and animals that looked a bit foreign but nonetheless, all gorgeously and lovingly carved. Oddly, there was still nothing of comfort. The inhabitants could have been a weird kind of ascetic, ones who had forsworn any physical pleasure, except that the carvings spoke loudly of enjoying the finer indulgences of life. But all the accoutrements of comfort were stripped away, just like the room below. Whoever was there had left long ago and from the looks of the outside, I would bet not by their own choice.

The sensuously curved walls were made of a translucent green serpentine stone that gave the room a gentle quality. Now that I think back, there were no corners anywhere to be found in the whole place. It all flowed naturally and effortlessly. The floor deserves its own description because it was so incredible. Keeping with the theme from the one below, it was laid out in a giant checkerboard mosaic but this time with organic swirls entwined throughout the grid. It was clearly a black and white theme but not with the harsh contrasts we usually see on game boards. These had a harmonious interaction, like former combatants occupying the same space, finally at peace.

I had to face the fact that I probably would never really know what was going on here or who was behind all the goings-on. Unless I miraculously manifested someone to explain it all, it would remain a mystery. Mysteries used to ignite my desire to know, but here I was at peace with not knowing it all. Well maybe I was still a bit curious, but at peace. There was a small bench in one corner that drew my attention because if I stood on it, I could reach one of the torches. I really wanted to see one up close and maybe I could figure out how to trigger it to light on command. To have another source of light would be comforting, even though the Temple seemed to be most cooperative. As I crawled up on top of the bench, the upper part rocked ever so gently. You know when a lid is not fully replaced on a jar and it wobbles. Easily I grasped the staff and just as easily it came off the wall. Surprisingly light, I could hold it with just one hand and quickly jump down to look at the bench now turned box. The lid was about an inch-thick and made from solid stone. It took most of my might to push it. Push I did, and ever so slowly it began to move aside to reveal its treasure.

Inside was a garment meticulously folded and carefully placed. The fabric was unlike anything I had ever seen. It shimmered like an exotic metal was woven into the fibers. What came out was a magnificent cape with a hood. It must have come to the inhabitant's mid back because on me it reached all the way to the floor. The earthy colors vacillated from greys to browns with the hints of metallic threads shining throughout. It must have been made for the outdoors, for some amazing adventure. While mine wasn't exactly amazing yet, it did not stop me from putting it on. It was the most exquisite piece of clothing I ever had the privilege of adorning my body with. Trying to figure out the kind of fabric was tough. It felt like a combination of all our most prized creations – from delicate silks to fine woolens to the softest of cashmeres and yet, it was like none of them. My mind boggled. Tinky, who had followed me the entire way, liked it too for no sooner had I put it on then she assumed her perch on my shoulder while purring her approval.

Under the cape lay a pouch made of soft leather from a hide I did not recognize. It was grey and had the patina of a tarnished silver vessel. The top was cinched in with a long leather cord. It was full of something, that much was clear, what it could be I had no idea. Throwing any caution that may have lingered away, I dumped the contents on to my lap. With a delicious clunking and clinking, out tumbled four stones. I will do my best to describe each one since each deserves a special acknowledgment.

The first was square in shape with softened edges. Like a garnet only denser in hue, it reflected a viscous like quality within its dark borders. It reminded me of blood, thick and lustrous, the substructure of life. This probably caught my attention first since garnet is my birthstone. A magnificent small sphere caught my interest next. Semi-opaque yellow with a hot white core, it glowed and pulsed as if it were alive. It was like holding the sun in the palm of my hand. Next was a spectacular purple crystal about an inch and a half long. It looked like the love child of an amethyst and opal, conceived with the intent to purely delight the world. As I turned it over in my hand, streaks of white fire seemed to travel throughout sending a palpable electric current into my body. Since everything about my situation was a bit suspect, maybe these stones really were alive. I liked that idea. No matter what they were, I saw what I saw and to me they all were larger than life, even though they fit into the palm of my hand.

Finally, the crème de la crème, a crystalline geometric shape that hung from a simple piece of grey leather that matched the bag. It looked like two tetrahedrons, mirror-images of each other and intertwined. It reminded me of the Star of David in a way, except this was three dimensional. There was something about the shape that spoke of pure truth and power. I was not sure what that meant but I was sure that I had to remind myself to breathe as I slipped it around my neck.

One did not have to be a special initiate into the yogic realms to feel the power these stones held individually, much less all together. There wasn't a second thought as to whether I should take them or not. I pushed the lid of the chest back in place and prepared to move onward and upward. There was more adventure waiting that day, even though I felt more than rewarded already. With the pouch added to the treasure already around my neck, the cape on my back and the staff in my hand, I truly felt like I had just walked straight out of Gandalf's world. He would have been proud.

Last, but not least, by any measure, was Tinky. Regally perched on my shoulder, we went looking for the next secret to be revealed. And revealed it was. Finally, the end of the stairs was in sight. Had this been a castle, I would have been nearing the top of the highest turret. I was the master of this realm. Proudly I scanned my kingdom and found another room hiding off to the right! This time the stairs did not light all the way to the top nor did the room respond with illumination. Instead there was an ominous glow coming from within, easing its way into the darkness of the hall. Mustering up some courage, I stepped inside. What I saw almost knocked me to the ground. I let out a gasp if not a small scream. Tinky flew off my shoulder and disappeared down the stairs.

Meet Thy Makers

Below me was a large sunken chamber that emitted a strange light. As it glowed upwards, it displaced the air in a way that warned one not to come too close. I could sense that something unusual was going on - maybe supernatural, maybe even dangerous. It was as if the parameters of this dimension were being bent to accommodate another. Very carefully I stood on my tippy toes and leaned over just enough to peer within but not enough to be entranced and potentially captured within this light. That is when I saw them for the first time.

Arranged in a pentagon shape was a ring of five open wood caskets, simply made with no apparent decoration. Even though they must have been ancient, they looked like fresh pine recently hewn into their perfectly balanced shapes. Each one contained a being, but there was nothing ordinary about them. They were large - very large - men, in perfect human proportion. In the center of the pentagon was a gigantic smokey crystal point. It would have taken at least two of these giant men to wrap their arms around its entire breadth. The light was radiating from this stone and at each of the corners of the pentagon were foot-high crystal columns that seemed to anchor and amplify the three-dimensional field. Four of the beings looked almost identical. They wore simple tan robes with a brown vestment over the top and golden cords tied around their waists. Their arms were carefully placed over their chests with elegant fingers purposefully interlaced. They all had long wavy auburn hair and long red beards. Around their foreheads were wide bands of copper with half suns and moons peeking out along the upper edges. Each band looked slightly different from the others, but all seemed part of the same celestial series.

The being farthest away was not like the others. I could barely see him from where I was standing, and I was certainly not going to lean in to get a better look. With only the very edge of his face and body in view, I saw his pure white, almost translucent skin and no hair. He was also wearing a simple vestment like the others but his was all white. None of them looked dead in any sense of the word. Their skin was not preserved like with mummies, nor had they deteriorated in any perceivable way. Instead they looked like they had simply fallen into a deep sleep and were waiting for the magical moment to be awakened from their slumber. How long they had been there, I do not know. But gathering from the age of the ruins, these were beings from a past so distant we have no record of their existence. Undoubtedly, they were in a deep homeostatic state, placed there to withstand the hands of time. The last thing I wanted was to be caught in whatever was holding them in suspension. Even though that is how I felt most of my life, not quite dead and certainly, not quite alive, it's not how I felt right then and not how I wanted to be remembered. That is if this place was ever found by another human. That did not seem to be in the realm of possibility, so chances were that I would just be stuck in limbo with no one ever knowing or coming to the rescue. Stuck for an eternity or more with these strange men. No thank you.

I shuddered at the mystery. It was all so disconcerting that I felt physically ill. I had been rocked by so many unexpected experiences; this was just one too many and one that I was not able to digest at that time. I quickly turned around and fled down the stairs as fast as I could, with my cape flapping hastily behind. I did my best not to panic or to think about them in fear that my energy would somehow be the key to awakening them. Thankfully, that did not happen.

When I reached the bottom, I raced to the fountain to furiously splash water on my face, as if to wake myself from a dream. I gulped down as much as possible, as if that too would pull me back to some semblance of reality. There I was, standing with water dripping down my chin, cape on my back, magic stones around my neck and Tinky patiently waiting for my return.

Lovingly wrapped up like an infant in a papoose, I curled up in my new cloak and fell into a deep sleep. I dreamed of strange places and strange men with long flowing beards. Red of course. Graceful women in regal gowns, holding colorful streamers in their hands as they danced and danced. The rest was a blur, but I would recognize the feeling forever. They inhabited a place of joy and power. Not a world I was familiar with, but one that answered a universal longing for coherence and harmony.

Freedom

By now you know that time was irrelevant and irreverent to my situation. I simply had no idea of a day or a week or a month and time did not care that I did not know. It kept passing as I spent it in utter silence and all alone. That was a good test of sanity for anyone, especially a modern human who has been indoctrinated with technology and the constant flow of information streaming in. It is easy to read this and think no big deal, but I am here today, still having a voice to say that this was a big deal, a very big deal. Silence and solitude open opportunities that the bustle of daily life does not. Once you get past the curse and horror of being disconnected, the blessing of having time to go within yourself in absolute quietness can sink in.

It was there, in my prison, that I could move beyond the human bounds of place and time. I learned to simply turn the conscious switch off and allow the magic to happen... or not to happen. Sometimes there was a *whoosh* and out I went and other times I just sat in deep thought and communion. Occasionally I just went blank for a time. Thank goodness when I did take flight it was always out to the surface. Mostly I travelled to majestic snowy clad peaks of some spectacular mountains, somewhere. I was free from any bounds or bonds. Out of body travel, at that point, never included anyone else. I was still completely alone but I was free, and the latter was more important than the former. The price of my freedom always came due with a thud as I reentered my physical body and my tomb.

My waking meditations varied from reliving the precious moments in life, with love and gratitude and much affection for all involved, to just floating in the vastness of peace, that which I considered my Universe, my God. I was becoming familiar with Him but not in the way you do with a personified version. (Please forgive the use of the masculine, it is just for ease of dialect and not meant as a gender description). Unlike my old choices, this new God never had anything other than an all-encompassing love for His creation. I was still not sure how it all fit together but just knowing that God was not judging me or anyone, helped to relieve a huge burden. It was time for me to lay down that mantle of judging myself so harshly. I was starting to get it. *Maybe life and God is knowable? Maybe there were some answers to the mysteries of life?* I liked that thought and I loved being in the feeling that it brought forth, even though I still had times of struggling with the way I was learning the lesson.

And of course, Tinky joined where and when she felt the need. On her perch, in my lap, along my side or simply disappearing to somewhere I could not see. She was mostly cat, after all. With each conscious endeavor or mood explored, the room would adjust to match. The walls would glow in delighted shades of gold when I was awake and feeling happy. They would then shift into serene shades of blue as my moods would shift into the things that still troubled me. As I went to sleep, they would fade into content shades of darkness. On extra inner-calm nights, I could swear there were stars trying to sneak out. I tried to point them out to Tinky so she could understand something magical about the world I had left behind.

△

One day I knew that the end of my time as a captive had finally come. I had filled the space both externally and internally to the point where there was no room left to grow. My horizons were ready to expand, and a new adventure was ready to be born. I am not sure how to explain it, but for those who understand and trust their intuition, they will understand what it means to just *know* something. I knew there were still untapped resources left within me that only new circumstances could bring forth. I was ready. I closed my eyes and set a clear intention of walking out the door that was no longer there, the one that had let me in. When I opened my eyes, as if by cue, there was a large rectangular shape materializing on the wall right in front of me as if it were being freshly cut by a powerful laser beam of light. It was exactly the size and shape of the one that allowed me entry. Knowing without question that it would continue to manifest, I grabbed my backpack, adjusted my cape and grabbed my staff. Tinky was on my heels and ready to go. As we approached the door, it effortlessly swung open on invisible hinges. Easy as that. Out we strode to the edges of the platform. The light was probably as dim as when I entered but my eyes had adjusted, or maybe they had changed, all I knew was that the faintness did not bother me anymore. I could see very well.

It was not easy exploring ruins of what was once a fully intact city. Not surprisingly, its building blocks were made from huge stones, not like our tiny cinder blocks. This meant that as they lay toppled, there was plenty of crawl space to explore within. Obviously, I needed to be very careful not to disrupt the balance, but hopefully it was well settled by this time and would not easily cave in. Tinky and I roamed in and out, not finding much of anything except for occasional shards with tiny remnants of color still attached. Maybe from a fresco, a tile or a pot, it was hard to tell. Whatever had caused the exterior destruction had also obliterated the interiors. I felt a deep chord of sadness running throughout the cavern. There would be no heart hard enough not to feel the sorrow of what was lost. While there was much area to explore, there was no indication that we would find anything of value. My hopes of discovering something to reveal its secret origins or more information about the inhabitants, seemed as faded as the light.

As we went to the back of the cave, the very far end opposite the Temple, there was a three-story wall still partially intact but leaning heavily against the side of the cave. Tinky and I were able to carefully squeeze our way into the wedge created between the two. Tinky noticed it first. Alerted by her loud sniffing, I too saw a large crack at the bottom of the cave wall and a slight air current moving into our space. Tinky was the first to go in. I wasn't sure I would be able to fit except for the fact that my small frame was now even slighter. With nothing to lose, I made the attempt and was able squeeze in with room to spare. After crawling for the distance of a short hallway, I stood up into a completely dark, cobweb encrusted space. I knew there were cobwebs because I could feel them sticking to my face. Not a comfortable sensation considering the large size of everything around this place. Hopefully, the spiders would not be equally as impressive.

You would have thought that a cave would be full of all kinds of weird insects. The only critters I had been in contact with were Tinky and her lot, which oddly had not made a second appearance - not yet. Maybe I was down so deep into the earth that even the smallest of creation had never ventured this far. Smart bugs. Tinky ran off to explore and left me standing in the dark. My vision had not adjusted to the complete absence of light. Knowing it would work, I grabbed the staff tightly and willed it to light. The crystal obeyed by bursting into a soft white glow. Lucky for me there weren't any spiders to be seen but even luckier was something truly unexpected.

The Library

I was surrounded by shelves made of stone. Lots of shelves. They went from the floor to as far up as the torch would light and my eyes could see. On the shelves were books, books and more books. Everything imaginable was bound in every conceivable way. They all sat there waiting to be enjoyed but untouched for eons. Along the floor were giant clay pots and crates full of rolled up parchment and various papers. Some in tubes of leather, some unprotected as if trusting the hands of time would be gentle. In the center were simple pedestals and tables made of stone. This was once a library, no doubt. A secret stash that only gave up its location because of a crack in the foundation. Clearly, whoever ravaged the city had not found this either or its treasures would have been confiscated or destroyed. Nothing this valuable would have been left behind, no matter who inflicted such violence everywhere else. Certainly, they would have recognized this trove of knowledge for what it was – priceless. Tears welled up in my eyes as I felt the gravity of it all. These were the remnants of a long-lost civilization. The mysteries they held were mind-boggling. The keys to enlightenment, to advanced technologies, to who knows what, was beyond my mortal grasping. My mind scattered in many directions with all the possibilities. Truly this was a treasure beyond measure, beyond time and beyond space. Undoubtedly there were secrets contained in the texts that held the potential to change humanity. If only my people could be here with me or I could take the knowledge to them. They would never be the same again, I just knew that they would be better.

With light in hand, I started scanning the books. They came in every shape and size. Most were very large, not surprisingly. Some must have been miniatures because they were in perfect proportion to my stature. The materials they were created from were vast. Some were made from leather, some in what looked like thin sheets of stone, some in clay, some in metals and others in materials that I did not recognize. Some spines had writing, and some did not. I felt overwhelmed with the variety and scope of it all. I was hoping some of the printing would be recognizable, but nothing was familiar. Then one by one, I pulled the smaller books off the shelves and carefully opened them. They were in varying degrees of deterioration and the last thing I wanted was to defile them. I was standing in the middle of something sacred. Beyond what we know is contained in any museum, whether it was on display or held in secret. Even our libraries paled in comparison. I was probably the only human, modern human that is, to ever witness this spectacle. The thought crossed my mind to get my phone and take a picture to prove that it really existed.

Strangely, just the thought of cataloging the library brought a weird sense of comfort and at the same time discomfort. It was like a tether still existed to the surface, beyond my heart strings to Daniel, yet the very thought of taking a photo or making a video was met by resistance. Modern technology had no place there. The use of a cell phone would only make light of the rarity and weight of the find. Like much in our world today, being seen on a screen seemed to turn people and places into caricatures of themselves. Technology has a way of separating the viewer from reality and ultimately, making it easy for them to trivialize and dismiss what they see. I would not be the purveyor of a cliched treasure, watered down for the masses to ingest and then ruthlessly discard. No, I would not be the provider of the next sensational headline. Sacred things would be held sacred while I was still graced to live. I would keep those precious gates intact. The library would remain safely hidden with me.

The cool dry air of the cave combined with the lack of light must have helped to preserve the treasures thus far. My hopes of finding something that I could read, some language that I could understand, were being thwarted one by one. Even though there appeared to be many, maybe hundreds, of different languages, there were none I could recognize much less decipher. That was disappointing. But there were books with drawings that allowed me to get a general feel for their meaning. Some contained maps of land masses, even though they made little sense to our world today. Some were instructions about the stars with arrows and geometric shapes pointing to special areas in the heavens that I knew nothing of. Some were in color with beautiful borders and designs much like our illuminated manuscripts of yore. And some even had interesting images of peoples and animals, all a bit strange to my limited eye but they were obviously life forms! The rest contained lots and lots of writing. These people had much to say about many things. I could not help but think that most of the topics were things we no longer thought about or, even more likely, things we no longer remembered existed.

Tinky and I must have been there for hours. I carefully sifted my way through the trove of books and manuscripts, barely making a dent. Tinky sat patiently by my side, as if she too were a bit stunned by our discovery. Her only requirement was the occasional acknowledgement by way of a snuggle or two. At some point I began to feel an odd pressure building in my head. I thought maybe the fine dust in the air or the use of my eyes in such a concentrated manner, which was not something I had done in a while, was the cause. As it started to grow in intensity, I decided it was time to make our way back to home base. I knew exactly where this hideaway was so we could easily come back another time. I would love nothing better than to spend time surrounded by this secret cache of wisdom. For now, I selected three books to bring back with me - one having to do with maps, one to do with the stars and one that caught my attention. It was wrapped in parchment paper with a seal of red wax holding it closed. The mystery of it was just too much to resist. No longer would I feel so alone. Those who have found refuge in the written word, especially during difficult times, will understand that quite literally, books can be treasured friends. I could hardly wait to get to know my new acquaintances, even though I assumed that we came from vastly different times and places.

△

On the way back to the temple my headache reached a critical level. It felt as if something had it in a vice or, even more accurately, that something was trying to hammer its way in with a spike. From time to time, I had to squat down and hold my head in my hands to try and relieve the pressure. It was the first real physical discomfort I had felt since the crash landing. I could not have formed a thought if my life depended on it. Luckily for Tinky and me, our lives would depend on that very thing *not* happening.

Close Encounter

As we rounded the final corner, to my absolute horror there were three large creatures standing on the platform of our Temple. It looked like they were trying to figure out a way inside but that wasn't what was so horrifying about the situation. It was who they were or maybe I should say, *what* they were, that sent shivers down my spine and made my head want to explode. I quickly ducked out of sight and tried to catch my breath. The pressure was still increasing and for some reason, I knew it was coming from them. They seemed to be probing the area and trying to penetrate my mind. Maybe they had picked up on our scent or I had left some clues, something that had led them on to us. Tinky was long gone, hiding far away from even my sight. She was at least as terrified as I was, and for good reason.

The *things* looked like something straight out of the Creature from the Black Lagoon - part lizard and part humanoid. They had similar stature to the beings in the homeostatic state. They probably stood an easy 10-12 feet tall and were very muscular. While they had arms and legs, they did not have skin like ours. Instead they were covered in a greenish hide like an alligator with a pronounced ribbing down their spines that ended in short powerful looking tails. They were wearing some sort of technology because I could see what looked like dials and gadgets on their chests, but it all blended so well with their bodies that I wasn't sure where one began and the other ended. Maybe that was on purpose or maybe that was their biology. Their chests were a lighter and slightly varied color. I was too far off to tell exact details with any certainty. But most alarming were their heads. They were shaped more like reptiles than humans with pronounced jaws like lizards. I could only imagine the size of their teeth and what kind of appetite they quenched. There was a reddish crest that ran down the back of their heads to the top of their spines. Their eyes were located towards the sides of their heads, dark and large, and even from this distance, I knew they did not hold any warmth. I took another peek to make sure I was not having a migraine hallucination. But they were still there examining the Temple wall. Shivers went clear down my spine as terror took hold. Like Tinky, my new sense of Zen was nowhere to be found. As if they sensed my fear, they all turned and looked in my direction.

Since this journey began, I had faced the possibility of death many times. Never in my wildest imagination would I have thought that this would be the way I would take my final leave of this planet. This just could not be written in the book of my life – *"E sadly was dispatched by giant reptiles. Our hearts go out to this untimely and unseemly departure..."* My heart started racing even though I knew that these creatures could probably sense the disturbance in the field. It was my biology taking over once again. Suddenly I was aware of the stones around my neck. They were trying to get my attention. I swear they started pulsating with a regular slow rhythm, much like a heart. Slowly and steadily, my own heart started to calm down as it entrained itself to their pattern. It was exactly the help I needed to regain my center and move into a place of calmness as I could hear and feel the creature's presence approaching. I knew they were trying to feel my presence too. *Who was this intruder and where was it hiding?* They were vibrationally scanning the air for me.

Something took over as time slowed down. My heart was kept in check by the stones as I controlled my breathing and cleared my mind of any thoughts. It was not easy but there was no other choice except for the one written on an epitaph that I was not interested in receiving. I carefully placed the hood over my head and wrapped my body with the cloak, being sure not to let anything show. It reminded me of when I was a child and would wrap myself tightly in my covers, making sure nothing was exposed for the evil spirits to grab on to. My mind snapped back into reality and turned to a single thought. I am stone. That was it. I knew how to do that! Just like in the Temple, I let my atoms slowly unwind so that they could repattern with my surroundings. Eventually I was no longer even aware of my breathing. I was one with the stones. As the creatures grew nearer the pressure began to dissipate. Their probes were passing right through me. I hunkered into as tight a ball as possible as they slowly approached. When they got within a few feet of where I was crouched, they stopped. Not only did they stop, but they too stilled their minds, as if to try and sense even the subtlest of anomaly in the air. But there was none. After what seemed like an eternity, they gave up and started walking away. Once they had gotten far enough, I mustered the courage to look.

No wonder Tinky had run in fear. She knew who they were, and they were not on friendly terms. Hanging from the back of their belts were several of her kind. Limp and lifeless, they had been caught and tethered. My heart broke at the cruelty. Whatever Tinky was, she was a kind soul but to them, she would be dinner. With sadness I reflected on how my species treated animals. We were no different from these creatures, at least not in this respect. While some cultures hold certain animals sacred, others mercilessly cage and slaughter the very same without giving their precious souls a second thought. At that point I lost any appetite for meat of the flesh, ever again – if ever I would get the privilege of a choice, of course.

After they were out of sight, I slowly stood up and gently called Tinky's name. But she did not come. Keeping a close eye on my surroundings, I headed back to the Temple hoping that my little friend would eventually come out of hiding and join me. But she did not. I imagined she was curled up deep within the bowels of the ruins, trembling in fear and not wanting to test her fate. I could not blame her. I did not want to either. At least she was safe, so I headed back to the only safety I knew. There I could collect my thoughts and plan my next step. This was a game changer and it was not over.

Peace Out

To my great relief the door to the Temple reappeared when I arrived back at the platform. I entered still shaking from the experience and all alone. I didn't realize how much I had come to rely on my Tinky. The lack of her presence took the joy right out of the air. There wasn't anything or anyone to console me or be consoled by me. As with all my emotional challenges, the waters of the fountain called. Once again, I answered by indulging my thirsts. Trying to reassemble a sense of inner peace, I sat for a time to collect the fragments shattered by fear. Eventually I came back to a place of calm. The time had arrived to leave this remnant of a civilization and the Temple, leave and never come back. The lizard men would return, and I would be no match for them... *at least not yet*. Things would end badly next round. Unfortunately, that would mean that the library would never be explored, at least not by me. I had three books and that would have to suffice.

I wasn't sure why I was so sad. Maybe it had to do with leaving the safety I knew versus the potential challenges to come. At least I had several things to remind me of this experience and hopefully they would help somewhere down the line. I would wear my cloak and carry my staff and the stones would rest safely around my neck. As for water, in the pack was the water bladder I had entered my journey with. I hadn't given it any thought since I was gifted with an unending source. I had come to rely on the font's special properties of mending many broken wounds and keeping hunger at bay. The idea of going into the unknown without being able to drink from it was unsettling. But I had an idea. . . Maybe by placing some of the special stones from the fountain into the bladder, they could continue to charge the water with their magic. Maybe they could even energize new water going forward. It was worth a try. Feeling no resistance, I reached in and took several handfuls out and carefully placed them inside. I then dipped it in best as I could to fill it as full as possible.

There was nothing left to do but to say goodbye to a space I had initially cursed but had eventually grown to trust. If I was honest with myself, I had grown to love this space in a way. Not in the way a hostage can eventually bond with their captors. My affection was for someone, something, that showed infinite mercy and focused on my true betterment. While I did not necessarily agree with all the terms, the transformation taking place was exactly what I had wished for my entire life – to become who I was made to be. And that was exactly what was occurring. Contemplating my release felt like I was in the process of dying and being born again, all at the same time. I was being cast out to make my way in a world I was clueless about. It was a world contained deep within a world I once knew. I was as ready as I would ever be. With tears in my eyes, I turned my attention back to the door, held my staff and walked out.

Standing on the platform, I surveyed the landscape. I knew if those creatures where anywhere nearby I would feel them. Thankfully the air was clear and my way was open. Before I reached the last step, Tinky came running out from the rubble as if she were waiting for me. We had come to know each other very well and she knew I would never leave her behind. I wanted to shout in delight but did not want to scare her. Surely, she was feeling rather delicate, as I was. I leaned down to greet her. This time she allowed me to hold her tight. I could feel her tiny being relaxing in my arms. I held her until things felt right again. When we were ready, she crawled under the cape, rested her little rump on the backpack and placed her front paws over my shoulder. With only her sweet eyes peeking out, we moved forward into the big unknown.

∆

Finding an exit was key. What I was not going to do was follow in the direction the creatures had gone. No way. Instead we went in the exact opposite way. Skirting along the outer edges of the cavern, we had to carefully climb over a lot of rubble. Picking our way along, we eventually came to a place where the air began to change. Tinky got excited and ran ahead. I guess we both were familiar with what that meant. Another open space had to be near. In the next pile of rocks, the air was clearly moving in through all the openings. Like someone had a fan blowing towards us from the other side.

"This is it," I told Tinky, *"we found our way out! It's going to be all right my Sweet One. I am going to take care of you."* There is nothing like feeling responsible for another and having that other rely on you. We were a team and I was in charge of our safety. Her presence carried more weight than if I had been by myself. Her life increased the value of mine, as only a true heart connection can.

Tinky picked a path through the rocks for us. Eventually we were able to squeeze through to the other side and stand on solid footing. In front of us was another tunnel. Nothing extraordinary. We could easily see our way with the light from the crystal torch. By now I knew a thing or two about underground tunnels since I had traversed many miles of them. This was a short one. As we approached the end, the air changed again. I knew something big was coming. This time it came as a complete surprise. The air was filled with moisture and smelled like a new spring shower. At the mouth of another large cavern, I stood frozen in disbelief. My mouth hung open as I gazed at a sea of green.

Into the Garden

Imagine being lost in a desert for many moons, longing for redemption and release. Always hoping but never fully believing on some days and on others, losing all hope but somewhere inside always believing. I think most people are well acquainted with one of those feelings, if not both. Whether you are experiencing the angst of physical distress or just sitting at home watching your life dry up and slowly slip by, we all go through our time of trial and in the end, there is redemption. Always redemption. It may come at the last second, on the very last breath, or it may come with enough time for you to enjoy a new beginning, a new life. Of all the trauma and distress that I had been experiencing, I was still alive and that counted for much. I had no idea how long I still had to live or how it all would end. I finally had hope even though there was no promise. I was in my power like I had never been before because I knew that this was not all there was to me or to life. It was so much bigger and better than even my few excursions into the other realms. I knew those were just a glimpse of a truly large and magical universe. Right then, looking into that cavern of green was like taking a glimpse into a land of milk and honey, it held much promise and I counted my blessings.

The unexpected garden was contained in a large domed cavern. The largest I had seen so far. It glowed like the previous one, but this old sun was not as tired as the one that shone above the Temple. Unlike the other, this one still had enough energy to care for its charges. And these charges were living. They were plants. Lots of plants. Trees, vines, tall grasses and such were its responsibility. Even though it was all long overgrown, a pattern was still apparent. This had once been a productive orchard of many foreign delights. On the nearby trees I could see apples, or what looked like apples, all hanging quietly and serenely, knowing that they were now there for their pleasure alone. No longer obliged to give of themselves for another's delight… except for now, since I fully intended on indulging!

Around the perimeter were waist tall grasses, clumps of very bushy bushes and viney vines all weaving their way in and out of everything. Between the lanes of trees were more grasses, providing a gentle frame around each one. It all had a soft but vibrant feel. And the smell… ahh the smell. Growing up a midwestern girl, part of my DNA is wired to love moist air, something I had not enjoyed in some time. I stood for a few minutes trying to take it all in and to carefully listen. Even though I was feeling connected to the love and kindness of all, that did not mean that creatures did not exist that felt differently. In this strange universe threats existed so I had to be wise and careful. Down there was not much different from surface life, in that respect. Tinky stood on my backpack, front paws on my head, fully extended and nose high in the air sniffing. With nothing to lose and only an adventure to gain, I took the first step into this new terrain. The ground below softly gave way about an inch or so. I reached down to feel what I suspected. There would be no way for actual rain to come down, so the moisture had to be coming from somewhere. I was willing to bet that this entire cavern was either naturally placed or carefully constructed over a high water-table. The water table was in fact so high that the ground was moist to the touch. The plants would have had an endless source of water regardless of the lack of anyone tending them.

As we approached the first line of trees, Tinky let out a combined wail and scream followed by the teeth chattering that I had observed in our first encounter. Caught totally off guard, I almost jumped right out of my skin. In response to her strange call, the branches of the trees began to come alive, then I not only wanted to jump out of my skin but to leave that skin far behind as I bolted to the safety of somewhere. Tinky was obviously very excited. Her hind end and tail wiggled with anticipation. I didn't sense a threat or warning from her, as I knew how that would end. She would bolt to protect her skin and leave me to my own defense. But this time she stayed right with me, so I kept walking forward until we were under the canopy of the trees. That is when I saw them again. No wonder she reacted as she did. Out from the thicket of leaves poked pointy noses, bright eyes and little white teeth. It was her tribe! I had often wondered what had happened to them. This must have been their home, and they only curiously wandered into the cavern because they heard me coming. It was quite the reunion as I would imagine mine would be if I ever made it back to my tribe. Strangely though, Tinky did not join them. Instead she stayed attached to my back… and head. Clearly there was a specific social greeting going on that I finally began to understand. Lots of cackling and chattering of teeth, striped tails wagging and little feet running about. All I could do was laugh. There was nothing menacing about them, they were perfectly unassumingly adorable.

Timing of the feast was also perfect; the trees were just on the outer edge of harvest. With many of the fruits on the ground starting to rot, there were still plenty left to be plucked and gobbled. Considering I had not eaten in a very long time, going straight to gorging was probably not the best approach. After carefully picking a perfect specimen, I took out my pocketknife to carve a big slice. There was not much choice in the size of a slice considering these fruits were bigger than my entire hand, about three times the normal size of an apple. Not surprising considering the size of mouths they once fed. The skins looked almost translucent with colors that transcended the natural spectrum of reds. Delicious does not give the experience justice. The taste was phenomenal. Like a combination of apples, peaches and strawberries all rolled into one. It was like the fruit we know but put on steroids to enhance size, taste, smell, all the necessary phenols for delight. Tinky eagerly extended a paw my way so she too could partake. I had yet to find anything she did not like to eat but we did not have much to go on yet. I took note that my pack could easily handle a few specimens for the journey ahead. Not that I needed food at this point, it was more for the sheer enjoyment of their exquisite taste.

We kept moseying along, taking our time and enjoying the feast. The space between the trees was wide enough for the waist high grasses to grow and to make passage easy. Occasionally there were large clumps of bushes fully loaded with giant berries but since I could not identify them with any certainty, I decided not to push my luck. Our companions were scuttling from tree to tree, playing and romping all the while keeping a watchful eye on us. Everything seemed to be going smoothly. Finally, I was in an environment that I understood. I felt carefree and happy. Like when I was with Daniel exploring new lands. He had it all under control, all I had to do was to relax and enjoy the surroundings. Of course, up until that fateful day in the canyon. It seemed like a long time ago at that point in time. But it didn't take long for things to shift sideways, once again.

Suddenly, as if on cue, all the frenzy of fun stopped in the exact same moment. Tinky's pals all disappeared. *Where did they go? Why did they go?* Not a good sign. From somewhere behind us, from many places behind us, came rustling noises through the grass. A rustling that only large things can make. Whatever they were, they were coming and I did not feel like standing around waiting to see what emerged. Tinky's kindhearted friends did not want any part of them, I assumed I would not either. She held on tightly to my shoulder with claws piercing in a tight grip as I took off sprinting. The noise was getting closer and closer, so I ran faster and faster.

Growing up one of my favorite movies had an aerial scene where you saw the main characters running through fields as the stalks behind them bent down from the deadly creatures in hot pursuit. If memory serves me correctly, they were the illustrious raptors brought back from a time long lost. Maybe from a time such as this. In the film you could see the end of the field fast approaching but the creatures were closing in on the characters even faster. *Would they make it out in time, would they escape, would they be overcome at the last minute? Would I?!!* The tension mounted on film and in my reality... I didn't know if these things would stop at the end of the field or if they would charge out into the open and gobble us up right then and there. The hope that whatever shared living quarters with Tinky's tribe would be vegetarians was not something I was willing to bank on. Nor were my new Zen abilities to redirect or calm savage beasts something I wanted to test. Nope. I ran like a crazy woman as though our lives depended on it – and they very well could have.

As we approached the end of the tree line something very unexpected happened. Tinky's buddies had not vanished at all.

Instead they must have been waiting to spring their plan at exactly the right moment. They had all congregated on the perimeter trees and began shaking the branches and making a ton of crazy noises. I did not stop nor turn around to see what was happening, I just kept running with lungs ready to burst. We made it past the trees, but I did not stop. We made it to the edge of the dirt, but I kept running. Right up to the large pile of rocks along the wall, which I quickly ascended. It was only at the top that I stopped and gathered the nerve to turn around.

Whatever had been chasing us was gone. Gone and with no sign as to what they were. My mind could certainly find something terrifying to latch on to, but I was too winded to even imagine. Within minutes, the grasses started to gently rustle as the posse of our little friends came forth. My heroes! I would have loved to have gone down and hugged each and every one of them but alas, they were wild creatures and just because Tinky had taken to me, I was not sure that a close encounter was the best for any of us. Like at the foot of the Temple stairs, they gathered around, looking up with teeth chattering. It was more than a simple greeting, it seemed like a way of paying tribute. I finally understood. This was a cross species recognition of friendship and deference.

Looking down at my flock, I raised my staff high in the air. From the tips of my toes, up through my spine, gathering energy as it came out through my vocal cords was a primal scream of triumph and power. Tinky followed and then her whole tribe burst into a uniform cry of acknowledgement. It was at that very moment that I knew that I was finally the hero in my own movie.

Exodus

While I was ready to move on, I was not sure Tinky was ready. There was another tunnel directly to our left but as I turned away from her pack to leave, she quickly spun around to face them. Her little claws dug in tighter as if a part of her was saying *'No don't go!'* and another part was saying *'Let's go!'* She was deciding whether to jump down and run to join her kind or stay with me. I certainly hoped she would choose me but if she did not, I would understand and while sad, I would forever be grateful for the companionship she had blessed me with so far.

Without another reservation, Tinky relaxed her grip and settled back on to her perch, my shoulder. It was only a fleeting thought for her and one I understood very well. Thankfully, she chose to stay with me.

△

Onward we traveled, but not always upward. There were many paths to choose from and I always tried to pick the one that looked like it went uphill. Not many did, unfortunately. I had a sinking feeling that we were traveling deeper and deeper into the earth. Many choices ago I stopped marking the trail where we had come from. It seemed like a silly ritual considering I would never turn around and go back. There was nothing to go back to. Occasionally we would come across various sources of water. They were always pristine, but just in case, I would put my nose in close to see if I could detect any foulness. Once the bladder was filled, I would give it a good swish to make sure the water fully merged with the stones and it would be ready to sustain us. Something about having a part of the Temple moving through me was comforting. The bag of stones stayed around my neck and the necklace remained safely buried under my shirt. The three books were now wrapped in the space blanket after I realized my sweat and the condensation from the water could potentially damage them. I did not want my lack of mindfulness to have an adverse effect on their longevity. After all, they had survived for eons by that point. Having them destroyed was not an option – especially not by my hands. My staff lit the way beautifully. The cape was spectacular. And Tinky was simply my best friend and confidant. These were my traveling companions and for each I was extraordinarily grateful. With every breath and every footstep on solid ground, I appreciated still being alive. I had lasted far longer than I had initially thought possible. But in these circumstances, I never knew when something would go wrong. Bad luck only needs an instant to change a fate forever. It had done that once in a spectacular fashion, I was not going to bet my luck on it not happening again.

△

Being kept in a perpetual state of nighttime is not natural to our kind. Darkness is a game changer. I had no idea what all was changing, but I knew things were shifting in profound ways. Besides my hair growing out and skin looking a bit pale, I figured I still looked pretty much the same. But inside, I could feel things rearranging including my senses heightening. It was probably a similar process to what occurs when someone becomes deaf or loses one of their six senses. The other senses rally in response with greatly intensified abilities that seem to make up for the loss in clever ways.

The first apparent change was a heightened ability to hear. This environment was completely still and quiet. Other than the few close encounters we'd had, there was nothing but Tinky and me. Forget the expression *'It was so quiet you could hear a pin drop.'* Here it was more like, *'It was so quiet I could have heard the slight sucking noise of fingers starting to pull apart <u>before</u> the pin* *dropped. Heck, I could have heard the person thinking about dropping the pin long before they dropped it!* It was nice to know that I hadn't totally lost my sense of humor.

Another sense that most of us do not know we have but was quickly becoming apparent, was extrasensory perception, otherwise known as ESP. Sending my thoughts out like a radar tracking any abnormalities in the field was starting to feel like a real thing. Like how the lizard men were trying to track me down. Surely if I did encounter them or someone, I might just be able to read their minds. That is if they thought like us. Not all two-legged creatures do.

My sight was also changing. The further we progressed, the less I relied on the brightness of the crystal. Eventually just a dim glow from it was plenty to see far distances. Anything more hurt my eyes. My vocal cords got very little usage. I was still on high alert for any danger, so I kept as quiet as possible. Not that I had anyone else but Tinky to talk to, which I did more often than I care to confess, but it was usually in hushed tones. After the lizard men, I was not going to take any chances. You know that biology of ours... *survive at all costs*. I was determined to see this adventure to its very end and hopefully it would last a while longer.

When I felt tired, I would look for a safe place to tuck us in and rest. Often I would have to wait for a long time to find one. Sometimes it was nestled behind a large boulder, sometimes it was in a tiny alcove and other times it was down a small opening leading to nowhere. Typically, I would sit down and lean against the rocks, wrap us up in the cape, beckon the crystal to turn off and then close my eyes all the while hoping that Tinky didn't run off. She never did. Rarely did my rest entail lying down. That position felt too vulnerable at that point. I still had no idea what to expect around any given corner. The first thing I did when I closed my eyes was to be thankful for all I had and then very quickly, since there wasn't a very big list right then, I would drift into a deep meditation and light sleep. I did not always remember where I went or who I spoke to while asleep, but I always awoke refreshed and encouraged to move on.

BURIED

CHAPTER IV

The Claws of Life

At some point in the traverse that never seemed to end, we rounded a corner only to find a deep pit looming right in front of us. To test the theory of bottomlessness, I picked up a large stone and threw it into the abyss. I could hear it clattering its way off the sides but never heard it thunking at the bottom. Bottomless theory tested and proven. There hadn't been any other options or alternative routes for some time so circumventing its edges seemed the best choice. The path was about three feet wide and split to both the right and the left. I chose the left route by no other means than my feet just started moving in that direction. Tinky was on high alert as she always seemed to mirror my state. We were a team and that is what teams do. I picked up on her cues and she on mine.

The path started out wide and easy to maneuver but after some time it narrowed dramatically. The shift was subtle, so I didn't realize the changes for some time. It was not until the path had shrunken to about a foot wide that I started to become nervous. Unfortunately, I had mindlessly been moving for too long so too much terrain had been covered to want to turn back. Even when the ground started sending small rocks down into the crevasse, we kept going. That was probably a mistake.

There was a sharp corner in the wall where the path wrapped blindly around to the other side. I could not see but trusted that a ledge would be there, despite the path almost disappearing at the turning point. With my belly towards the wall, I tried to find a handhold on the other side while keeping a tight grip on my staff in my left hand.

It was rather tricky, but I was not going to let go of my only source of light. Been there, lost that before. I did not feel like repeating that scenario. Slowly and very carefully I slid one foot around the corner. It seemed to land on solid ground, so I shifted all my weight... thankfully. As soon as my weight was counterbalanced on the other side, the entire path crumbled away under my left foot. With lightning fast reactions, Tinky jumped off as I started sliding down. Her cries shattered the silence as she called out for help. I am not sure how it happened, but my right arm was able to keep a firm grip while the other hand clung tightly to the staff. With death on the line, I still didn't want to let go of that prized possession. Even though I was rather light, I was not sure how long my arm could hold on. As my body swung out, I glanced downward to see a vast pockmarked opening in the earth that disappeared into complete darkness. Swinging back towards the wall, I knew I had to make a quick decision. The choice was between holding on to the staff and possibly losing my life or letting go of my only light source and possibly living. Before I could decide, my right foot made the decision for me. It slipped off its ledge in a very unpleasant Déjà vu experience. It reminded me how this whole situation began. My foot slipping off the rock and my hand being ripped from Daniel's grasp forever.

Hanging by just one hand, my other hand did what it needed to do to keep me alive. It let go of the torch. That blink of an eye reaction, not consciously made, sent my staff tumbling into the chasm. With both hands firmly gripping the wall, I peeked through my arm to see the light getting smaller and smaller as it kept falling downwards and downwards and downwards. But then suddenly... it stopped! It stopped as if hanging in midair. Suspended until it slowly started to move upwards towards me! Before I could even react, something latched on to my right wrist. It felt like I was being placed in a shackle or tight-fitting hand cuff. Something cold and hard had a hold and was pulling me up at the same time my light was moving up from the void. Tinky must have quieted down because I could not hear her anymore. All I heard was a light clicking of something solid hitting hard stones. *Click click click*. Up came my light and up I went until suddenly I was held high in the air by some strange thing examining me.

As if in a slow-motion reveal, the first thing I saw as the light came close, was the big oval face of a creature. Please do not laugh at this description or be afraid because I was neither amused or scared. I intrinsically knew that this odd being did not have a malicious intent of any sort. While I could not read its mind, I could sense something rather gentle and kind in its nature. As if drawn right from a cartoon, what held me looked exactly how I would picture an anime ant. As in black ants, red ants, fire ants, the tiny insects that crawl around. Only this one was well over ten feet tall with highly stylized large eyes and rounded features like the much-loved Japanese characters. It stood tall on two legs and had me in the clutches of its upper arms. Quickly the clicking turned into one big explosion of noise that was either the loudest and most intense echo I had ever heard, or a sign that I was about to be overcome by the entire colony.

My benefactor gently set me down on the path so I could stand on solid ground. It was then that another ant man appeared and graciously offered me back my torch. I instinctively bowed my head and did a semi-curtsey to the creature, as if that were a universal language. I do not know why I bowed, it just felt right. They then turned and started walking down the path as if nothing had happened. I on the other hand had a racing heart and shattered nerves to deal with. But not wanting to get left behind, I followed. As they turned their backs to me, I could finally stare and get a good look at their entire bodies without the risk of being rude. I had no idea how sensitive giant ants would be about being stared at. Typical to the species of ants, they had trisected bodies, three distinct bulbous areas with the largest being at the base. Their legs were very long and very delicate looking. They had four arms, two on each side, just as delicate as the legs but a bit shorter. On the ends of the arms were claw-like features, the ones that had grabbed my wrist. Their big round eyes were set on either side of their heads but far enough forward that they could look at you straight on. For mouths they had small pincers like mandibles. On top of their heads were two very active antennae. The rest was a smooth exoskeleton the color of shiny obsidian. These were literally giant ants with unexpectedly human qualities.

The loud noise had in fact been a good part of the colony coming up to greet us. Or so I hoped it was a simple greeting. As we walked down the path, they all found their place in line, adding to the growing procession. I called to Tinky in hopes that she had not run away for good or was too far gone by now and would get lost. Losing her would have been unbearable for my already broken heart. Soon I could see her black and white tail weaving and racing through the long legs, finding her way back to her roost, my shoulder. My big sigh of relief that Tinky was back was immediately followed by immense curiosity as to where they were taking us. Not knowing what else to do, I kept walking with the ant-like creatures, away from the chasm and out into a large tunnel. They continued marching in a single file line that was by now very long. I tried to quiet my mind so that I could tune in to their communication and maybe understand something about them. The only thing I could sense were waves rippling up and down the line, from ant to ant to ant. The ripple contained neither emotion nor visual impressions. They were such foreign life forms that it wasn't surprising I simply could not lock on to anything identifiable in their communications. Nonetheless, I tried to converse by projecting a picture of life on the surface of the Earth. The sun, moon, trees, dirt (maybe they could relate to that!) wind blowing and so forth. I hoped that they could understand that is where I wanted to go. That was where I belonged. That was my home.

After some time, the ant in front of us, I assume the one that grabbed me, but I was not entirely sure since they all looked very much alike, stopped. The rest kept moving in a half circle right around us, without missing a step. To the left was a small tunnel heading upward at a sharp angle. The creature turned to Tinky and me, with its upper arms it pointed in the direction of the opening as if to say, *"This is where you get off."* I took the invite without question and made another deep and hopefully grateful bow before turning away.

Climbing up was not a problem since the sides of the passage had enough texture to hold on to, and it was not steep enough to tumble back if I missed a handhold. I had had enough adrenaline rushes by that point. We scrambled up rather quickly as I was eager to see where it would lead. Tinky must have been excited too for she jumped off my shoulder and raced ahead with her tail held high in the air. At the top she stopped to wait for me. Her body was lit in silhouette by a bright light behind her. I crouched down and quietly crawled to the opening. What I saw would forever change my life. The end of the tunnel opened into another world. Literally.

An Opening

Luckily, I was lying down for if I had been on my feet I would not have remained upright very long. Peering over the edge lay an immense cavern. A large city could have easily fit inside. And in fact, that was exactly what we were staring at, a giant city. Between blinking several times and catching my breath, the magnitude of what lay ahead was beyond staggering. So far, I had seen many things that jostled my senses and upended my world view. But this took the grand prize.

The city was a mixture of futuristic and familiar looking buildings in all different shapes and heights. Some had giant spires, some wound around like they were made of saltwater taffy, others arched up in bubble-like domes. There were too many varieties to adequately describe. Lots of glass, lots of reflective materials and then in contrast, much that looked like it was hewn right from the ground. Despite all the technology, the city appeared like it could have sprung up quite naturally from the beds of this cave. It was a most unusual combination of organic and man-made, with the man-made part paying homage to nature and working with her perfect artistic sensibilities. I was too far away to discern much detail about the life forms that inhabited this magnificent place, but I did see things moving about. There were lots of vehicles flying around. Some were obviously space crafts, but others were hard to distinguish. Close to the ground were lots of tiny dots of colors moving about. It was impossible to tell if they were flying or if they were some sort of automobiles or what. Then suddenly everything went dark.

I woke up in a fetal position on a very softly padded bench. The first instinct that came back was one of protecting what was mine – a real mother bear type of attitude. *Where was my Tinky and my belongings?* I roared inside. With a sigh of relief, I found her curled up at the end of the bed, fast asleep. I had never seen her out like that before. She was either fully exhausted, completely at peace or totally drugged out. I felt rather groggy myself and for no apparent reason. My backpack was at the foot of the bed along with my staff. My cape and clothes were still on my body along with my necklace and pouch of stones. After a deep breath in, I let out a big sigh of relief. I was glad the few items in my new world were still intact, since the old world had been completely lost. That world already seemed like another lifetime ago.

The room I found myself in was circular with walls made from a soft hued malachite. Like all the walls I had been finding, at least the intact ones, they lit the room with a beautiful glow from within. There was a large fountain in the center with gently flowing water. The air was filled with an even softer aroma of jasmine and patchouli.

As I slowly sat up, I noticed a man standing off to the side next to a doorway. At the same time, he noticed I was awake and approached. He politely asked me to take off my clothes and to wash myself in the fountain. He handed me a small jar that I presumed was to be used to cleanse myself, along with a towel and fresh clothing to wear once I was done. There was no greeting or any pretense of an introduction. There was no awkwardness coming from him or any actual words spoken. This was all conveyed through thought. I was rightfully alarmed about a strange man in my head and then having him ask me to take off my clothes! My reaction teetered between being shocked and being appalled. Sensing my feelings, he bowed his head and stepped back to where he had originally been standing. I spoke out loud without considering whether he would understand or not.

"Thank you but I am not going to take my clothes off with you standing there. I am fine the way I am. I just want to talk with someone! Who is in charge?"

It all came out a bit more defiantly than intended, but after all they were the ones who had absconded with our bodies and brought us here without asking. Even though a good cleaning sounded incredible, I was a bit ticked off about the whole idea of being taken somewhere without my permission. Fresh clothes upped the temptation, but I was not about to get that vulnerable. At least not quite yet. The man kept looking straight ahead as if I had not said anything. There was something very elegant about him and quite normal compared to the life forms I had seen so far. His height was on the taller side but nothing of super-human proportions. He wore a long pale green robe with a darker green long vest over the top that were completely in sync with the magnificent walls. There was a golden chain with some sort of medallion hanging from his neck. His hair was a dark brown with golden streaks running throughout, sort of how I remembered mine looking.

Clearly, he was not going anywhere, nor did he seem to care much for looking at me in all my naked glory. In the end, the allure of water pouring over my ragged body was more enticing than hanging on to any vanity. Aside went my indignation and indignity, off went my clothes and in I went. The water was luscious and warm. I let it flow over me for a long time before I decided to try the contents of the jar. It contained a clear jelly-like substance brimming with speckles of light. It felt like thousands of live enzymes swirling on my skin searching out all the dirt and grime, pain and trauma, and breaking it loose. When it was done working its magic, it all washed easily away and only I remained. It was the first time I had had a good look at my body since this strange adventure had begun. As I gazed down, I noticed that I had become quite lean although not malnourished looking in any way. Perhaps a bit on the boney side though. Most surprising was the color of my skin. It had become quite pale, bordering on chalky white. After all, I had gone without sunlight for a considerable length of time. My hair fell in silky wet locks about halfway down my back. I had not realized it was that long as it was a rather tangled mess since this all began.

The clothes I was given were made of fabric that felt like a light silk and linen blend. Like my cloak, it was unlike anything I had ever seen or felt. The pants were a light lilac color and gently wrapped around my hips and tied at the waist. The over tunic was a delicate blue that skimmed my body to perfection. There was a long scarf in lilac with a wonderful pattern in blue embroidery. I felt quite lovely and ethereal. As I finished dressing, the man walked over to my belongings and started to gather them up. Tinky did not move even as I called for him to stop. I was not going to let any of my meager possessions be taken out of my sight. They represented the entirety of my world. Quickly I went over and put my necklace back on, being sure to carefully tuck it inside my tunic while the pouch of stones hung visibly on top. I grabbed my cloak and was about to put the pack on when *she* entered.

There are pivotal times in one's life that revolve around the meeting of someone extraordinary. This was one of them and more. The woman who entered the room was quite frankly the most beautiful person I had ever seen. She stood several inches taller than me with long white hair and porcelain skin that glowed from within like the walls that contained us. It was as though her very essence could hardly be contained inside her body. Her eyes were deep pools of blue that seemed to move and flow with the tides of thought. Her nose was perfectly proportioned to her perfect face. She wore pure white robes and an inner sheath with delicate sparkles woven in. It shimmered outward through the layers like stars might at the end of a clear day. Her hands were clasped in front of her with fingers long and graceful. Around her neck was a beautiful silver chain and a large amulet that matched her eyes.

"Please do not be worried about your possessions. We have no need for them." She said this in a smooth silky voice, inside my head.

When she first walked up, I had caught her looking at what I thought was the pouch around my neck but would find out later that she was looking for something else. She wore an expression I could not quite put my finger on. It was ever so fleeting, but I caught it. So even though she parlayed these kind words, I was not fully sure what was really going on. As if knowing this, she smiled and tossed her head ever so slightly back. *"I give you my word that all your belongings will be safe right here. Including your furry friend. She will sleep for a while and will come back to you when the time is right."*

"My name is Urda. We have been awaiting your arrival."

Urda

Her very presence began to put me at ease, and so I followed her without question. We entered a small simple room. When inside the Earth, simple should never be confused with anything less than extraordinary. The adornments we use to clutter our spaces did not exist there because they did not need to exist there. Below the surface, beauty comes from nature in raw and powerful ways. The walls always set the stage with a specific ambiance according to the type of stone they were made from. In this room they shimmered like moonstone, one of my all-time favorites. The stone of the Goddess. It was like being back in the womb once again. Only this time in the womb of the divine.

Urda invited me to sit down on a beautiful, colorful cushion. Staring eye to eye, especially with someone you do not know very well, is usually an uncomfortable experience, but this was not. I was doing my best to keep my mind in check since I was well aware that she could read it. My thoughts wanted to run wild with questions. So much had happened and most of it was a great mystery. Patience was never my strong suit before, but I was willing to develop a new talent right then and there. I would be patient.

In her hands appeared a cup of hammered gold containing an opalescent liquid that gave off a delicate mist. She held it to her lips and drank before giving it to me. I hesitated slightly as I held the cup. My reservations melted as she gave me a warm reassuring smile. The liquid alternated from warm to cool as it made its way in and through my being. I was sure it was some sort of a psychotropic for instantly my consciousness pushed through the confines of the room, then through the confines of the Earth and onward past its celestial orbit. Dancing in a multicolored universe, I once again felt no bonds to physicality or to a limited identity of self. I was growing to love the freedom of this other dimension as it felt more and more like the real world than did the one my solid body resided in.

Eventually I returned to find Urda calmly holding her gaze at me. In my head she greeted me and said that we were ready. If I were to say to you that I asked her such and such and she answered with such and such, I would be doing the interaction much disservice. Our conversation was not like anything I had ever experienced. Ordinarily we are used to words going back and forth in a linear sequence, one building upon the other. This way of conversing was more like blocks of thought and feelings being exchanged all at one time. My mind would then have to unpack them into a framework that my consciousness could interpret. I do not think she needed that extra step. Since I have no adequate way to convey this sharing of the minds, I will simply share it the best I can using our conventions.

"You have many questions for me and rightfully so. It is not often we have a visitor from the surface."

The first block of questions went something like this, *"How did you know I was coming? And why has all this happened? Who are you? Where is this place? What is this place? I am confused. Are you saying that it is not an accident that I am here? What was that tunnel I was sucked down?"* My thoughts rambled as I am sure my spoken words would have rambled as well.

"We sensed your presence below a long time ago and have been waiting for you to find us. We did send some help though, just in case." My mind wondered what help they sent but before that thought went far, she continued, *"The tunnel that brought you to us was created by the ancient builders, the architects of this planet. They would retreat below at times of great turmoil and climatic changes, as had most civilizations since the beginning of time, except for yours. They were masters of the elements of nature. They created all the initial structures, both inside and out, and resided here for millions of your years. They are the ones that made the hidden openings into the underworlds. There are many more than the one that took you and all are quite different from the others."*

"Above their water supplies, they created openings as a means of infusing the waters below with the waters from above. They are rarely ever seen as they are made to simply replenish their waters with fresh life-giving microbes and nutrients. Typically, they would open in times of flooding and then quickly disappear. The openings were shut down long ago when the ancient builders totally left this planet. For you to see an opening, much less be swept into one, is no mere accident and is very rare. Your harmonics must resonate closely with who they are since they have strict protection around all their creations. Nothing foreign that could be destructive is allowed. Simply put, you were permitted access."

The idea that this was not totally random but rather something special just for me, rewrote my entire victim narrative in one stroke of the pen. *"But why me? There is nothing that special about me."*

"That, dear one, is the question that plagues your kind. I am sure the answer will be fully apparent at the proper time. For now, it might be best to let that rest."

"I can do that," I had already had some practice on that one. *"You are referring to the builders in present tense. Who are they and where*

are they now? I think I was in one of their cities, but it was demolished beyond recognition. Something bad had happened. How could that be if it was protected? Who would have done something like that?" My mind was wide open but that did not mean that I had lost reasoning or critical thinking capacity. More than anything, I wanted to know what was going on. Why me, could wait until later. There would be many layers to understand and it would take some time. For now, we danced around the most obvious.

"They are the master builders and even though they are not here now, they very much are. Their story is long and sacred. One for another day perhaps. They left this planet voluntarily, many moons ago. Well past your reckoning and your history. In more recent times, still long before your awareness, other races infiltrated the caverns within the Earth and fought over their leftovers. I see that you found one of the rarities intact. There are few, if any, left."

It took me a moment as I was not sure which of my treasures she was referring to. Perhaps the stones around my neck, the cape, the Temple... Eventually it was apparent that it was the library she was referring to. Her mind was blending and probing into mine, seeking out the memories of where I had gone. I pulled back in defense when we came to the library part. For some reason I felt very proprietary about the library, like I was charged to protect it. But how could I keep her from finding out, she had far superior abilities. Her gaze grew brighter and more laser like as she continued to explore my mind. Fear started to build and that immediately broke the bond.

In a flash she regained her composure and nodded. *"All is well. I meant no harm. You do not have to share what you do not want to."* She gracefully stood up and said, *"Enough for one day. You deserve much needed rest in a place that I hope you can feel safe. For you are safe here, I assure you. You are my guest."* She bowed and led me back to my room and my Tinky, and my treasures. They were all there even though Tinky was still fast asleep on her watch.

Before Urda departed she asked, *"You have been partaking of the waters and you may not be hungry yet. If that should change, please let us know. We are honored to share some sustenance with you. I am sure you will find it most pleasing and uplifting. For now, rest and we will explore more together upon awakening."*

With that she floated out of the room but not out of my life. We were to spend much time together and, under her guidance, I would never be the same.

The Kingdom

From a deep peaceful sleep, I awoke to find a small bowl of honey colored liquid next to the bed. I hesitated again but sleep had eased the tensions of resistance and so I partook. It tasted just as it looked, like liquid honey. Surely this must be the nectar of the gods. It was refreshing and mind clearing. Just then two lovely women entered the room. Clearly of the same ilk as Urda, only with softer, less intense energy. In their arms lay my clothes for the day, towels and various jars. They walked to the fountain, slid off their garments and beckoned for me to follow them into the water. I did.

A long-lost ritual in modern life is being cleansed and cared for by other women. It felt perfectly natural to participate in this act of love. In our world it would be judged with tawdry minds. In their world it represented pure kindness and unapologetic service. Afterwards one gently dried my body before anointing it with oils of sweet orange and frankincense while the other combed my hair and pulled it back into a soft bun. The finishing touch was a simple grey floor length tunic that was covered with delicately embroidered vines and leaves. Their loving touch traveled deep within my being, smoothing the rough corners cut by life. I provided them a perfect opportunity to give and they provided me an equally perfect opportunity to receive. In that moment I knew that both were equal in value and that one could not exist without the other.

Tinky stood up, arched her back, let out a sweet little mew and promptly curled right back up. It was weird that all she wanted to do was to sleep but she seemed unbothered by it all, so I let any worry go. On that day I decided to wear my cape. Maybe it was a slight vestige from the night before, feeling the need for an extra layer, an extra buffer to help me adjust to my new surroundings. Or maybe I just wanted to have something of my own on. The pouch of stones hung in its usual place, on top of my clothes and in front of the strange geometric shaped necklace that lay hidden underneath.

A different man came into the room, looked me over and gave me the slightest of smiles, almost a laugh. Maybe I was not quite as put together looking as I thought. He was also very kind and similar looking to Urda with long white hair and elegant features. He guided me into a different chamber. Another round room but with walls of matte metallic grey. Not dull and lifeless or bright and shiny by any means, these were more like a soft burnished pyrite. The room was otherworldly calm, like the energy was simply absorbed by the walls and cleared before returning to the air.

Urda appeared looking as spectacular as before. This time she was also robed in subtle tones of grey, lighter shades than what I was wearing and in the same color family as the walls. I had a strange feeling of being accepted and belonging. The day's block of discourse came in smaller chunks and was a bit easier for me to track in consecutive thought. It was probably harder for her to communicate with me because it required much more patience on her part. Her information came in seconds and was infinitely more complex and comprehensive than mine. It took me a while to figure out what she was conveying much less to formulate a response. That took a lot longer to do and required sitting quietly while my mind whirled. Eventually I asked Urda if we could just talk. She graciously nodded and then said the following out loud.

"I trust your rest was regenerative. I have many exciting things to show you today if you are ready. But first there is something I must do. I was remiss at not extending an official greeting from all last night... Welcome E. Welcome to the Kingdom, we are pleased to have you as our guest."

I did not remember telling her my name and certainly not my special name, but she could read my mind after all. I bowed in return and she followed in kind. *"I appreciate the warm and generous welcome. I am honored to come into your world. And thank you for helping me. I am sorry that my mind is struggling to keep up with your form of communication."*

"Do not worry. This is all very new for you. In time it will become easier to communicate in our manner. For now, I do not mind simple speak." She gave a genuine smile that reassured me that she understood and was telling the truth. She was not being condescending in the slightest. Had I known how to fully read minds it would have been confirmed instantly.

Urda turned and with a sweep of her hand the walls became transparent, like giant windows revealing their world in unvarnished Kodachrome, except that it was not a reel of film, rather it was their world in all its colorful reality.

◆

The Kingdom was magnificent beyond measure. My initial glimpse did not hold a candle to what I could then see. We were still high above the city, so precise details were not totally discernable yet. Mostly what I saw was stunning architecture that defied a sense of gravity but always in perfect balance. Nothing seemed impossible. There were buildings that towered up into giant spires while others were the inverse, they rested on fine points. Others twirled around like ribbons fluttering in the hands of nimble dancers and some looked like billowing mounds of living clouds. And the green, there were more shades of green than I knew existed. The plant life was abundant and combined seamlessly with the buildings. Massive aerial walkways connected various structures and wound around giant trees while an assortment of vehicles scurried through the air. A river was the finishing touch as it meandered lazily throughout the city. Still odd were all the tiny colored spots moving around close to the ground.

Reading my mind, Urda responded with a delightful laugh, *"Those are the means of individual transport, of course when one has more things to carry than just their bodies, they use carpets."*

She made it sound so logical and like people could just fly around at will, and on carpets. Flying carpets. Seriously!

She responded to my thought, *"Yes they can. It is quite elementary. Even children can do it. But let us not get too far ahead of ourselves. Please come and sit with me. You look lovely today. I hope you enjoyed your wakeup visit. Morning brings one of my most favorite rituals of the day. And I see you have on a very special cloak, how perfect. You might need it today!"*

Always cordial, she continued, *"I would love to hear the story on how you received it."*

I could not help but think that she already knew, but I complied as a good guest should. I had missed having someone to talk with, someone to tell my story to. After all it was quite the story, even if it was still just beginning.

"It wasn't exactly given to me, rather I found it in the city I told you about. The one that had been devastated. There was one building still intact but well hidden. I think it was a Temple of some sort. In one of the rooms there was a carved box. Inside was the cape and this bag of stones." Carefully I touched my chest where the stones hung, strategically not including the other one around my neck. For some reason that one felt too personal to share. Like everything though, I felt like she already knew about them all.

"Was the box sealed?" Not the response I was expecting.

"It had a lid and when I went to stand on it, it moved ever so slightly. I had to work hard to get it to slide open. Inside I found these."

"My dear one, those boxes are sacred, and they are sealed save for the initiate who knows the secret. Do you wonder why these were left behind when the Temple had been carefully cleared?" She was not at all taken back by my story nor did she ask me for all the other details, and there were quite a few. Instead she seemed to know exactly where I was and what had happened. *"The Masters would always leave behind various signs and treasures in hopes that someday someone special would come and find them."*

"I did not do anything special. Trust me. I did nothing special. I am not special in any way. I am just a girl who was unlucky and then had some luck. A little bit, I guess." That did not ring particularly true at this point. I was feeling special, but the old habit of self-deprecation was still intact.

"You are funny and stubborn, and that is an old narrative. One that does not suit you anymore. Come let us move beyond that." I understood exactly what she meant even though it was a bit hard to hear coming from another. *"Nothing is just there to be stumbled upon, not in the Sacred Abodes. They present themselves to you.*

They choose you. Just like your access into the Temple. It was not by accident. You will understand more, eventually. Do you have any idea what your beautiful cloak is?"

I was touched by the acknowledgement that maybe there was a reason behind all of this and that maybe there was something special about me. And of course, I had no idea what my cloak was, beyond just super cool!

"It's called a cloak of 'confusion' for lack of better terminology in your language. But even more importantly, it serves as a reminder."

"Confusion, a reminder? I am sorry, but I am really confused. Ha, it must work!" I laughed at my own joke and Urda let a small smile pass her lips as I went on, *"How can a cloak be a reminder? I know nothing of its history to remember."* I genuinely had no idea what she was inferring.

"As for confusion, maybe you have had a glimpse of that already?" It was a purely rhetorical question. *"Your cloak has the ability to change its molecular structure, to come 'unglued' as your kind would say, and then to reunite to give the illusion of a different form. All to confuse the outward senses. In harmony with the person wearing it, it can be willed into anything, such as blending with one's surroundings for protection."* Now I was certain that she knew what happened with the lizard men.

"Of course, the one wearing it must be careful to keep their mental vibration perfectly aligned to fully blend otherwise to a more advanced being, you would stick out like the proverbial sore thumb. Did I get that one right?" We both laughed. I was relieved that I didn't have to relive that memory and Urda chuckled because she made a joke.

"One day, given the right set of circumstances, you will understand its

true purpose, that of a reminder." With that the conversation of my cloak was over. And she was right, one day I would understand why it was a reminder.

Counterbalance

I really didn't care to talk about me anymore, I wanted to learn about the Kingdom and its inhabitants.

"Who are you and how long have you been here? This place is breathtaking! I would never have imagined that something like this exists in the earth. We are never taught that anyone lives underground. Does anyone else know?" I was too excited to wait for any one answer. Maybe they were on to something with their method of communicating in blocks of thought.

"We are like you in many ways but have been around for much longer. Like so many before and after us, we were looking for refuge and found it in the inner realms."

"Are there more cities hidden in the earth?" I asked, considering that if the Kingdom were possible, anything could be.

"There are many things 'hidden' in the earth, you have discovered a few of them on your own. Haven't you?"

A bit sheepishly, I nodded my head.

"Our Kingdom serves a very important role for your people. Without us, you would have long ago been gone from the face of the earth, and probably not relocated down here or elsewhere for that matter. Most likely you would have utterly destroyed yourselves by now. Our role is to provide a counterpoint. We hold you in energetic balance." My

quizzical look alone must have told her that more explanation was needed.

"Your world is focused on fear and bent on destruction of that which is not understood. And you understand so very little. If it is foreign, it must be bad. If it is bad it is out to get you and it must be destroyed. That is your first and only response, destroy. And so, it goes on and on. You seem to be bent on repeating the same sad history over and over again, even though it continually proves that it does not work. Hate never works, war never works, division never works. Those lessons from history are somehow overlooked. But alas it is not entirely your fault, it has been wired into your genetics and sold to you as a bill of goods for hundreds of years now."

"It is in the vibrational realms that we work. Those are the realms of real creation. Adjustments made there change the flow of what comes into the physical dimensions. There is not a moment in time that we are not actively seeking to balance that which you set in motion. Call it a different view, call it inspiration, we make that available to those who are ready to hear. This is all done without violating the Prime Directive of Free Will."

"How would that not be a violation of free will?" I really didn't know much about free will except for my prime directive - *I will do what I want!*

She went on, *"In the Universe all things are acceptable. This is an observable truth. But that does not mean that all things are taking a generative route back to communion with our Creator. The Creator of All is the God of Love, Light and Truth, in the process of growing and expanding and rediscovering itself. Sometimes civilizations, just like people, entertain strange bedfellows before deciding who they want to wed. So to speak."* She gave me a knowing wink, *"Sometimes it takes some pain for a world to wake up. Sometimes it does not happen and the civilization must be started all over again. For a civilization to destroy itself is a loss on a tragic scale. Sometimes that start cannot happen again for a very long time. Sometimes the cycle is not right for another million years."*

As Urda shared these revolutionary thoughts, I did my best to follow along. It was difficult at that point.

"Please do not worry, I will explain in more detail very soon." Urda reassured me. *"For now, just let my words sink in. Do not try to figure it all out. It will come in due time."* She then continued right where she had left off.

"Ultimately each person decides what they want, they make choices and they receive consequences. Forcing one to take a certain route is not acceptable and not allowed. Unfortunately, the aggregate of the decisions made by all creates the trajectory along which your countries and your world will move. However, decisions can be changed through outer or, in our case, inner influences. There is nothing wrong with inspiration. Unbeknownst to most, you are heavily influenced at all times, in all ways. If the veil were to be lifted right now as to what is really going on, people would lose their minds, quite literally."

"The problem we are faced with now is dire. Our time is almost up. As a civilization we have evolved to a point where it is our time to transition to another level of existence that is off this planet. Our time in the third density is closing rapidly. We are doing all that we can until the last possible moment, in hopes that your kind will finally wake up and see. When our time has come, we will have no choice but to go. We are running out of subtleties. The gentle coaxing has not gotten the necessary results. I am afraid that more extreme measures will need to be taken if our work isn't effective. Mother Nature will have to deliver in quite spectacular and most likely painful ways. Much will be lost."

"Like you, for instance. Why do you think you are on this journey through earth? You like to think you are a poor victim, but you are

not. None of you are. That is another problem with your kind. Constant victimhood to avoid the responsibility for your actions."

The courting was clearly over. Urda was not going to be a motherly type figure. This woman was in the fullness of her power, the likes of which I had never seen. She spoke her truth, period. There was no messing around with that or with her. Catering to any delicate sensibilities in me was not going to happen. In a way it was most refreshing and nothing like my experience with my mother, or any other woman in my life for that matter. Luckily, I have always had a penchant for the truth, even if it was hard to take. And luckily, I was not looking for a motherly figure. I was looking for the truth and would take it any way it came. I had gone through death's door several times to arrive right there, right where I was standing. I was not going to let any bit of the opportunity slip by.

"Tell me more Urda, please. I want to know." No truer words had ever come from my lips. I was desperate to understand, even if it was hard to hear. I had to know. Earth was my home, and even though I never really related well to my fellow inhabitants, I did not want to see it or them laid to waste. *"What can I do? Can I do anything? Can I make a difference?"*

"It is time for me to show you more of our world. You are going to have to wake up to what is really going on with your people if you are going to do anything about it. Are you ready?"

⇔

There was no direct sense of the room moving or stopping but my suspicion was that we were in a craft of some sort. The walls had slowly returned to their original opaqueness while we were talking. As we finished our conversation, they cleared again to reveal that we were in the center of a large atrium. It was like being in a glass elevator, seeing everything as we gently floated downward. Floors spun off the center column, like spokes on a wheel. Each level held hundreds of floating white chairs that looked like open pods. In every pod sat a person, also dressed in white, with some sort of contraption on their heads. It covered their eyes and ears as they sat crossed-legged and slightly reclined. They looked to be in a deep meditative state.

Reading my mind, she said, *"You are correct. Each person is in the deepest meditation state possible, without being asleep. They are in what you would call the theta realm. They are connecting vibrationally with your world, typically with individuals or groups, but only if the group is in unison. Some of your organizations, religious establishments and such, have members who are on the same page, so to speak. It does not matter what their belief pattern is, just that it is based in love and harmony and open to receive."*

"The process is simple for us. We never look for dissonances or darkness, there is far too much of that and it never leads to the upliftment or enlightenment of anyone. Instead we look for points of light and seek to help those people grow. Just like the analogy of opening a door so light can naturally move into the darkness. There is no point in trying to inspire the dark to change into light. It just cannot happen. The minute you give the dark attention, it gets bigger. We simply focus on what is real, the positive. This is done by enhancing and inspiring the light so that it outweighs the dark."

"Every member of our society partakes in this service. We each have an allotted time to sit and connect. This act of service is our solemn honor and highest calling. For every victory we all celebrate. Helping just one person to move into their divine consciousness makes it all worthwhile. Of course, we are aiming at a threshold amount to tip the scales but that does not mean that each life saved isn't of tremendous value. We know exactly what we are doing, we have done this for thousands of years without ever missing a second

in time."

"Do you ever make appearances on the surface? Like talking directly to people?" I asked.

"We have, but not that often anymore. We have found that this can create more problems than intended. When, and if we do, we tell them that we are aliens from some distant planet. They understand that. It is not as threatening as saying we are right under their feet. The challenge is that people then overlay the many UFO and alien misconceptions on us, but they tend to be less complicated than if they had to contend with the full truth. The last thing we want to do is to hinder a soul in the waking up process. Knowing how much Truth a person or society can handle must be carefully gauged. You get only one good shot. If there is a misfire, the gateways in consciousness can quickly close with overlaid concepts. It may take another generation or another era to open them again and sometimes, sadly, they never reopen. We then must find an entirely different route. It is a tricky matter and happens more often than we would wish. We also need to protect our home. Telling people directly about us rarely, if ever, happens."

"Protect the Kingdom from what?" I wondered.

"It is more from whom. We have enemies in the inner realms that try to create problems, but it is mostly from your secret military factions that the biggest threats come. They have been covertly waging war on the interior for some time. Not just with us, but with many of the other civilizations. Unfortunately, they have help from some of the more unsavory denizens of inner Earth. The last thing any of them want is to lose power. Power is their god. The power they are stealing from others. If people understood the truth of what is going on, it would all be over. The overriding goodness of the Universe has more power than they could ever accumulate or hold. The belief that power could be seized and used for their selfish ends is but a dream – a rather nightmarish one at that. They have forgotten that we are all

connected and in forgetting they try to make others forget so that they too can enter into that nightmare. It is most unfortunate, but that is why most of our service is done in secret. I get ahead of myself. I apologize. There will be more on that later. For now, we have covered enough."

I was feeling quite drained. This was a lot of new information to take in at one time, so I did not resist Urda calling it a day. On the way back my mind shut down and I went delightfully blank. Quickly we were back at the place I knew, wherever that was. I was escorted to my room to join Tinky and my belongings. They were all there, waiting for me. Tinky was still fast asleep so I decided to curl up and join her in dreamland. I am not sure if it was a whole night or just a cat nap, so to speak. When I finally awoke the room was in its night mode of soft darkness. I was filled with a sense of deep gratitude for where I was and what I was experiencing. My life was no longer the story of being lost and forgotten. I was waking up into a reality of such magnitude that it was quite frankly beyond my imagination. I never could have made any of this up, like being welcomed into a magical hidden land. Appreciation and gratitude filled my being to a level I had never known possible. At that moment I noticed the hammered gold cup on the side of my bed. My evening elixir had been carefully placed and awaiting my attention. I drank without reservation and then slid into a deliciously altered state.

⇔

There are many stories of paradise found and paradise lost. Shangri La, the Garden of Eden, Atlantis, Lemuria, Agartha, Shambala, the list goes on. We chalk them up to myth created by simple societies or allegories created by poets, but I can tell you with certainty, they can be real. Some have existed and some still do. I am sure of that because I have seen one such place with my own two eyes. While I would love to share all the amazing things I witnessed in the Kingdom, I am sorry to say that I will be leaving much out, for now. How I spent my days, what I saw, was for my eyes alone. Putting the details on paper as part of a story would never do it justice and my story deserves justice. Timing is everything. It is not that time, not just yet. What I can say is that this is a place where the fundamentals of beingness are the foundation. Everyone from a young age is taught the 'mysteries' of life – who they are, why they are here and how to be. The very things that we do not teach our children. One must dig deep to uncover these mysteries in our world or they have to let go in blind faith that someone else will handle it for them – namely a religious leader or guru of some sort. We have by and large lost the compulsion to seek out the mysteries of life, to discover the Truth for ourselves. To boldly go where few men have gone before.

I came to learn that in the Kingdom love prevails as the number one directive. No one has forgotten that we are all part of the One Creation. That what we do to another we do to ourselves. They are in service to their true selves and they know who that self really is. They love and honor themselves as sacred beings that are greatly cherished. This sets the platform to be able to truly love and cherish others. There is no strife or striving. Everyone is fed, everyone is clothed, and everyone is educated. Their lives are not monotonous or similar in any way whatsoever. Just like us on the surface, not all people want the same things nor do they all have the same drive or talents. Everyone has something to contribute and is appreciated for their intrinsic value and contribution to the whole. There is a hierarchy of sorts, more like a structure, but nothing or no one lords anything over another. Everyone is governed from within so that the law does not have to be enforced from outside. There are some who love to garden, some who love to sew, some who love to teach, to heal, to build and some just love to dream. There is a place for everyone because everyone is a part of the whole. Nothing is monochromatic or boring. It is more vibrant and dynamic than anything I could have imagined. Our societies pale in comparison. If I ever got back to our world, this would be my singular focus - creating a harmonious community based on the principles I learned from the Kingdom – based on the Truth. Maybe we can get it to work for us.

Fundamentals

This is probably a good time to interject a bit about telepathy. Even though Urda and I did not always use it to communicate, feelings and impressions were always being picked up and integrated with the words that were spoken. The most important thing to realize is that when you are with someone with telepathic capabilities, nothing is hidden. Absolutely nothing. You think it, they hear it. This manner of exchange works very well in the Kingdom because of the level of personal development the society had reached. At their point in time, they no longer had any desire to lie or manipulate much less to cover anything up. It can be most refreshing when you know a person is being straightforward with you, that what you hear is what you get and when you yourself can be totally honest in return. It amazed me to reflect on how much energy I had spent in my past trying to portray myself as this or that instead of just being me. This expenditure of vital energy was totally wasted on play acting and trying to convince others of the reality of my machinations. You can imagine how odd this manner of communicating was at times, how refreshing at other times and how downright scary it could be at still other times. There was no hiding in the Kingdom. There was no hiding anything from Urda.

I came to learn that there were basic principles that made up the foundation of understanding in the Kingdom. In this highly evolved society these are considered the Fundamental Truths. People have been taught them from the very start of their lives. All of what we would call primary education is based on these principles. The higher realms of education move forth from their understanding. Science, art, technology, economics, ecology, astronomy, mathematics and more, have all reached heights that we are unaware of because of this common platform. In our world we are taught a curriculum of stuff, none of which relates to applicable knowledge on how to live your life, such as: who you really are, why you were created, what you are supposed to do with your life and, most importantly, how to get along with others. Much less the biggest question of them all - *Who is God?* The nature of the universe and why things happen the way they do is skipped right over. None of the things that would help make living a whole lot easier and much more enjoyable are ever taught.

During my time with Urda she always stressed that having an open mind and being able to engage in nonjudgmental conversation was of the utmost importance. She said that instead, most people in my world have blinders of fear and shame placed on them from a very young age. They are groomed to obey and to follow along without questioning. I understood exactly what she meant. I had noticed this from a very young age. She said that in order to be free of these influences, one must ask questions from outside the box and then be willing and able to hear the new answers. Especially if the 'new' ideas vary significantly from the 'old' understanding. From her vantage point, we are told a mixture of truths, half-truths and downright lies about who we are and who God is. Maybe I should say from her 'advantage' point instead, for she and the Kingdom as a whole, had a definite advantage over us, by a long shot! It was a civilization that had evolved well beyond where we currently exist. It was obvious to me that they were doing something very right, sometimes painfully obvious to see. They lived in harmony with each other and nature. There were no wars. They had technology that far exceeded ours and they could do things with their bodies and minds that we don't think is even possible. Even though I was seeing these apparently miraculous things on a daily basis, I was still finding resistance welling up inside.

There was in fact a war going on where one part of me wanted to fly free and embrace the seemingly impossible while another was clinging hard to the old ways of thinking. Ways such as: *Who do you think you are to deserve to feel this good? Do you really think you could fit in here? There is something special and different about them but not about you. Their God is not your God. You don't belong. Who are you trying to kid?* I was used to having a war of worthiness waging inside but the part of me that had been winning the hard battles while inside the earth, had now grown much stronger. It became much easier to stake another claim into the ground of my being during those challenges. *ENOUGH!* I would need to say. *I am worthy of happiness!* I would need to declare. And then I could move on with my learning. And then I would be able to hear more with an open mind.

Urda understood what was going on within me. She knew I still fought private battles. Yet, I always felt her great compassion like an alchemical elixir of love that traveled deep and wide, healing and transforming everything in its path. From the base metals of surviving into the gold of thriving, my life was transforming. I often thought that her magic did not stop with me. That whatever was going on was much bigger than just my life or contained just within me. From her level of understanding it was easy to see that most people feel they are not worthy of an intimate relationship with God or with the Truth. We are told that we must rely on others to intercede for us. And that it is all an unknowable mystery. To take off the blinders and be open to learning takes real courage. While indictments about my world were often hard to hear, Urda was very adamant that I understood the differences between our worlds. She said one day I would uncover the truth of how we got to be so far off course but for now I had to be satisfied with knowing that we are being fed many falsehoods by various groups for various reasons, none of which are with our highest and best interests in mind. That what is going on is not random or the result of natural progression. Probably the hardest thing of all to hear was her assessment that we are devolving instead of evolving. And that my reeducation would need to start with the basics and work its way upwards. I was already quite aware of that need. Unfortunately, and fortunately.

One casual afternoon I finally broached the subject with her. I finally felt strong enough to hear the answer. Once out in the open, my question lifted a million bricks off my heart and allowed it to feel ridiculously light.

"Urda, why is it so hard to change? I feel an intense resistance welling up inside of me that does not want to change, even when that is what I so desperately want to happen. I look around at your society and want to be a part of it. To really understand and to be able to be at peace. What is wrong with me?" My long overdue question finally came out into the open.

"Resistance is typically in place to protect areas of awareness that are closed off because one is afraid. At the root of all the dysfunction and separation is simply fear. Fear is what you are facing, and fear is what everyone has to get past." She easily answered as if this truth should have been self-evident to all. And without question, self-evident to me.

"But what am I, are we, so afraid of?" I knew my fears but was

afraid to say them to another, even when I knew that other did not judge me. Maybe I just didn't want to hear them spoken out loud.

"The fear you are asking about is the fundamental error, the base lie, that you are fed right from the start of life. It is simply that something is wrong with you. The original sin doctrine that states you are fundamentally flawed and because of that you are unworthy of a relationship with your creator. With God." Urda sure knew how to cut to the point. She went on.

"Flawed and unworthy yet desperately craving a relationship with God, you fall prey to those who are motivated by lesser impulses to intercede on your behalf. Once they intercede, the power is theirs and they will never voluntarily give it up. It is quite simple. You are now one step removed from your Creator. The lie always includes lots of rules and regulations, concepts and beliefs. And it doesn't stop with that one layer. More and more lies are easily compounded on top of the fundamental lie. All they really do is cover up reality for a time. That is how things get so complicated and you become compromised, distorted and controlled." She chuckled softly but I was too far lost in thought to pick it up. Never was her lightness about serious topics disrespectful.

⇌

Still, in spite of her light delivery and delivery of light, Urda would often have to assure me that while things would need to change within me, nothing was fundamentally wrong with me nor would I ever be punished by a vengeful God. Instead, I was a valued part of creation, to be honored and cherished throughout eternity. Knowing that did not necessarily make it easier to hear certain things. Still I remained open and willing, and above all, I was utterly curious! Those qualities worked very well for me. The Truth only needs a small opening, a tiny crack for the light to start shining in. From there it can begin to work its magic. And magic is exactly what it works. One miracle after another, if given the smallest of chances.

Some of her lessons were not hard to hear at all, in fact they were quite delightful. Like how the Kingdom approaches religion. Quite simply, there are no religions because none are needed. The Kingdom's understanding of God is a humble perspective, one that everyone is worthy of knowing. In no way does any individual or group of individuals claim to know everything about the Creator. In fact, it is an absolute that the Creator of All is not knowable in Its fullness by any single person or group. Yet it is in the seeking to understand and the meeting of others with another perspective, sometimes entirely different from yours, that creates an ever-growing understanding of the nature of reality – the nature of God. Just like in our world, there are differences of perspectives in the Kingdom. But unlike us, those differences are not at odds with each other. That is what makes it so dynamic and quite frankly, enjoyable. No matter if you venture out into the unknown or go within to explore new horizons, your job is to come back to report to others what you have found. This one thing is encouraged above all else. Through different perspectives everyone grows and learns more about the Creator and, at the same time, learns more about who they are as individuals. Instead of holding on to self-limiting belief systems that claim to know it all or clinging to others to lead the way on their behalf, each being's journey is one of mutual exploration and collaboration for the benefit of all. Having said that, Urda made it very clear that all our religions are sacred unto the Creator. They all contain levels of truth and love. And because of that they are honored. The unreal that is woven within does not defile the sacredness of the real. She cautioned me to tread lightly on other's beliefs. I need not be afraid of those who feel differently. Just like the people in the Kingdom, we too are on our individual journey of discovering God and who we really are. We simply have not yet reached the point of seeing clearly or mutually respecting different perspectives.

"All in good time," she assured me. *"With the help of those brave enough to clear the way."* With a twinkle in her eye the conversation ended.

Ripe Fruit

Some of my most cherished memories while being a guest in the Kingdom were the occasions when Urda brought me to the gardens to help pick fresh fruits and vegetables for our meals. Meals were always deliciously otherworldly tasting, delightfully presented and deceptively simple in preparation. Food was either lightly cooked or eaten raw, and always served with lots of fresh cut herbs and other naturally harvested seasonings. My favorite meal was their spectacular flower salads. If you have never had a salad made entirely of flowers, you have no idea what you are missing. There is no way one could partake in even the tiniest portion and not be filled with pure joy. It is just not possible. Urda often used the times in the garden to teach me more.

One day while we were harvesting some rather familiar and at the same time odd looking fruits, Urda caught me off guard with a surprising question. A very simple one but probably the hardest to answer of all possible questions.

"Who is God?" Urda casually asked without shifting her gaze away from the task at hand, harvesting large bulbous fruit hanging off

strangely scraggly trees.

I almost tripped over an exposed root as I reeled backwards. I was not intending to be melodramatic in my response, it was just that Urda never led with a question much less THE mother of all questions. Quite honestly, I was glad she broached the subject.

"Urda, you caught me off guard with that one! I have been meaning to ask you that very ...." Well silly me, she knew what was on my mind all along. I just had not mustered up the courage to tackle that one openly quite yet. I guess the time was as ripe as these fruits in my hand were. It was fleeting but I did manage to catch one of those sly little smiles sneaking across her lovely lips.

"My question is genuine. Who is God to you? I know you have struggled with this for some time. Would it not be nice to gain some clarity once and for... all?" There was a slight pause before the 'all' so that it would be clear that my understanding God was not just for my sake. Like in the Kingdom, we learn for the sake of everyone.

"I am not sure where to start...?" My thoughts started to trail off into a whirling haze of discomfort as I grappled with trying to come up with a smart explanation. I wanted to show her that I had been learning something.

"My dear, try starting with describing the nature of God. What it is or what it is not. Either way works just fine." She was right. I could do that.

"When I first came down here..." The words started pouring out even though I knew that they were not really needed for her to understand me better. It was more for me to understand myself better. *"I struggled with who God is. I mean... I really struggled. It was painful. All the things I had been taught about God did not work for me. I just couldn't follow a God that was vengeful, nor could I quite fathom a*

God that wasn't present. Nothing was really adding up. But then, in the Temple, I started remembering my childhood and the magical time when I left my body, but I did not know how that fit in with the God from the religions I grew up with. Then I had a series of experiences in the Temple that opened my mind and my heart to something much bigger. Now that I am here, I am sure there is an even bigger story, but I am not sure what that is. The peacefulness and harmony I experience here has been so inspiring that it has shifted my idea of what life can be like. I understand some of the reasons why you are like that but quite frankly I am not sure how it all fits together with God."

"Inspiration is a good thing. In fact, it is a perfect place to start anew." Urda reassured me, *"It is alright not knowing... tell me what you do know."*

"What I now know is that God is completely about love. He loves us, He loves me, He loves all of creation. The stories of an angry God seem so silly in hindsight. More like how you would describe mankind than the Creator!" I found myself struggling more than I thought I would with describing God. But I pushed forward, *"What I know for sure is that God is not vengeful. He is not mean, and He certainly doesn't like to torment and kill people. God is not evil!"* I proclaimed, pretty happy with myself.

That about summed it up in my mind. Truths that were self-evident to anyone with half a brain. God was good and God was not evil. My pride did not last long. Urda burst that bubble rather quickly and nonchalantly.

"You are right and absolutely wrong on all accounts." Still she did not look up. She just kept casually examining fruit to see what was ripe for picking. Clearly, I was one of the ripe ones.

I must have let an audible *'ughhh'* slip out. Not that I needed to in order to be understood.

"Urda, I need some help here. Please explain how I could be wrong about that. Everyone knows God loves good and hates evil....?"

My solid understanding was slipping sideways. Sensing my struggle, Urda calmly turned towards me and handed me one of the fruits she had just picked. The minute it was fully in my hands it burst completely apart. It was so ripe that its skin could no longer contain the liquid interior. I looked down in shock as the orange and pink juice rushed along my forearms. Clumps of seeds stuck to me while others scattered about the ground. I was a complete mess! We both burst out laughing as I stuck my face smack dab in the middle of the squishy chaos that had once been a nicely contained object of oral delight. Looking up at Urda, I licked my lips with self-contentment, as if intending this all along. It was rather funny. I took a big breath. Finally, my inner clown felt at ease enough to come out and play.

"Who created that fruit?" Seemed like a silly question but there was no sarcasm in Urda's voice.

"God did, of course." I knew that could not be undermined.

"Now then, who created the mess that you are holding... or should I say, trying to hold." She said with a smile. *"Is this turn of events a bad thing?"*

"Well Urda, it's just fruit. It is meant to have a short life span and its meant to be eaten. This has nothing to do with God." I knew I was caught in a logic trap but didn't know where she wanted to take me.

"It has everything to do with God. God is the Creator of ALL things. If the fruit did not break apart and scatter its seeds, it would not propagate itself. It would die and that would be the end of that kind

of life." With that she beckoned me to sit down with her in the soft grasses of the orchard.

"The basis of everything is knowing who God is and who God isn't. If it's alright with you, we will start there." And so began the most important lesson I was to learn. The single most important Truth that all others rested on and in. The following is what she told me as I sat there completely captivated by what she described...

"God is the creator of all things. God is ALL things and in ALL things. There is no separation. Everything that exists in the Universe is part of Creation and therefore a part of God. Everything was called into existence by the Creator. It is very important for you to understand that nothing, absolutely nothing, exists outside of the Creator and Its Creation. Good people/bad people, kind acts/evil acts, happy times/sad times, times of victory/times of defeat, vibrant health/sickness - it all exists in God's Creation. There are no mistakes. NONE. There is no saying 'God isn't this' or 'God isn't that' because God is everything. There is no saying 'God isn't here" or 'God isn't there' because God is everywhere. It is just not possible to separate anything out because everything, absolutely everything stems from the Creator. No matter if you like it or not. Whether you can reconcile your life experience or your world view with that or not, it does not change what is true. GOD IS ALL THINGS, and all is allowed for very specific reasons. This means that there are roads that are straight and narrow and lead to abundant life <u>and</u> there are others that can lead one astray and into sadness and disharmony. No matter, all journeys are a part of God and eventually lead back to Oneness."

While it seemed obvious and so simple, I wondered how this one fact, the prime fact, had slipped by our religions. Most declare that

God created everything but then proceed to separate out what they want God to be associated with and attribute the rest to... to something other than God. Without missing a beat, Urda went on to explain why God created the Universe.

"In the beginning, before anything was brought forth into creation, God had a thought. With that one thought God began to create the Universe. The thought was initiated by God's desire to know itself. What came forth was the first question ever asked - "Who am I?"

I sat stunned. Those were the very same words I asked the universe when I was a child, floating high above my body on the banks of the river. She smiled at my inner realization and went on.

"On the quest to discover and riding the currents of Love, God took a breath and began the journey of self-discovery. That one act of Love initiated ALL of creation, ALL of the universes, ALL of the dimensions and ALL the consciousnesses contained therein. The desire of the Creator was to explore Its own beingness. To answer the question "Who Am I?" To learn about itself through Its ever-expanding experiences, on all levels of existence. For there are many levels you do not know about yet. There is simply no end to what was and what is being created."

"In that singular moment, off went the sparks of creation that differentiated into other consciousnesses, other parts of the original God-Head – so to speak. These aspects of the One could be considered as co-creator gods. The co-creator gods were on a mission to continue the quest of the Prime Creator to know itself. In turn they created more dimensions, more galaxies and more sparks. The co-creator gods created the demi-gods and they in turn created more depth and dimension to the ever-expanding universe. Solar systems and more sparks came into being. The magic of Creation, as awareness, danced across the heavens in a multitude of solar bodies and divine beings, differentiating and multiplying out into infinity. All on the same singular mission to know themselves. Each perfect

and each on the same mission of exploring who it is. Who am I? *Is the only real question."*

Urda paused and looked at me. She knew I needed a moment to let this all slip into the freshly created opening in my consciousness. A lot of things would need to be rearranged and many things simply thrown out to create room for this new vantage point. After a few moments she continued.

"God in all of Its perfection, knew that to really understand who It is and for It to grow, all things must be allowed. Its children, all the divine sparks throughout the universes, would be given full range of creative powers and full range of time and space to explore and to learn. This meant that they would need allowances to make mistakes, for errors in thoughts, words and deeds, for self-enlightenment to fully work. Hence the creation of Free Will. It is not that God condones what we would consider the negative or evil works. It is allowed so that we can learn all that is possible to know. God loves everyone so much that all is allowed. The ultimate goal of our Creator is for ALL of Creation to remember who it is and to enjoy what it is capable of doing. And to learn from their mistakes."

Once again, I was stunned by her simple explanation. It made perfect sense. I was open to considering a completely different perspective. In fact, that is what I had yearned for my entire life. She knew that too and so she continued.

"This is the very process of an ever-expanding Universe. First there is oneness and from this unity creation explodes forth. Much like God taking a giant breath in and letting it all out. The one job of the differentiated aspects of the God is to explore who it is and how it fits into the Whole. When all the pieces remember, they reunite with their Creator, with God. This coming back to the Source, this

reuniting, creates a new, wiser more expanded version of the original creation. A new expanded starting point. From there God takes another deep breath and it begins all over again. A new creation that is more expanded and even more magnificent than the one we have. This process will continue through all time and all space and beyond. As some correctly proclaim, God's way is glory unto glory."

Urda continued, *"One of the biggest differences between our civilizations is that the people of the Kingdom lead from the heart on their journey to understand the mind of God. They know the mind of God contains their minds, but the access point is through the heart. The access point is through Love. Love for us is not an empty platitude to be voiced mindlessly in empty repetition. The people of the Kingdom are a living manifestation of Love, of Truth. They live the Truth because they know they are a part of the Truth. They know that as a part of God, we are all encoded with the quest for self-discovery and expansion. We are all imbued with the same desire to discover who we are, what we are and how we are to serve, as a microcosm of the Creator's magnificent journey. They honor every other part of creation as part of the sacred soul of God. They know that each and every one of us is fulfilling God's desire in all that we do. The good and the bad. It is all part of discovery. Having no parameters allows for the maximum potential of growth and understanding. All is acceptable in this game of being and discovery. At some point people evolve to a place that the baser level of lessons is no longer necessary. I sincerely wish that for you and for your people."*

Her words washed over my heart as my mind wondered what my life would have been like had I known these things from the very start. *What would I have done differently? Anything? Would the sting of so-called bad decisions have softened my inner voice of condemnation? Would that have allowed me to pick up the scattered pieces more quickly and move on? Surely, I would have been more gracious with myself and therefore with others' seemingly bad choices. If only I knew we were all part of the One on a journey of remembering and growing. If only I had understood those simple two words that were told me a long time ago...* I AM.

"This is enough for one day, wouldn't you agree?" I gave her a feeble attempt at a smile. She knew my plate was running over, just like that delectable fruit had a short time ago.

◆

After enjoying a simple meal consisting of the day's harvest, I excused myself and headed back to my room for some much-needed quiet time. Tinky was exhausted as well. While we were picking and discussing ripe fruit, she had been a busy little girl frolicking in the garden. I was sure that eventually I could once again frolic open heartedly in the garden with her. Eventually the shock of realizing all the wrongs of our world would wear off. Before I slipped past the Earthly bounds of wakefulness, I wondered if morning would bring any relief from the indigestion I was experiencing. It was not my belly that caused concern, it was my entire being that felt stuffed. There had been a lot to assimilate for one day.

A Lady Never Tells

The next morning, I awoke feeling wonderful. I was filled with a feeling of completeness and peace that I had never experienced before. The weight of the world had been lifted from my shoulders and out of my belly. Before I got out of bed, the two women returned to help me prepare for the day. A warm shower with the caring touch of these sweet beings would start anyone's day off on the right note. It did for me.

When we were done Urda appeared as lovely as always. On that day she was dressed in brilliant shades of cerulean blue that ranged between the azure of a pristine ocean to the dark blue of a mountain sky on a cloudless day. Typically, she adorned herself in white or soft tones. To see her dressed so brilliantly made me think that something special might be happening that day. I tried my best to remain calm, but it was challenging. If the day before had set a standard, this one portended to be quite interesting. Tinky understood and greeted Urda with an exuberant rub against her shins and then quickly jumped on mama's shoulder. We both laughed in acknowledgement to her unwavering loyalty to the one she was given to watch over.

"Where would you like to go today?" Urda generously asked.

I was not expecting it to be my choice and was a bit disappointed that there was not already a big plan in place. Quickly I adjusted my expectation and allowed something to come to mind. There was a tall spire on top of one of the rolling hills that I had always wanted to climb. It was made of beautifully wrought iron and stone. At the top was a lookout platform that I was sure would give us a spectacular view of the city. Urda was pleased with my suggestion and off we headed. Once we got to the tower Tinky quickly disappeared up the stairs. Another sign that she was truly part of the feline persuasion was her love of heights. I am sure this predilection was part of the reason her species was used in the Temple.

"You are right about them." Urda read my thoughts.

I was sure that I would never get over someone inside my head.

"You won't." She replied again and with that we both broke into a carefree stream of laughter.

It would turn out to be quite the funny day as we considered more solemn subjects. Humor is always a great way to ease one's mind open. Urda ascended the stairs with ease and without losing her breath. On the way, she effortlessly asked if there was anything that I would like to discuss that day. I, on the other hand, was quite breathless and had to wait until we reached the top to finally be able to answer.

"Yes, there are a number of things I would like to talk about. Mainly picking up where we left off yesterday. I want to learn more about the principles of the Kingdom that make you so different from us. I really want to understand where my people have gone so far off track."

We settled down next to Tinky who was already fast asleep in the afternoon's warm summer glow. At least it felt like it should be summer. What season it was did not matter to me anymore. Neither did the time of day. I had slowly become untethered from the constructs of the surface's time-governed reality. Urda gave me a moment before realizing that she would need to take the lead. That I really had no clue where to take the conversation.

"The next big challenge for your civilization will be coming to terms with the true nature of time and cycles. Simply put, that time does not really exist and that your life is really part of a grand cycle of lives that you, as an individual entity, are privileged to live."

"You are talking about reincarnation, right?" As she nodded, I continued, *"I can wrap my head around having many lives but time not existing? How is that and how do they fit together?"* This took me right back to when I had the vision about the tapestry of lives and

the conversation with my wise old man.

"It is simple, my dear. First, all of creation happened in one moment and still exists in that one moment. Always has been and forever will be. A way to work with that moment, in the processes of self-discovery, is to wrap it in time. Wrapped in time it can be stretched out to be enjoyed and to learn many important lessons. Through that process the entirety of Creation has a chance to explore their beingness. Because time is an illusion, it is quite flexible. Time can be manipulated quite easily. It's like putty in the hands of one that understands. In the pause between your lives you understand this much better. But in this physical form you do not and for good reasons. Until you reach a higher level of consciousness, its best to leave the processes of sequential time as they are currently set. The fabric of the Universe can get messed up quickly if one doesn't know what they are doing."

"What do you mean they are like 'putty'? What can you do with time – theoretically, of course." I was excited to zoom right into the uncharted grounds of my knowing.

"You can jump around in time. You can jump forward and just as easily as you can jump backwards. And if that is not crazy enough, you can also jump sideways into what is known as probable realities." Urda was clearly enjoying this lesson.

By then my jaw must have been hanging open because Urda let out a little chuckle, *"Are you sure you want to know?"* She lovingly chided me. Not waiting for a verbal response, she went on.

"Let us start with your many lives. In between lifetimes is where you decide what is in your best interest to experience in the next one. Questions are considered like – do you need to go back and relive

an old decade? Would jumping forward be more advantageous? Or, wildly enough, does one need to relive that same life again so that they can make different choices to experience different possibilities. Even more crazy, do you need to simply download another's life and encode those lessons before reincarnating once again. No single life ever goes to waste."

"I have never heard of reliving a life! Can that really happen?" I wondered out loud.

"That possibility mostly comes into play when things go astray but not too far. If the lessons are still within that spirit's range of understanding, they can repeat that life. If things get too far off track, veer too much off course, that spirit might need time to heal and learn in the astral planes before trying again with a fresh start, a new life. Simply put, there are no rules with time. It is there as a tool to further our development."

"Wow. That is refreshing and at the same time sort of terrifying!" I loved having my mind expanded in dramatic ways even if my response was often at odds with itself. *"Living a life over and over again reminds me of Groundhog Day...."*

I never got the rest of that sentence out before Urda burst out laughing. I was completely shocked. I had NEVER heard an unbridled laugh come out of her typically poised self. And she kept right on laughing, clearly at her own private joke.

"Oh, my..." She shook her head as she looked down, lost in thought.

"You know that movie????" I did not think there was anything else left in my mind to blow, but I was clearly mistaken. They knew about our movies, but once again – *no way!*

"Yes, we do follow all your popular culture. It is quite entertaining, but for different reasons than you may think. Your creations are a direct reflection of where you are as a society and where you are headed. That movie just so happens to be one of my all-time favorites. And my darling Bill..." Once again, she trailed off deep in thought.

"YOU KNOW BILL MURRAY?!" I was astounded at that possibility. I knew he had a reputation for showing up in all kinds of strange places, totally unannounced and to the delight of all. Places like random family reunions, weddings, fraternity parties and more. But showing up in the Kingdom - *no way!*

With a devilish twinkling in her eye she said with all seriousness, *"Darling, what happens in the Kingdom, stays in the Kingdom."*

With that we both fell over roaring in uncontrollable laughter. There was so much more about reincarnation and time to consider but it would have to wait for another day, that is if the right day ever came. Clearly the moment for such discussion on this day was past. On the topic of Bill Murray, I knew enough to leave that one alone.

There are some secrets that you just never ask a lady to reveal.

Grace of God

Bright and early the next day, Urda led Tinky and me back to the metallic transport room – for lack of better words to describe it. We enter it and then we end up in another place, hence the transport room. How it happened, I did not know, not even to this day. Regardless, we would go inside and when the walls finally cleared, there we would be. Somewhere else. This time we ended up in front of the most beautiful dome I had ever seen. It was made entirely of small triangular crystalline shapes. The soft light of the dawning day shimmered across the surface as it broke into an infinite number of tiny rainbows. We both stood there for a few moments entranced as the magical spectrum of light washed over us. Even Tinky held perfectly still on my shoulder as its spell captured her too.

Urda bid me to follow her as we began walking towards an underground tunnel. The path was paved with large illuminated tiles. Each glowed with rich shades of plums and teals but as we followed it down into the ground, the colors began changing. Like the spectrum of the rainbow above, the colors of the path progressed accordingly. By the time we arrived at our destination, the tiles under our feet had turned to rich blood reds. In front of us was a large archway with thick double wooden doors that looked like they were enameled in the same blood red as the illuminated tiles. The hardware on the door was ornate shiny black wrought iron. It made for a very impressive entrance, to what, I could barely imagine.

As we stood facing the doors, a strange energy started emanating from Urda. I had never felt her doing this before. Either I was not sensitive enough to perceive it in the past or it was something unique to this special place. Either way, she sent out what must have been a secret energetic command for the doors to open and of course, they obeyed. Slowly they swung inwards to reveal the treasures within. It was readily clear that what we had seen on the surface was just the top of the building, the tip of the iceberg so to speak. Looking inside I could see why it needed to be contained within the earth. This was the very bosom of Mother Earth, the place where she nurtured her precious children.

My first impression was that I had walked straight down into heaven. My own heartfelt version of heaven. For it was at this very same altar that I had worshipped many times before this journey and many times during this journey. The room was filled entirely with Mother Earth's creations – crystals, gemstones and rocks of every sort. I stood absolutely spellbound. It was a few moments before I could take in any more details. When I finally came back to the moment, I noticed that the room was round, and the walls were draped in intricate tapestries that told of ancient stories and adventures. The walls rose almost two stories high and were held in place by the mighty dome. Distracted by the treasures below, I could have easily missed the giant glowing orbs suspended near the top. They seem to float in mid-air and magically glide along preordained paths. It looked like a solar system with a center sun and planets revolving around but as hard as I tried, I could not fit it into what I knew about our planets.

"It is not this solar system. That is our home." That was all she said as she stared upwards. There was a distant longing in her voice that, once again, I knew came from a private place and that it was not for me to ask any more questions. I let her be and began exploring on my own.

The variety of stones was astounding. They came in every shape and size imaginable. From delicate ones that I could balance on the tip of my finger to giant crystal points that literally soared into the upper reaches of the room and then every size in between. There were giant amethyst geodes that were so large you could step inside them. Some even contained small benches where you could sit and meditate. *Imagine that, sitting inside a giant geode and meditating!* There were many other shapes that looked like they would lend themselves to higher pursuits as well. The smaller specimens rested on gorgeously carved wooden tables and glass shelves that seemed to be illuminated from a secret source. It was hard to fathom that some of the formations were made of stone. Like the ones that looked like bowls of jiggly jello cubes or clusters of spiky sea urchins or spun filaments of delicate glass or even piles of squirmy earthworms… the list could go on and on. There were too many varieties to describe in one book. Suffice it to say that Mother Earth works in mysterious ways and has no limit to her imagination nor to her pride in her creations. For they all unabashedly flaunted their beingness. *A lesson we could all learn!*

At some point Urda and I found each other again.

"Urda, thank you so much for bringing me to this very special place. I feel like I am being allowed a glimpse into Heaven." My heart was truly overflowing with gratitude for being right there. Even though I was not sure where 'there' was or why it was. I was there and that was all that mattered.

"I am sorry to have to tell you this, but there is no Heaven." She smiled, clearly enjoying setting me straight, *"At least not in the typical sense that your religions like to promise. They simply leverage an innate longing in people."*

"So why do people so desperately want to believe in a Heaven? It seems for some that is the only way they can make it through their life, knowing that a Heaven waited at the end. The promise of it has played a powerful role in all the civilizations I know about." I was careful to add in that caveat since I was clear that there was much more about our history that I still had to discover.

"The promise of a Heaven has held sway over man because he is lost. He lost the knowledge of who he is. Had he been in touch with his own divinity, he would know that Heaven is truly at hand. Instead it is relegated to some far-off dream and one with a dangerous hook. It is exactly here that people are imprisoned with the fear that somehow, they might not be worthy of such a gift. Even though we have covered this subject in many ways, I want you to be completely clear. Heaven is at hand. Heaven is your divine right. It

is the place you are created to dwell in. Not in some possible future on some far-off plane of existence. Heaven exists on all vibrational levels, in all dimensions and across all of time. You are birthed in Heaven and you die in Heaven and all your in-betweens exist in Heaven. It is there waiting in each and every one of your your moments - in the Eternal Now. Waiting to be recognized and waiting to be claimed."

"Allow me to teach you something about the power of now. Would that be agreeable to you?" Urda asked, acknowledging my right to choose a lesson or not. I had enough time for a quick smile before she began.

Urda walked over to a table and held up a piece of flat wood about a foot long that reminded me of a ruler. Down the center was a perfectly carved groove. Urda proceeded to balance the wood on the tip of a small pyramid made of loadstone, as if it were the easiest thing in the world to do.

"Imagine that this ruler represents time - past, present and future." She said as she pointed from the left to the middle and then to the right. Urda then carefully placed a round marble made of pure lapis lazuli in the center point, right above the tip of the pyramid. A perfect representation since it looked like our beloved planet. Of course, she balanced it perfectly. *"Now imagine that this is you, the marble, balanced perfectly in the present moment. What do you think the moment of now represents in the timeline of things?"*

"It's just the now, it's not the past nor is it the future. It's the only moment that we are truly alive. It's all that there is!" I liked my answer and thought I was getting a firm grasp of things until she asked the next question.

"This is true. The present moment is the only thing that exists. If you extend your thoughts into a future or dwell in a past, you throw the

whole balance off. That is easy to see, right?" Urda said, stating the obvious. Without waiting for a response, she continued, *"So then how do you change your future?"* Even though it felt a bit like a test, I didn't mind taking the risk of being wrong again. But that didn't mean I didn't still take a bit of joy in being right!

Still feeling full of myself, I replied, *"To change your future you simply start changing your present moment. Because that is where you are! Then voila!"* And then voila, my grasp slipped away again.

"Not exactly. What you are experiencing right now is a reflection of all that has been. All your thoughts, dreams and actions have led to the present moment. They are all perfectly represented in the Now. The Now is a testament to the past. It is the place where you can honestly assess yourself. It is not the place to start moving around the pieces of what has been. You may have heard the joke that moving stuff around in your present moment is like rearranging the furniture on the Titanic?"

I wasn't sure it went quite like that, but it was close enough for the point to be made. The expression went by quickly, but it was there. I had caught Urda in a tiny self-satisfied grin. Guess someone else was prone to bouts of being proud of themselves. And it was a pretty funny joke.

Without missing a beat, she went on, *"In order to change the future you need to start creating a new one in the now and that is done in the invisible. Don't get caught up in the reflection of things seen in the now. Use what you see as a springboard to adjust your intentions. Dream your dream, make it as big as possible and then be sure to let go and have the confidence that it will be. Be so confident that it will be, that you can give thanks as if it already is! Remember you are a creator. A chip off the proverbial block…"* another quick self-congratulatory grin.

"Someone is on a roll." I said with the utmost of deference.

"Good lead in, now watch this…" she moved the marble to the right and into the future. With that the balance was thrown off, the marble began to roll, and the ruler began to tip. *"Now this."* She moved it to the left and into the past and it began to tip in the direction. *"You cannot live in either direction, future or past, without creating an imbalance. The larger point here, the point at the tip of the pyramid, is that everything hinges on the point of balance. Or said another way, on being balanced in the now."*

She went on, *"It gets even better. Are you ready for more…?"*

"Yes, of course. You really don't have to ask me. You know I want to know everything!" It was strange to have her ask me this question over and over again on that day.

"But I do need to keep asking. It is not my place to impose anything on you. It is your place to want to know and to agree to the consequences. It is one of the laws of the Universe. You call it Karma."

"How does me being asked whether or not I want to learn something have anything to do with Karma?" As soon as I said that, I knew I was being set up perfectly for another lesson.

"Action and reaction. Nothing can be done in the Universe without causing a reaction." She paused waiting for me to respond and when I did not, she continued. *"Karma can be looked at as the Grace of God freely given to us, a testament of the Creators' Love. It is THE overriding law everywhere. It is there to ensure that someday we all return Home, using the only route that is available. The straight and narrow road of Love. Karma keeps us on track. It is the road sign, the traffic lights, the entire map and more. In every now we can look to see what we have created. Our circumstances will not lie. Make no*

mistake, our life reflects us and our choices. It does not bear witness to anyone or anything else. The reflection is not there for us to feel badly about ourselves, not to feel shame or unworthiness. It is there to help us learn and then to adjust what we are creating."*

While simplicity won the day again, I still had questions.

"But Urda, if the point is to remain balanced, does that mean that we must sit there and Zen out all day and night, so to speak? For to move would certainly throw the whole thing teetering off."

"Enlightenment is not inaction. Rather it's right action for right action's sake. Life is in constant motion and so are you. You don't have to worry about being perfect, at least not yet! What you need to focus on is being honest with yourself about what you are creating. And if it is not right, be thankful and change. While the change is still in thought-form, be thankful like it has already manifested and then it has a path to come into reality."

"That is the simple version." Always in Urda style, she proceeded to pull the curtain back just a bit more each time so that I would not get too comfortable thinking I understood it all or get too overwhelmed with how much I needed to learn. *"Let us use another example to see how Karma works. E, if a man decides to donate meals to the local food bank, would you not say that was a good deed?"*

"Of course, it was." I answered.

"Exactly." She began to turn away before pulling the old Columbo move of turning quickly back around to address me again.

"But what if that food was tainted and a bunch of people at the shelter died? What would happen to his Karma?"

"I guess nothing since he intended well. He did right action for right action's sake but simply got the wrong reaction. I think his Karma

would be ok."

"What if instead, that man did the same thing but did it simply to get much needed publicity for his flailing business and no one dies? Would wrong action creating the right outcome be ok?"

"Quite possibly." I was doing my best to keep tracking Urda, but I had a sinking feeling that that wouldn't last too long.

"What if he did it for self-aggrandizing reasons and they died?" That one seemed like a no brainer. And she kept right on going with another layer.

"What if you knew that in a previous life the woman running the shelter had been running an inn where the man and his family had come to find food and shelter. They had no money, so she cast them out into the cold night where they all perished. In the current life it was reversed in a way. She corrected herself by providing free shelter and got to see firsthand what it would be like to have people in her charge die. Is he not simply helping her to balance her Karma? Would that not be considered a good thing? Does that change anything about his current actions being condemned as good or bad?"

"This is getting rather complicated. I am not sure what to think or how to judge the situation." I got the picture that things are far more complex then what we can see.

"What if one of the destitute people that died of food poisoning in a previous life was a rich landowner who had taken the food from his tenants for taxes and ruthlessly left them to starve. Would you say that that action clearly delivered him Karma? Is that a bad thing or is it now a good thing? Did their motivation matter?" Urda was on a roll and I was sure that she would have just kept on going with an endless stream of examples that further complicated reality. I on the other hand was ready for the point.

"You got me, I do not know how to fairly judge any of those situations."

"Exactly." This time she did walk away and left me standing there to draw my own fine point.

The Choice

The thing I missed the most from my old life was staring up at a starry starry night. I thought of all things to imitate below, the stars in the heavens would be the on top of the list but obviously, to the people who lived there it was not a priority or maybe they visited them by other means. That was quite possible. There was much about them I didn't know. I, however, yearned to see the heavens. They were my steppingstones to the universe, and I longed to share them with Tinky.

Often, I wished that I had a pen and paper to write down everything I was experiencing and learning in the moment it was happening. I did not want to forget anything. Urda reassured me that nothing would be lost. Even though I may not understand some things right then or remember what was told or even be conscious of receiving it, at some later date an event would occur, and the knowledge would be made available. Much of what I was learning would be time-released in the future. She assured me that what I remembered would be perfect and that given the right time and right circumstances, the right stimulus, I would recall more.

One day Urda came to me with a choice. We sat down in my room for what would become the most difficult conversation that I would ever have. Urda straightforwardly announced that it was time for me to decide to stay or to leave.

While I had been shown many things and witnessed many things, I was never allowed to fully integrate with the people. Urda explained that to become a citizen of the Kingdom required one to go through a sacred initiation process. They obviously were extraordinarily careful on who they allowed to enter their domain much less to become one of them. It was a very difficult choice. Everything hung in the balance. Their world was so far beyond anything I had ever experienced or would be able to experience on the surface. This was the first time I truly felt at home. Harmony with others, education on the meaning of life and how we fit into the cosmos, clean food and water, advanced healing techniques and so much more... *who would not want this for themselves?* I wanted this for me. But on the other hand, this was not my home. I was still an Earthling from the surface and that is where my people dwelt. The good, the bad, the inglorious and the noble. If I chose to be initiated, Urda told me that I would be fully committed. The Kingdom would then be my new home, I would never be allowed to return to the surface. I would be too spiritually and psychologically changed to survive there ever again, and it would definitely not work for my new biology. Even a short visit would not work. The link to their world would be too strong within me. I could potentially lead the unsavory powers above right back to them and that would not be good. I would never want that to happen. But the real bonus, if I chose to stay, would be to leave with them when they departed from this planet and be able to travel up in the stars with this physical body. That made it all very tempting. All my dreams could come true – *Tinky and I, space warriors. Amazing!*

I was honored to have a choice and it was a very difficult decision to make.

⇔

Eventually I knew what I had to do. When I finally told Urda, she seemed already prepared, as if she knew all along that I would choose to return to the surface, to go back home. She told me before departure day could arrive, there were things that needed to be done to ensure I was fully ready. Urda said the next phase in my development was the most important part. It would include heightened sensitivity training along with desensitization exercises. That sounded like a paradox, but it was not. Those specific processes would allow me to fully integrate what I had become and ensure I could accomplish what I needed to do next. The first step would be surviving the journey home. It meant having the skills necessary to fulfill my destiny once I made it back, assuming I did. There were no guarantees and if my journey so far had taught me anything, it was that one never knew what would happen next - no matter how enlightened they were. The lands in the depths of the earth, right under our feet, are full of unknowns. Many of which are quite dangerous and do not honor life as the people of the Kingdom did. If my training had anything to do with acquiring similar capacities as these people quite naturally had, I was fully willing. Reading minds, levitating, walking through walls and translocating made bending spoons and remote viewing seem like child's play. Quite literally since these capabilities were nurtured in them as children. Urda said that we all have the same abilities, it is just that they usually lay dormant. Resting until a time that they could be ignited. I had a strange sense that somewhere therein lay my destiny. At least I hoped so.

My ability to read minds had vastly increased since I arrived even though Urda and I continued to use 'simple speak', as she liked to refer to our verbal communication. It was easier for me to understand what she was 'saying' and I could respond more quickly, plus Urda didn't have to sit for long periods of time waiting for me to unravel her messages. Using words took a lot less energy on both our parts. We still used the psychic parlaying of information to enhance our words with deeper feelings and other sensory impressions. By easing the pressure on trying to communicate via telepathy alone, it allowed for me to more slowly develop ways in which to compensate for the things I lacked. The most important thing I learned was how to let my mind relax enough to be able to release many of the tensions that interfere with mind reading, especially the ones caused by trying too hard and then being frustrated with failing! Those adept at advanced meditation will understand. Imagine if being able to sustain a deep relaxed state of mind were your natural state, not just for a short period of time but on a continual basis. *What could a relaxed mind springboard you into? What new doors of awareness were just waiting to be perceived?* I loved pondering these types of things.

Emotional sensitivity was another important skill that was developing. Having always been empathic, I thought my senses in that area were fairly developed. I was wrong. Being able to identify the general emotions of an individual or the basic atmosphere of a room was just the beginning of perception. Moving into more advanced ranges, the emotional overlays in people start to take on a three-dimensional quality. Going even farther you find that emotions quite literally create separate entities. They have a personality, a temperament, depth and color. Our emotions, like our thoughts, create realities. Albeit they are not as fully formed as we are nor do they live in a reality as dense as ours. Nonetheless they do live. Make no mistake about it. We create other worlds through our emotions. Knowing this, I felt a growing sense of accountability for what came forth from my being. That sense of accountability was a reflection of the increased level of responsibility that comes with spiritual maturity. I was finally growing up.

What made me most nervous about the final lessons to come, were the parts centered on how to overcome my fears. Urda stressed that fear is what keeps us all in bondage and until I could be free of mine, I would not truly be free. And to be able to help others, I would need to be free. Even though I had experienced some serious wins in this area under Urda's tutelage, desensitizing myself to my fears was still a scary thought.

CHAPTER V

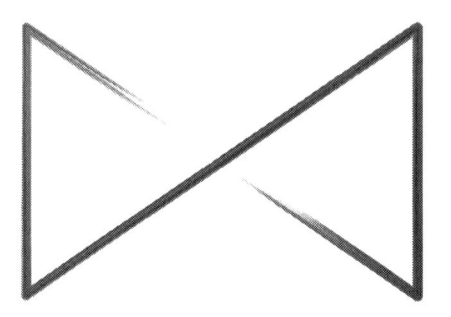

The Three Visions

The first night after I made my decision to leave, Urda returned to my room with her golden bowl in hand. I hoped it would be more of the sweet nectar that initiated my time there, but it was not. This mixture looked like the sienna of raw earth, tasted like the sourness of a land long forgotten and was as thick and slippery as mud. Enough said. When I was done drinking, she instructed me to focus all my attention on one single point, the point of gratitude. She instructed me to ride the waves of gratefulness without pause to see where they would take me. With that she left the room.

Earth Story

While my eyes felt heavy, my mind was fully alert. With Tinky by my side, I laid on my back, shut my eyes and let the process begin. At first my thoughts started flowing slowly. My mind went over each and everything I could possibly think to be grateful for, but it did not stop there. The more relaxed I became, the more I let go of my mind. The more I let go of my mind, the more blessings to be accounted for came flowing in. And they kept right on flowing in, at an ever-increasing speed. At some point I could no longer consciously follow the stream of gratefulness, but it was all known to my heart. Faster and faster the thoughts kept coming until they reached the speed of light. At that point I started to vibrate to match their speed. Then it came again, *w h o o s h …* and there I went again, out of my body and into a state of pure freedom and beingness.

I saw planet Earth spinning in the velvety blackness of the universe, surrounded by billions of twinkling stars. In all Her spectacular beauty, the Earth hung as a precious jewel like no other. Had I any breath at that point, it would have been caught. I was utterly captivated by the sight. No wonder being an astronaut is a coveted job and one that kids dream of becoming. Somewhere inside they still remember this celestial perspective from before they were incarnate. To be able to view Earth from a heavenly distance is truly transforming, beyond words. It is a sight that one never truly gets over seeing.

Before my inner eye, the whole of Earth's creation, her entire story, the alpha to the omega, opened like a book. Page by page, Her history turned and revealed itself as if it were being downloaded into my very beingness. Once again, it went so fast that my mind could not track it all for the volume of information was immense. But still, it made absolute sense as it all poured into me. I understood everything that had happened, what was happening and all that was to come. It was all there. The history of Earth was one thing and it was all contained in our beautiful sphere of life. Our Mother, our Gaia. She and I were now One. She had all of me in Her and I had all of Her in me.

I gently slipped back into a sleep of deep peace. Upon awakening I remembered everything that had transpired. While I did not understand what it all meant or why it happened, it did not really matter. I belonged on Earth, I belonged with our Mother and I belonged to Her.

Homecoming

The next day I was left alone. Tinky and I went outside for a walk to enjoy the surprisingly fresh air that this world provided. The green grass was as lush as the most well-loved and manicured lawns above. Tinky loved the grass! She ran and jumped but never went very far from me. We were well-attached by then. That night Urda came again to my room with her golden bowl. This time the liquid was dark and inky, tasted of bitter herbs and cherries and was as slick as oil. Ironically, all things I loved individually, but together not so easy to swallow.

This time she simply said, *"Enjoy your resting."*

> Soon after lying down I found myself in a child's playground sitting on a swing. I began moving back and forth. My legs and body were pumping to go higher and higher, moving faster and faster until I reached the very top and was about to topple over to the other side. Instead of falling over there was the *w h o o s h ...* I was out again. This time the rate of vibration was faster than I ever remembered feeling. I thought how exciting, I must be going really far. And that I did. On my way out of the boundaries of our planet, I had to pass through many strange layers. Each one I moved through felt like I was shedding an old heavy worn out coat.
>
> The first layer surrounding Earth was a dense field of large tablets, like enormous oversized playing cards. Each one represented something about Earth. I don't clearly recall what exactly was on them, but I do remember that each made sense as it pertained to a belief structure or paradigm associated with life. It was as if all the substructures of our society were being exposed and had to be left behind.

As I moved out layer by layer, there were fewer and fewer cards and while their meanings got simpler, they grew more profound and more encompassing. They were refining down to the core beliefs of those who inhabit the surface of the Earth. Eventually all the cards went away, I had passed out of the influence of humanity and was truly free to roam the Heavens unencumbered. At that moment, I knew what it was like to be a cosmic being. I was a cosmic being.

I was experiencing pure freedom and unbridled exaltation as I made a direct line through the cosmos, intent on a destination I knew not but not knowing mattered not. I traveled past the speed of light and very quickly arrived at a place very very far away. After arriving, I immediately felt completely and utterly at rest. In my heart I knew that this was where I had originally come from. My celestial origin. I curled into a fetal position and rested in the womb of my Source. The womb of pure Love.

My celestial rest effortlessly slipped back into the realm where my body lay and I enjoyed the most peaceful sleep ever.

Before Birth

The next day Tinky and I relished being outdoors, alone again. That night Urda returned with her golden bowl. On this night she offered a translucent liquid with silver streaks running through like tiny sperm on a heat seeking mission to somewhere deep inside of me. The taste had hints of peppermint and sage and slid down my throat like a glass of warm milk. Before Urda departed she asked me if there was anything I would like. I told her that I would like to meet myself before I was born.

Urda sat down on the bed next to Tinky and me. She instructed me to take short inhales followed by deep long exhales, one in quick succession to the other. I followed her voice. Soon my head felt dizzy and my feet began to cramp. One would naturally stop at this point of hyperventilating, but I kept following Urda's lead. Eventually everything went dark and I was sitting in a long tunnel with a bright white light off my right shoulder. To the left was a dark void. I was with another, but I could not see them. I just knew they were there. The presence felt like an angel, for lack of a better word. We were having a conversation, the words I could not hear but I remember having reservations about what was going to happen –having second thoughts about my birth into the world. My mother appeared before my eyes and I felt a profound love for her and excitement that we would be together once again. My father was in the background and I knew him well. My brother was there and many more who would be part of my life. There was nothing but the purest of love between us all. A camaraderie of spirits in cahoots for a grand adventure. The adventure of me becoming me. That is when I must have decided to go through with it for in the very next instant, I was rushing through the birth canal and coming out into the bright of the world. I shouted with pure joy along with several hearty whoops and hollers. *I had made it!*

If anyone ever tells you that being incarnate on Earth is a mistake or a curse, I recommend you seriously question their knowing. At that moment I knew that it was the highest honor to be born into a physical body.

As I came back into the present and opened my eyes, Urda was sitting next me, unmoved and with a soft smile. Ever so quickly I fell back into a trance. This time I went back even farther. The angel was back and had three things to show me.

First, we were looking at an almost completely dark world. The only lights were a few spots scattered here and there. As I stared at an ominous looking Earth, I remember thinking that it was going to be very lonely going there with it in such a condition. The condition was mostly darkness. I felt much reservation. My guide told me to watch. Very slowly a few more lights began to appear. Then a few more. Each time the amount of lights increased exponentially, small gains at first but then, reaching a tipping point, the whole of Earth exploded into one giant powerful light. It was magnificent. The Earth had turned into a brilliant new star right before my inner eyes.

Next, I was concerned because it would be a dangerous place to try and live. Bad things could happen. The world seemed to be full of people doing unkind and evil deeds. Without sufficient light, there would be many dark influences. I was terribly worried. *How was I to stay safe? How could I protect myself in such a place?* He proceeded to show me a column of bright white light piercing down through the heavens and right through the top of my head. All I had to do was to keep remembering that this column of light is always there and that it would surround and protect me. I could roam about the Earth knowing that I was shielded in Love.

Lastly, we stood before the Earth once again. Beside me stood the same splendid being. In one hand was a large sword and I was told to watch. The angel took the sword and starting at the top of the world carved a giant figure eight that encompassed the whole of Earth, top to bottom inside and out. Everywhere the sword cut, it burst into flames. I watched as immense power was wielded and unleashed. When it was all finished, the Earth stood burning. I was told the cycle was complete. Earth had fulfilled its destiny.

The following day I spent with Urda. We discussed, in our special way of sharing, what had transpired. I knew I had been uplifted and enlightened regarding many things; I just was not sure what they all meant yet.

"Your first vision was the story of Earth being downloaded into you. Literally. Everything that has happened, is happening and will happen, in all dimensions and probable realities, are now part of your being. You can access these records whenever you need to. Just make sure that you understand your needs. You never want to ask of Her with a mixed heart or with mixed motivations. Keep it pure and She will be available."

"How will I know how to get back there?" I genuinely wasn't sure.

"Have you already forgotten the route? Do not deny your experience. You were shown the way." Urda's way of reassuring was always rather pointed. But I knew her bluntness was always meant to empower me.

"You now know your Celestial Home. You have rested in Her womb. Never forget that feeling for it will be there to comfort and to ground you throughout your travels. It is a gift to help you to fulfill your destiny. And never forget what it took to get there. You still have much to leave behind in order to be truly free and walk the surface unencumbered."

I think this was the very first time that she said specifically that I would have a future, that I did have a destiny. I would be returning to my Earthly home. My heart leapt as she read my thoughts.

"Yes, there is a high probability that you will make it. But in all things, in all ways, there are no absolutes. And certainly, no guarantees."

Great, no guarantees and more surprises. My sarcastic thought was met with a serious reply by Urda.

"You will be alone, but you do not have to feel lonely. That is a choice of interpretation and ultimately one that signifies forgetting. Over time you will find the others that incarnated at this time for the same purpose. Your traveling companions."

"You can stay protected, but it takes much practice to sustain a state of remembering. We have some work to do in that area before you leave. It will not be easy, but you are not about easy, are you..." She tilted her head back with a splash of glee. I loved her laugh, even if it was at my expense!

"Above all, always remember that the Story of Earth is written in the Heavens and sealed with fire. All is well. It always has been and always will be. You need not be afraid. You are an eternal soul on the great journey of remembering and expressing the Creator." With that the lesson concluded.

Overcoming Fear

The next phase of training was specific to overcoming fear. Like always, Urda was direct in her assessment of life on the surface and with my people.

"Your world is bought and sold on the currency of fear. It is what ties you all together in unholy alliances while it binds your minds into isolated realities. It is what sentences your hearts into the prisons of matter. Ultimately it is the gateway for being controlled. It is the opening for destruction to enter and to take over. It is vital for you to learn to overcome your biology and your oppressors. Above all you must overcome your fears"

"But fear is something that happens so quickly, like it was

hardwired." So far on my journey fear had been the biggest challenge. Even though I was feeling good about all those I had overcome on my way to the Kingdom, I knew there was more fear to face. *"I thought that our physical make-up is about two choices, either fight or flight. Which one do I choose when I am confronted?"*

Intrinsically I knew it was possible to not be subject to fear. After all we have stories about masters who transcended the world but it always seemed those accomplishments went with the life of an aesthetic who denied everything about being flesh and blood, not that of someone interfacing with life and people on a daily basis.

"That is exactly it." Urda replied. *"Everything you said is part of the problem. You have not been told the truth from the very start of your lives. This has left you ill-prepared to be who you are designed to be. Remember our Fundamental Truths. Why do you think we teach them to our children from the very start? It is so they can be free, and no fear can penetrate and take that away from them. We are not open to being bought with lies and fear. We know who God is. We know we are His children created in Love. We know we have forever to explore His Creation. You have forgotten, we remember. It's that simple."*

"Our first lesson is going to be remembering that there is a third choice. A part of your biology that you have forgotten." Urda declared and with that we moved on with the lesson.

Fight or Flight

Urda began by saying...

"You have been taught that in the face of a threat your body will

respond one of two ways. It will either stay and fight or try to flee the situation. Typically, this decision is made in the blink of an eye. Your mind rapidly thin-slices reality to see which choice presents the best odds for your survival and then off you go, or not. Fight or flight are just two ends of the same stick, with the operative word being the 'stick'. Picture the other option as a third point above the stick. A point that creates a triangle when they are all connected. It is the point above the two that will provide other options than just listening to and reacting with your biology. The third point is transcendence. To transcend a scary situation requires you to remember. You need to remember what the truth is - who you are and where your power comes from. You are an eternal light being clothed in a body. You cannot be destroyed. You are born in light and sustained in light. Not sin. Always remember the column of white light. When you remember that, you cannot be harmed. Your body may be hurt but your spirit will never be touched. It is a living symbol of reality. You have power over that reality. When you remember that suddenly there are a host of options to entertain."

"And you are right about it happening fast. That is a challenge to overcome. You have been trained to go immediately into the fight or flight response. The save-your-sorry-ass-response." That was the first and only time I heard a swear word come out of Urda's mouth or in her thoughts, and it was a bit shocking. Probably part of her goal. *"Your dials go from zero to ten in an instant, not allowing you time to choose. You need to create space to choose, to transcend and remember. You need to create more time."*

"Urda, it makes sense. I know that if I had more time to remember, I could make the right choices but how in the world do I create time?" I asked.

"Time is quite flexible. It is not an absolute. You are not told this

either. But you have experienced it, you just did not know what was going on. Remember the times when you have been in a very intense experience, with your life quite possibly on the line? Remember how time seemed to slow down and your thoughts became crystal clear? That is your innate ability shining through. You quite literally slowed down time so that you could survive. You created time so that you could transcend. You just forgot the remembering part."

I absolutely knew how time slows down in a potential death situation. There had been many times in my life where I experienced this very thing happening. You probably have as well. Learning to control it consciously, now that would be very interesting and most helpful.

"If I understand you correctly, you are saying that I can learn to manipulate time?" My question was a big one and for the first time Urda took a pause before answering. Clearly, she wanted to be sure to say the exact right thing.

"In the days to come, you will become very adept at it. For now, let us just work on getting enough space so you can remember your options." She gave me that small smile that told me everything was going to be fine, even though my question would not be answered. We were only touching the tip of this very large iceberg of Truth and I wasn't going to see any more right then.

⋈

The rest of the day was spent in leisure, enjoying being in the Kingdom. Knowing that I would soon be leaving made everything that much sweeter as I relished in the abundance that this world offered. Everything was life affirming. On the surface, we have no idea what that would look like, much less feel like. While I was excited to return to my people, I felt a sense of foreboding. I knew that it would not be easy. It is one thing living in a state of not knowing, as hard as that can be, but quite another thing when you do know. I was waking up but that did not mean things would get easier. They most certainly would not.

When it was time to retire for the night, Urda came to my bedside. As I lay down, she gently touched between my eyes, a spot that is known as the third eye – the gateway into the subconscious. She told me to think back to all the times that I thought I would surely die. To remember how it felt when time slowed down. She instructed me to dive into those stretched out moments so that I could begin to get a feel for what was happening. That is where the magic lay. The secret to changing time lay in between the moments.

To find near death examples to explore, I did not have to think very far back even though it felt like a lifetime ago that I was spat out into the underworld. As I delved into each of those times of crisis where I was certain that I was one step away from the Pearly Gates, I began to understand the essence of what those moments felt like. Like all the things I had learned so far, they all were centered around feeling. You cannot think your way into Heaven or into knowing the Truth. You must feel your way into enlightenment. As the night wore on, I was entranced with reliving all the times in my life where I thought I was going to die. Reliving them over and over again until the feeling of time slowing became clearer and clearer. Until I understood its signature well. And then I dozed off into sleep as the training ended for the day.

In the morning I could not wait to tell Urda about what I experienced. Over a light breakfast of simple fruits, I tried to explain the unexplainable.

"Urda I think I understand! As I worked with my near-death experiences, I started to feel what happens when time begins to slow down. The flow of my consciousness stayed the same, but the physical plane slowed enough so that I became aware that it is really a pulsation. Our reality is like waves that oscillate from one moment to the next. That oscillation can be stretched out! As it stretches, time slows down. I started to feel how you could control that!" As calm as I wanted to remain, my excitement was hard to contain. Urda did not seem to mind a bit. She flowed with it beautifully.

"Exactly!" She exclaimed, like a proud parent.

Seldom had I seen her get excited – except maybe over Bill Murray but we will leave that one alone! Over time I had come to read her slight nuances of emotions and while they did not have as wild a swing as ours, they were still there. In fact, they carried more potency than our flagrant displays. For me to sense excitement in her was a big deal. I could not help but feel a well-earned sense of pride.

"As I told you before, it is the moments in between that are most powerful. Many things can be done within those paused moments that seem to defy nature. Like stopping and even bending time. As you master this you will appear to be a miracle worker to those less informed. You must be sure to use these new senses and capabilities very wisely. They will serve you well if done correctly and with great humility. If not, they can do great harm." Urda warned me and I humbly accepted.

This was another first. I had never heard Urda issue a caution as she did at that time. I knew that I needed to mark those words and never forget them. I remember them to this day, and they remain perfectly true.

"Will you teach me more about how to change time before I go?" I hoped so for several reasons – I absolutely wanted to know, but I

also did not want my time learning from her to end. I was the apprentice of a Master. *Who would want that to end?* I loved learning from Urda and I loved being in the Kingdom. I longed to go home and I yearned to stay.

"Your skills will grow over time. As long as you stay on the path." She said gently. That was all I was going to get for an explanation or for reassurance.

At times it felt like Urda could not only get inside my head, but that she was also at the control switch governing dreams. Far too many times did I have uncannily accurate dreams based on what we had discussed. I am not talking about out-of-body travel and visions, for those were no mere dreams. At those times I would literally leave my body while remaining in my full waking consciousness. What I am referring to is that wonderfully weird and convoluted state that we all experience every night, whether we remember it or not. No skill set required. Dreaming is part of the human package that comes with the physical terrain of having a body and consciousness. The next day Urda was to share with me a secret to unlocking some of the power inherent in dreaming. Power that can change your waking life.

Repatterning Dreams

Urda took me for a walk along the river's bank. I hadn't been to this place before, as I had not explored very much of the Kingdom. I never wandered around on my own, except in the beautiful meadows surrounding the city. I was careful to always stay within the boundaries of expectations. If I was not invited to enter an area,

I did not go there. But on that day, I was excited to be by a body of water, by something that I could relate to. It reminded me of my childhood up at our cabin. Maybe that is why she took me there.

The lesson began like this:

"Nighttime allows you the perfect opportunity to change reality through repatterning your dreams. While dreams are certainly rife with keys to unlocking your psychology, your motives, your thoughts and feelings, it is also a perfect realm to practice new skills. The time between thought and actuating is more in line with how things work in the spirit realm. You think and it happens. In three-dimensional waking, time is slowed way down so that you can learn about action and reaction. You can learn about the intricacies of finding and maintaining the balance point. It is still about figuring out how to find the third point of transcendence. The place of remembering. It just happens very quickly in the dream state. Think of it all as learning how to save time in the Karmic loop."

It was finally all starting to make sense. For most of us the things going on in our minds in the deep of the night are completely mysterious, yet we spend a good part of our lives in that state. You would think we would know more about it. Despite all the research, our scientists are still clueless, save for measuring some physical responses in the different depths of sleep. That is about it. While I was sure there was a lot more about this realm to understand than what Urda was teaching me, I was quite happy with these few new insights.

"The goal of repatterning dreams is to wake-up within the dream without stepping out of the dream. That way you are in position to take control of its outcome. It is the same thing that is being asked of you in waking life – to wake up and take control of your outcomes. Dreamtime will help you to get better at this in a very gracious manner."

She said it all in such a matter of fact way that it seemed so simple and obvious, yet I had never thought of dreaming in this way before. There is much we are not told about who we are and what we can do. I was privileged to learn some of that. Urda went on.

"The first step to waking up in your dreams is to set an intention before going to sleep. Then at the point where you start becoming aware, do not move your body or immediately start interjecting your mind. Lay with it for a moment and blend in with its natural flow. Typically, you will start to wake at the crescendo of a dream. The time of heightened emotional reaction triggers your biology, even in the dream state. People typically wake up frightened, angry, frustrated or with some intense feeling and immediately want to shrug it off. Do not. Stay with it and do not judge it."

"Once you have relaxed back into the dream state, slowly start to interject your consciousness. You are God in your dreamtime, just like you are in your waking time but here the perception of control is more immediate. It is simpler to understand your role because you are the only one energetically injecting into the dream. You have singular control of that reality. This is the exact moment where you can learn to pick the third option once again. The one that transcends fight or flight. Practice it over and over in dream time and soon it will spill forth in your waking realm. This I promise you."

She could sense my wonder tinged with a modicum of disbelief. Not that I ever thought she was lying because she never did, it was just sometimes the truth was a bit fantastical to digest wholly the first time heard.

"Tonight will be fun. We can start with all of the classics." Her head tipped back as a small but potent giggle ensued.

She was right, as always.

The Classics Rebooted

I am going to do my best to explain my first attempts to repattern dreams. What I will spare you is all the strange and twisted details that come with the terrain of my mind. The dreams that presented themselves on that first eve of attempting direct manipulation were in fact, classics from my greatest hits.

> *The air was thick and dank as a storm was on the edge of breaking. My heart was as well. Distraught, I was walking along the tall jagged cliffs of the Scandinavian fjords. Rolling grasses sloped down to the edges and then dropped precipitously into the roiling seas. Shivers went down my spine at the very thought of the angry waters. Then suddenly, without any warning, the soil under my feet started to move! My sleeping heart started to race in response. Within seconds I knew that the whole slab of vibrant grass would slip off its foundation and slide downwards towards the waters below. There was nothing I could do! There was nowhere to run since the whole bloody thing was moving and falling away. I was terrified. All I could do was to stare ahead and meet the inevitable. As I neared the edge of the cliff, my fear was reaching a breaking point. It was then that my body called me to wake up. I knew that I was dreaming, and this was my chance to rework the seemingly inevitable. All the dream hung in the balance, just waiting for my signal. I remembered that I had choices but what to choose? Every conceivable option was available. The thought of complete control that was not bound by reality was quite dazzling. Carefully I made sure to stay merged in the dream state and not to get caught in my head or other emotions.*
>
> *The obvious choice was to simply stop the grassy plain from sliding and then just walk out. But more exciting would be to fall over the edge and grab a hold of a rock to pull myself up*

or I could simply fly away to safety. The latter seemed like the most fun. So, I simply launched myself up into the air, like it was the most natural thing in the world to do. I then zipped through the sky until I reached the safety of solid ground, a far distance from the edge. It was quite exhilarating and empowering. Whatever circumstances had initially dampened my spirits, they had lost their hold. I overcame them by remembering that I had other choices. The fact was that I had every choice possible available to me, it was my dream after all. And in that domain, I was truly the master. My spirit was now soaring too.

Urda never said I had to stay within the realms of probability and realistic possibilities! After a few moments reveling in my win, I effortlessly slipped back into dreamtime.

Something about dark and stormy nights. There I was again but this time it was in my family home as once more a storm began to brew outdoors. I was in the basement all by myself, which used to terrify me as a young child. I was sure that monsters lay in the dark just waiting for an opportunity to get me. As I was heading to the stairs to leave, the lights suddenly went out all on their own. My back was encased in darkness as I looked up toward the light at the top of the stairs. It seemed like an eternity away and my life was in jeopardy if I didn't make it there quickly. I had to get to the top of the stairs before it was too late! I wanted to run while I still had time, but I could barely move my legs. It was like they were stuck in thick mud.

The presence of something evil was moving towards me. With painfully slow steps and a racing heart, I managed to get part way up the stairs until the thing, the evil thing, was on the verge of overtaking me. I knew it was intent on pulling me down into the fiery depths of hell from which it had emerged. That is typically when I would be yanked back to the reality of my bed, in a cold sweat. Taking charge, I told myself that this was a dream and I no longer needed to be in fear. I slowly turned around to face my attacker. Two beady red eyes stared back. In the biggest most authoritative voice I could muster, I ordered the creature from the deep to go back to where it came from and to never bother me again. I could see the moment it sensed my power and that I was stronger than it was. The light in its eyes went dim as it turned and sulked away, back into the depths. I knew that it would not dare to return either in the dream state or in wakefulness. I had commanded that demon out of my life for good.

While I was not sure the implications of these repatterning exercises or how they would affect my day to day living, I knew they were powerful. Whatever causes scenarios to be conjured up in dreams, whatever situations I needed to work out in my subconscious, they were obviously important. Changing the outcomes in such empowering ways would no doubt have spillover. I was looking forward to seeing what that would be when I was pulled in again.

It was the first day of high school and as a freshman I was obviously nervous and very self-conscious. Did I have on the right outfit? Would I look cool and fit in? Was my new haircut the right choice? I was having an episode of full-blown teenage angst. As I walked down the halls, I nervously stared into the faces of the other kids. They all seemed to be self-confident, happy and surrounded by friends. I was sure that I was the only one feeling alone, awkward and terrified. As I walked into my first class, I suddenly realized that I did not have on any clothes. I was standing there buck naked in front of everyone. I wanted to die. How could I have forgotten to get dressed? It made no sense yet there I was very naked and very afraid. A deep sense of shame washed over me in terrifying waves.

I was mortified to the point that it would have been humane to be yanked right out of the dream state. But I did not allow that to happen. Instead I seized the moment. Standing there in all my original glory, I changed my perspective. Instead I chose to stand confidently in front of the class and introduced myself, as if nothing were wrong. Instead of feeling shame over my body, I embraced it and stood proudly in all my natural blemished beauty. The room lit up and suddenly everyone was also naked and not caring one bit. We were all free and I felt triumphant.

I was going to love to tell Urda about that one in particular! As innocuous as naked dreams seem, I knew that they pointed to much deeper issues that we all carry around, without question. After that last dream I slid back into sleep from a place of victory and peace. The rest of the night carried on outside my conscious reach.

The next day Urda did not show up.

Truth or Consequences

In the morning instead of Urda greeting me, one of the men who I occasionally saw slipped into my room. Instantly I felt something was off.

Quietly he bent down to my ear and whispered, *"Follow me."*

I did.

Like two ghosts in the early dawn, ever so silently we made our way down several hallways without seeing a living soul. We came to a small niche and he beckoned me to step in. While spoken English was not his customary mode, his intent was very clear.

"Urda is not who you think she is nor who she pretends to be. She is not a revered sage or healer in our community. Not anymore. We tolerate her as long as she doesn't cause too much trouble."

I stood there in utter shock. At first, I was not sure if this was part of the training or if it was for real. Obviously, he sensed my reaction and was prepared for it.

The man went on in hushed tones. *"Have you ever wondered why she never lets you integrate with the others? That if you are allowed to enter public places, she is never more than a step away? What possible harm could come from your roaming freely? From your talking openly to anyone of your choosing. She knows you are not a threat to us. You are respectful and of good heart. You are just very curious, and that is what she does not want to happen. Your asking too many questions would not bode well for her game."* He already knew my next question.

"We would have told you long ago that you are on a fool's journey, but it all seemed harmless enough. Typically, when people get swallowed into the Earth, such as you did, they die. They either have already drowned when they arrive or they die soon after. It could be from terror, hunger or simply the elements. Even if they

were lucky to survive for a while, the other denizens of the dark would most likely find and kill them. If that didn't happen, they would likely go mad. We are used to gathering the bodies and giving them a proper burial. Do you wonder why you never saw any remnants of bodies? Did you really think you were the first to have ended up down here?"

Well that part was true, but I was not sure it proved his overall point. Before I could gather my thoughts, he went on.

"But then, there you came. Somehow you managed to survive and to find us. Urda was most excited to have a human from the surface in our mix. Most of us do not share that same enthusiasm. Did you really buy into the choice of staying and then never being able to leave? Did that not seem kind of strange? Well there is no choice!" He was very emphatic on the last point.

I was not exactly clear on what he meant by that last statement – *there is no choice?* That I could not leave, even if I wanted to or that I could not stay, even if I wanted to. I wasn't sure I wanted to know which one he meant.

"Urda lives on the fringes. Something happened long ago, and she has never been quite right since. We love her and honor her for what she once provided. She means no harm and if kept in check she causes no harm, but she can be a nuisance if not a challenge from time to time. Especially with the young who do not know better yet. Urda serves her own agenda, not the Kingdom's."

After a moment I asked, *"So why would you allow me to spend so much time with her. To be kept so busy with such… such amazing training? Why allow this?"* This was still not adding up but the possibility that it could be true would have devastating implications.

I needed to know, and he clearly wanted me to know.

He went on, *"Do not get me wrong, Urda is a very powerful woman and healer. She is just not quite right and not able to hold her place in the Temple anymore. You came along and provided a wonderful distraction. Much of what she told you is absolutely true, but it serves her goals – they may serve you to an extent as well. What is not true is who we are and what we are doing here."* And on he went, regardless of my feelings.

"The surface is already doomed and that is why we are leaving. There is nothing more we can do at this point to save your kind. Urda is just not able to let that go. She has her own delusional dreams and you are her savior."

The thought that any of this could be true was horrifying. I pushed back with a wounded hand, *"But I saw all the pods and people meditating on keeping us in balance. I saw that with my own eyes! You are helping us!"*

"And Urda was there to interpret all those things for you. Correct?"

There was no argument from me.

"We are continuing to keep you in balance, that is true but for a different reason. We do not need your people blowing themselves up before we are able to depart. We cannot take the risk of your destroying the vibrational field to a point where we are not able to penetrate it and leave. We have done all we can. Your people are beyond repair at this point and will have to learn their lessons in another iteration. This one is coming to a bad ending."

My knees wanted to give out. My mind was racing. *How could this be?*

"I am sorry. I know this is quite a shock to your system. You need to trust me. Urda will come to you shortly with wild tales of what will happen when you return to Earth. That you will accomplish great things. That you are destined to help change the world. I am sorry to say but you are just an average human, no offense intended. You accidently fell through a shaft not meant for you and then got lucky enough to survive. That is all. And there is no changing the world. If it felt surreal that you would be chosen to be the harbinger of Truth, there is a reason. It is but a pipedream. If you think that your return to the surface was guaranteed and that you would make some big difference, you are wrong. Do not fall for it. She is sending you to your death. You will never make it back to the surface alive despite all the fancy things she has taught you. The perils are too great, the journey is too long and you are barely a novice. Plus, we cannot take any risks."

Again, another very ominous statement. The implied threats were starting to reveal themselves, even though they were still very subtle. My skills of reading energy had grown immensely, to the point that even one as advanced as he was could not completely hide from me. *I don't have a choice and they can't take any risks...* that sounded like trouble.

"What do I do next?" I asked. *"It appears that I have little to choose from. Either I leave and die or... or .... You said I could not stay and go with you?"*

"That is up to the council. I can enter a plea on your behalf. But it is a long shot. Let me put it this way, it has never happened before. We do not allow your kind into our Kingdom. The reasons should be obvious to you. Despite anything Urda has said, it just does not happen."

"But look at all I have accomplished. I am not the person I was

when I arrived. Surely with all that I now know and my skills, I can fit in no problem." My pleading was almost a beg and that did not feel right on any level, so I dropped it. *"That is ok, I am sure I can make it to the surface. I have already survived against all odds, as you said..."*

This was not met with any encouragement, whatsoever. I sensed he was hiding something.

"Absolutely." He feigned a tight smile. *"I will ask the council. Just do not do anything until I return. I will be back and if you need to leave, I will help you to prepare."*

"But what about Urda? Surely, she will come to me again. What do I do?" I decided to go with this pretense even though things were still not adding up and I was feeling quite confused. My whole world just got tossed in the air like a bunch of playing cards at a slumber party. The only difference was that I was not having fun.

"Just humor her and do not do anything until I return." He bowed his head and slipped away as quietly as he had come.

⋈

My mind was spinning as I returned to my room. *What if it were true? What if Urda were half crazy? How could I tell with one so much further advanced than I was? Surely, I would have sensed something? Or did I not already have warnings but just never given them any heed?* There were things that seemed rather strange, but I always chalked it up to me not knowing enough of their ways to really understand. The not being allowed to mingle with others always felt a bit odd. I just accepted it all without question. *But if what he told me was a lie, what was his motivation? Was he the nut job and was I in danger from him? If I spoke to Urda about it and she was the nut job, then I might also be in danger from her.* Maybe I should just quickly pack up, grab Tinky and try to sneak away while avoiding them both.

I flopped back on my bed in frustration and confusion. I felt caught between a rock and a hard place. Everything was on the verge of crashing in, everything. Right then Tinky jumped on my chest, stuck her little pointy face right into mine and started to purr up her typical storm of delight. At least something in my world remained unchanged. There was someone I could count on.

A little later that day Urda buoyantly waltzed into my room. Something was different about her this time. There is an expression that says 'one is walking on air' to describe someone in a heightened state of excitement. That is exactly what she felt like and I knew that emotional highs or lows were not her style. Something had changed about her. *Was she just excited for me to embark on this final phase of my journey or was she excited about her goals coming to fruition?* Either way, this was not like her. It was unlike anything I had seen from her.

"E, I am so glad to find you…"

My hackles were up. First, rarely did she ever call me by that special name. And pretending that she was surprised to find me in my room, where else would she think I would be! I never went anywhere that I was not accompanied by someone, mostly by her. We were not off to a good start for reassuring my agitated heart.

"… you have passed all your exercises with flying colors! I knew you would. You are my most prized student. When you get back to the surface, world hold on, The Amazing E will have returned. Things will never be the same there. Great things await you my dear! You are truly the chosen one and very special indeed. I am so proud of you!"

I was not sure where to start with all of that. She never mentioned other students from the surface. And she never guaranteed my return but now she was emphatically declaring that I was going to make it. While my ego loved to hear how special I was and that I would save the world, I knew better than to accept that whole heartedly. *What happened to the measured and balanced woman I had come to know and trust?* This was not like her at all. Was this an act or had her true colors finally come out…

Just then her compatriot glided in with his head held down, the man who had warned me earlier that day. His presence seemed to startle her but she recovered and continued pouring out adulations.

"E, you must always remember that you are different from everyone else. You are the One. That you are chosen and everything of the world is for your choosing. You can have anything you want, whenever you want. You just have to stay focused and never forget your lessons."

Case closed. These last statements went against everything else I was taught. Flattery and a promise of rewards would not be a means by which I could be swayed away from what I knew to be true. Even if it came from the one that I had grown to trust so completely and had taught me those truths.

"Now Urda," the man interjected with a modicum of respect, *"we both know that this might be a bit of a stretch."*

"And what would you know of stretching! You who do nothing but comply with whatever they say. Never questioning, just following

along like a...." She snapped back.

"Urda, do you really want to have this conversation, right now, in front of your friend?"

That was exactly what he wanted to happen. His hopes of her revealing who she really was, was exactly what he wanted. I could sense it. My heart started to break. How could I be caught up in a game that seemed so lowly from those so highly esteemed.

"I will have whatever conversation I want when I want. You are not the boss of me nor can you change what already is." Urda shouted back, clearly agitated.

That sounded just like me and *my* old narrative...

"ENOUGH! Just stop. The both of you just stop!!!" I truly had had enough of this conversation and whatever game they seemed to be playing. I regained my composure and from a place of power I stood tall and spoke.

"The truth be known; I do not care what either of you think of me. I do not care if you think I will never make it or if I am the savior of the world. I simply do not care. I am going to return to my people, and I believe there is hope for them. I know there is plenty of love in the world and good hearts. All is not lost! I believe I can make a difference and so I will. I am going to leave first thing in the morning and there is nothing you can do to dissuade me. The only thing I need is for you to show me to the door. I am gone from here and will never return. Forever, I will be thankful for what has been provided. I am awake now. I am as loved as you are in the eyes of our Creator. So are my people. I am going to help them in whatever way I can."

The words I proclaimed held the entirety of the truth of who I had become. The beautiful thing about reading people's minds is that a few words can be embellished with a novel's worth of meaning. Through this journey I had learned the truth about who I was, where I came from and why I was alive. The very things I had longed for my entire life were now the story of my life. How I would serve mankind and what my destiny held truly mattered not. What would be, would be and it was all good in my heart's eye. No one could ever take my inner journey away from me nor did it any longer depend on anyone but me. I did not need to be cast down or cast upward. I AM, and that is enough.

With that Urda turned to the man and exchanged a knowing smile. She then turned to me and said…

"You are ready." They bowed to each other and then to me and left the room together.

Mission Ready

After they departed my head was spinning. It took a few deep breaths to realize what had just happened and to regain my sense of balance. When it finally dawned on me, all I could do was burst into a giant laugh of relief. That was the cleverest test ever!

Urda came back later that evening to help with my departure preparations. On the bed I had all my belongings carefully laid out. There wasn't much but it would be all that I needed. The minor accoutrements were still in the backpack. The three books lay on the bed. The one wrapped in paper and sealed with red wax contained a mystery that would have to wait. I was not yet ready to reveal it to myself. The water bladder was now empty but still held the stones from the Temple. My beloved cape, the staff with a crystal on top and the bag of precious stones were all still accounted for. All of them had been carefully set aside while I was immersed in the Kingdom. The clothes in which I began this journey with were all there as well, a bit worn. My strange geometric necklace remained around my neck and carefully hidden from sight.

In Urda's arms she carried a few simple gifts. First, she presented me with a fresh set of clothing to adorn the new me. I was glad for that since the old ones I started my journey with no longer fit who I had become. She gave me a pair of simple drawstring pants and a loose-fitting tunic that skimmed the top of my thighs. Both were in flaxen shades with the pants being darker than the top. She also had a large scarf made of a combination of the two tones. No adornments, no embroidery, just simple and to the point. I have to say that they blended beautifully with my cape. I was quite aware that this was not a fashion show, but my aesthetic eye still loved to be pleased, maybe even more than ever. The most precious gift was when she took off her necklace and put it around my neck. She wore it the very first time we met and every time after that. It was the one that matched the deep liquid pools of her wise blue eyes. Maybe someday mine would match too.

"You can add this to your powerful friends to take with you on your journey."

I was touched with her generosity. For surely this was not a gift she would casually give away. The following words I carefully listened to since the Urda I knew was the one now before me and when she spoke, her words were concise and for a purpose.

"There are many things for you to accomplish. The world will change because you have changed. Remember that not everyone is ready to be a part of the change. Some will say they are and yet they

are not. Others will pretend they are not ready, yet they are perfectly primed. Like people, some things will not be as they present themselves to be and yet some things will be exactly as they seem to be. Your staff will help light the way out, but your inner eye will be the most important light to shine. It will show you the truth of any given situation. You must be willing to listen and then to pay close attention to what your knowing tells you. Your inner light will never lead you astray if you trust it completely. Above all else, remember that your sovereignty is to no one but yourself, your true self. The God within you."

She went on to clarify my 'powerful friends', the things I would be carrying with me. *"Your cloak is an invaluable tool. At this point you will need it, at some point you will not. Remember it is a cloak of confusion but ultimately it is one of remembering. Your lovely bag of stones will also serve you well. Their uses were not needed here but, in the days to come, they will be important. Like everything else outside of you, for a time. These stones are aligned perfectly with the energy points in your body. They will also align with the energy points of the Earth. You will gather more as time goes on. Remember that Mother Earth is now within you and you can call on her. She will answer. These are her calling cards."*

"Above all else, keep an open mind. The books contain many secrets that you will have to rely on others to help you decode. Choose who you give them to wisely. In the wrong hands, their secrets can be turned to meet other ends. You will not want that. Please do not worry about the library. It is safely tucked away for eternity. It will never fall into the wrong hands. We have always made sure of that and will continue to do so long after you leave."

"And who can forget about the most precious of all!" With that Tinky gently rubbed up against Urda with an arched back and happy tail. She always seemed to know when the attention was pointing her way. *"Tinky is a special angel and she will always be with you*

in one form or another."

I hung on every word she had to say since I knew in my heart this would be the last time I would be in her presence. No longer would I hear her soothing voice and wise words. My heart ached at the thought of leaving. She knew that.

"Do not fret. There are other guides waiting for you on the surface. They will help provide direction in the next phase of your journey. You have many things to uncover. The truth has been hidden from you and your people. Sometimes it is hidden deep within, like us, and other times it is hidden in plain sight. Never forget that your world is run by tricksters. Their arrogance in thinking they are so clever will be their downfall. Do not fall into their traps. It is ok to act the fool, just do not be the fool."

Finally, the part I was not eager to hear. The spell needed to be broken for a journey needed to happen. Urda knew this and was the first to come back to the practicalities of my departure. We both blinked away the tears that filled our eyes.

"In the morning four men will come to your room. You are to follow their directions exactly. Do not question what they ask of you. There are specific reasons for everything. You do not need to know what they all are. The men will be carrying you to one of the farthest outposts. From there they will leave you to your journey. Start walking and never look back. On your journey, never look back. Do you understand?"

"Yes. I promise, I will never look back."

"Next, always take the road that goes straight ahead. Do not make a turn to the left or to the right or you will never find your way out and we won't be able to protect you anymore."

"Yes. I will take the road that goes straight ahead."

"I have one last gift for you to take with you." She handed me a beautiful wand made from a gorgeous milky crystal. I would later find out that it was selenite. *"If you get confused, allow this to show you the way."*

"Be prepared for things to be different when you reach the surface. Time moves at a different rate than it does here. In the Kingdom we spin more slowly than above. You may find that many things have changed. That is ok. Just move with them and know that all is just as it should be. Prepare yourself with no expectations."

"And finally, remember that everything you need to know is within you. It will be available when the time is right and when you are ready. Your real training is just starting. What has happened so far has been in preparation for now."

With that she stood to leave. My tears could not be held back as my heart felt like it was losing something irreplaceable. The love and compassion in her eyes were enough to totally ruin any notion of being poised and stoic. I fell into her arms weeping as a child. She held me for a long while.

"You have done very well, and I am most proud of you. I have always been proud of you. I trust you and I believe that you will do exactly what is in your highest of nature, for it is a nature I know very well." Her eyes sparkled unusually bright. *"Do your best in every now you are blessed to experience. The world can change from one single point of light. Be that light always and never get attached to outcomes. Remember always, right action for right action's sake, and you will do well."*

It was then that I noticed something else. It was small enough to hide in her palm. She was holding it in a rather strange way. I would say she held it nervously but that would not be her. Maybe it was more like thoughtfully. Then she stopped, looked deep into my eyes and carefully opened her hand. Reflexively my hand went up and touched my chest. It was still hidden there. *How could that be?*

In Urda's hand was a geometric stone exactly like the one I had been carrying around my neck since I found it in the Temple. It was precisely the same crystalline tetrahedrons woven together. It was the exact same shape, exact same size and exact same stone. It hung from the exact same grey leather as mine. No wonder I had to check to see if mine was still there. My eyes grew wide as I tried to pull together the meaning of our shared treasures. In another instant it began to dawn on me.

"Urda…. do…. do you…… do we…." I was trying my best to put a million revelations into a few small words. Finally, it came out in a small whisper, *"Urda do we know each other?"*

"I have known you since you were just stardust dancing throughout the Heavens. Before you were a twinkling in the eye of a distant galaxy." The tears welling up in her eyes made them look like distant oceans from a faraway planet of unimaginable depths.

"I have loved you since the beginning of time and will continue to love you to the end of time and beyond. You are a part of me and I am a part of you. Our story is written in the Book of Life and can never be undone. I have been given to watch over you."

"My real name Eurda. We belong to the ancient lineage of 'E.'"

There are moments in time that are beyond words and even beyond thoughts. If I said I stood there blankly, that would be wrong. My mind may have been unable to gather a thought much less put it into words, but my heart was soaring into realms beyond description. At long last I was in the presence of someone I knew, a kindred spirit from the stars.

Urda smiled and glowed, as she turned and walked away and out of my life.

BURIED

CHAPTER VI

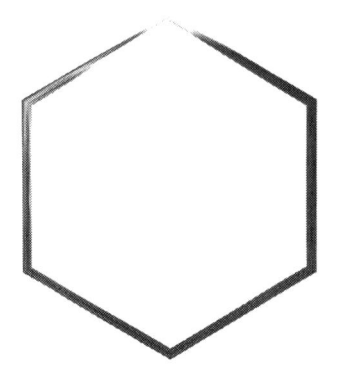

Point of No Return

The next morning my four escorts arrived as Urda said they would. It was early and I had hardly slept the whole night. You can imagine the emotional adjustments taking place as this part of my life was coming to an end and I would be reentering my old world. Entering that world but as a new person. I met those thoughts with both trepidation and excitement. There was so much to process as time seemed to be accelerating. That was alright by my account. Better to get this part over with sooner than later. Tinky and I were as ready as could be expected.

The men silently and swiftly led me through various hallways. They were on a mission and like me, were intent on it moving along without any delays. We eventually reached a beautifully carved archway that opened into a large ordinary looking tunnel. It marked a transition point that led away from the Kingdom. Resting in front of us was an unusual object floating about three feet off the ground. It looked like a large white egg, like the meditation pods I had witnessed earlier in my stay. This pod emanated a beautiful blue aura and carried a similar peaceful feel. It was just big enough to, well… to fit me perfectly. One man handed me a silver bowl with a warm milk and honey tasting liquid. I had tasted this one before and knew it was to help me to relax on the journey. I drank all but a small amount so that my sweet companion could lap up the rest. I figured she might need some calming too. With that, the top of the pod slid open to reveal what looked like a softly padded lounger. Since the beginning of this whole ordeal I had to confront my fears of being confined many times. Starting with landing in the cavern and then inside the Temple, each time the spaces got smaller and smaller. This would be the ultimate test of whether I had grown enough in my abilities to transcend this primal fear of entombment. This was the real deal. I either was going to make it out alive or I was not. No more pretending or practicing. I was willingly stepping into a coffin. Albeit a very nice one! With that last thought ringing in my head, I did exactly that. I climbed in, arranged my belongings and beckoned Tinky to join me. Not a bad way to exit. It was exceptionally comfortable, like it had been built with me in mind. Maybe it had.

The lid slowly slid back in place. The top of the pod was transparent so I could easily see the four faces of my escorts staring down at us. They, however, were not as clear. I couldn't pick up any emotion or thoughts. They just looked at me as their charge, as a part of their mission and nothing more. I was ok with that. I was not there to bond or make new friends. They were there to help me on my way out and that was it. The ceiling gently faded into an opaque shell as Tinky and I relaxed and slipped into a delightfully long nap.

Tinky was the first to start stirring. Her stretching and wiggling triggered my return to a semi-conscious state. As I lay there, part way between dreamtime and wakefulness, I remembered how in the beginning I felt cursed by some vengeful or distant God that was forcing this fate upon me. I had been angry and confused but mostly scared. I desperately wanted to know why this was happening. It was truly absurd and at the same time truly terrifying. The Temple marked the first of many blessings for it was there that the most serious journey of all began. The journey of going deep within myself and totally out of myself. That is where I discovered my true identity and real freedom. My time with Urda and living in the Kingdom was beyond my wildest of dreams. Urda would forever be imprinted in my soul. From what I gathered this was not our first time together nor would it be our last. It might not be in this lifetime and while that was sad, I knew I would be ok without her. She played her role perfectly this time. As for understanding my star lineage, that would have to wait.

How far I had come in time and through space. I was no longer the woman I once was. Not by any standard or any measure. The God I came to know was one that loved and cherished me. I knew then, without a doubt, that I was never cursed. This whole adventure was never done 'to' me. Rather I had been extremely blessed and all of this had been done 'for' me so that I could wake up and step into the real me. The I AM that I AM. I knew that once I was back on the surface the changes would become even more apparent. As the reality of stepping out into the fresh air and entering my old life was drawing near, I was feeling rather disconcerted. *Who had I become? How was I going to fit in? How would I feel about Daniel and even more importantly, how would he now feel about me?!* It could have been many months or even longer since our ways diverged.

Urda alluded to time being different in their world. What that meant was unknowable right then. It had been a long time since I had even considered how much time was passing. Early on I would contemplate that often. I was very concerned with how long I had been gone and what my loved ones were doing. Upon entering the Kingdom, the fixation on time completely left. I was single mindedly immersed in the experience. Totally living in the ever present Now. I am sure that is why the magic that happened there, the wonderous things I went through, were able to happen. The power of the present moment reigned supreme with the Kingdom's people and I finally understood why. Even though I lived just a short period of time with them, it felt like I had traveled light years to get there.

Right at the point of fully coming back into reality, I could sense the motion stopping as the pod slowly lowered and rested on the ground. I stayed very still while listening for signs of what was going on. But there was nothing, no voices or movements. It was strange but not alarming. But the lid was not lifting. *Were they just resting? Had they left?* While I wanted to be compliant and quietly do as I was told, sitting there waiting was tough. I bided my time for a while and then started to grow concerned. Tapping lightly on the ceiling I called out to see if anyone was there. Nothing. I tapped harder and called with more intent, but nothing. I searched around the inside but could not find a lever or a handle. There was no apparent way of opening it from the inside. Finally, I started banging on the container and shouting. Still no reply. Fear started creeping its way in. I knew that feeling well and it was an option. I wondered why they would carry me all this way just to leave me to die right there, in this lovely little coffin. Tinky sat there looking at me with her eyes and tail bigger than usual.

It would have been easy to succumb to fear, as I would have in the past, but I knew better. Even though I could feel it and taste it, opting down that path was an old road I did not need to travel again. Tinky had been with me long enough and knew better too. At that point she could easily feel my emotions and me hers. I calmed my heart rate and focused on the third point, transcending my current reality by tapping into the field, the source of All. Balance and options were all I needed. After a few minutes of centering, the space seemed to expand without moving. My head cleared and everything felt perfectly right again. Very calmly I placed both hands on the sides and saw with complete conviction the top sliding right off... *and so it did*. Surprisingly, there was nothing out there. Nothing. No men, no outpost, just the soft glow of the pod. As soon as we stood on solid ground the top closed as it gently rose up into the air and zipped off at a high rate of speed in the direction, I assumed, we had just come from. It was an odd and unexpected way of sending me off. Even though I was well indoctrinated into the 'odd' by then, an old fashioned sending off party would have been nice. Like being able to look into someone else's eyes and hear them say 'farewell' before I disappeared into the unknown again.

With the departure from the Kingdom complete, I lit the crystal torch and looked around. We were in the middle of a nondescript tunnel. To be honest I had been looking forward to seeing some cool high-tech outpost and maybe some equally cool badass warrior guards with lots of gadgets. But alas, nothing. Just Tinky and I standing alone and surrounded by darkness. That was an experience I knew all too well and had not been eager to repeat again. If I made it back, I planned on never going into another tunnel or cave again, ever, no matter what. All my future journeys would have to be on the surface... or above. I was done with the below part. Little did I know that those other kinds of adventures would be rife with an equal amount of challenges.

Tinky stayed close to my feet as we started the final phase of our journey, hoping it would be nicely uneventful. We walked for a while still basking in the aura of the Kingdom but eventually that started to fade. It was right about then that we came to a small open space where the path split in two directions, a typical 'T' in the road. Urda was very clear – *always take the path that leads straight ahead. Do not turn to the left or to the right.* There was no mistaking what she said. If I did take a turn I would be lost for good and they would not be able to help me anymore. Not wanting to incur the results of that option left me a bit perplexed because there was not a third choice. The road went to the left and to the right. There simply was not a road straight ahead. There had to be something I was missing. There had to be a clue. In the center of the open space was a rock pedestal that came up to my chest. This had to be it. I carefully walked up to the stand while making sure nothing was approaching from either direction. One of the things I had learned was to be prepared for the unexpected. I knew my safe arrival to the surface was still an open question. Thankfully, all was perfectly still and quiet. Yet, even with Tinky in tow, the quietness of the underworld was not something I enjoyed. It was not the kind of stillness that one savors as a respite from their busy life. No, this had a heavy oppressive feel to it. A vacation it was not. Quietness here simply meant no danger ahead.

In the center of the platform was a small indentation. I kept staring at it. There was something about the size and shape that seemed familiar. The answer was flittering around in my head as I tried to grab a hold of it. *Finally! The wand Urda had given me… that had to be it!* She said it would come in handy. I quickly retrieved it from the pack and, of course, it fit perfectly. Tinky and I stepped back to watch what would happen next. Slowly the wand started to glow from the inside out. First at the base and then working its way upwards. Upon reaching the top of the crystal, a bright light exploded like the beacon of a lighthouse to sailors lost at sea. The beam of light lit up the wall ahead of us. As soon as its beam touched the surface, the wall quickly started to fade away. Almost like it had been an apparition all along. And then there it was, the path straight ahead.

Tinky's eyes mirrored mine exactly – wide with happy surprise. Not wanting to tempt the fates shining down, I quickly grabbed the pack and the wand while Tinky jumped on my back. Forward we went, dashing as fast as I could. As soon as we got to the other side, the opening slowly dematerialized leaving behind a very solid looking wall of rock. Another reminder that we would have to remain on our toes throughout this journey - everything was possible and nothing was guaranteed.

Darkness All Around

We traveled down, or should I say up, the path for what seemed like a very long time. There were more forks in the road but never anything like the first challenge. Luckily, there was always a clear choice that went straight ahead. Occasionally there were sources to replenish our water and we ate our way through the dried fruits, nuts and small grain packs that were lovingly given to us for our journey. Drinking the water infused with the Temple stones slowly took away most of our need for food. I was grateful for that. As much as the foods of the Kingdom were amazing, having an empty belly was preferable when I needed to be vigilant and light on my feet.

We kept moving through an array of tunnels that never seemed to end. Nothing looked different, just more and more of the same. Rocks and dirt followed by more rocks and dirt. Even though this was a momentous time in my life, after a while things got rather monotonous and I must have let my guard down. It can happen so easily. Maybe it was fatigue setting in or maybe I started to drift off into sleep while still walking, no matter, I was not paying attention and things took a bad turn rather quickly. Unbeknownst to me in my half-tranced state, the terrain had been slowly changing. It was getting rockier and craggier. At some point I stepped on a rock the wrong way and my foot slid precipitously off to one side. It happened so quickly that it caught me completely off guard. I hit the ground hard without any attempt to break my own fall. The torch went flying out of my hand. Time slowed down as the nightmare of it tumbling through the air played out in painful detail. When it finally came down, it hit the ground even harder than I had. The crystal shattered like it had landed on a bomb. Our only source of light went out as I laid writhing in a state of pain. Mostly the pain was of the emotional sort. I was in the dark again.

My mind started careening to the edge. *How could this happen now?* I could not think of a possible way out of this mess. The unplanned can and does seem to happen but in this instance, it would be with devastating results. I reached down and held my ankle tightly. It was not broken, thankfully, but a sprain was not good news either since I did not know how much distance we still had left to traverse. With a little rest I would be able to walk well again but with no light, that would be a difficulty I could not surmount. Do not forget that these tunnels in the depths of the earth contain a blackness like no other. I called for Tinky and thank goodness she came right away. Losing her would have been the end of my journey and the end of me. I held her tightly in my arms as I began to sob. It seemed so unreal that it all would end this way. It was the ultimate of bad dreams and repatterning would not help me now. On the verge of giving up, I was startled by a small sound slowly making its way to us through the darkness.

Click, click, click…

Instantly I knew what it was.

It was the comforting sound of an old friend approaching. Soon I felt two hard and strange things sliding underneath me as I was gently lifted into the air. Our friend the ant man was there to save the day, once again. Holding me carefully in his arms, he gently cradled me against his chest. Though it was cold and hard, it gave me the warmest and best feeling ever. With Tinky held tightly in my arms, we allowed ourselves to be carried away.

Our friend patiently and lovingly covered many miles, traversed through many tunnels, all on the path towards my home. You may wonder how I could say lovingly, how I could know its emotion. I certainly could not get a read on it or its thoughts, it was still so foreign to me and I was not that adept yet but I knew that one, no matter what one was, does not perform an act of generosity such as this without having a good heart. Somewhere in the matrix, a call of distress must have gone out. Maybe Urda felt it and called on him to come to our aide. She had mentioned a long time ago that she had sent us help before. Maybe these beings were connected to the Kingdom or maybe it simply felt my distress on its own and decided to come to our rescue, once again. I really did not care how or why. I was back in full acceptance, trusting the bigger picture that all would work its way out to the right ending.

During this time, I was able to rest and recharge my being. Eventually it stopped and we were gently set down. Tinky and I both said a wholehearted thank you and bowed goodbye. I think it understood us by instinct too as it also gave a slight nod before turning away. Ahead we could see the end of the tunnel and a small glittering of light. I knew what it was. We were almost there, and I almost let out a scream. I was glad that I did not.

Monsters at the Gate

If I could have, I would have run towards that light. Instead I hobbled along with Tinky perched on my shoulder and my cape lightly fluttering behind us. Like an old pirate hobbling back after being at sea for too long, we made our way down the path as quickly as we could. Nearing the light, I heard the murmuring of voices.

Voices, actual voices! As we drew closer and closer it became clearer and clearer that the language being spoken was my language. My heart almost skipped a beat. The end was certainly near, it was hard to believe that it was really happening. I would really be returning home! While I could not hear the words yet, it was becoming quite clear that it was a heated conversation. Then came the screams. They were not the screams of excitement but rather of terror. Utter and complete, unhinged terror. I stopped in my tracks as pressure started to build in my head. Something was wrong. Very wrong. The only other time I felt pressure in my head like that was on one other occasion. I shuddered while remembering. Tinky knew it too and grew understandably anxious. She tried to get under the cape and around to my back. Her little claws felt like sharp needles against my skin as she grew more and more frantic. She desperately wanted to hide so I opened the backpack for her to jump in. And jump she did. The very thought of seeing the lizard monsters again sent a cold chill through my entire being. Of all the tests I could imagine having to endure to make it home, this was not one I wished upon myself or Tinky for that matter.

With Tinky carefully hidden in the backpack, I drew the cape around us so that we would be completely concealed. The only path home was forward so there I had to go. I took a few minutes to get centered in our surroundings and to allow my presence to begin the process of blending in. After all I had on the cloak of confusion. I completely trusted that it would work, just like it had before. No one, no creature, nothing would be able to see us if I were able to maintain the correct energy pattern. I needed to stay in alignment and not to succumb to fear. That is if I ever wanted to get home. It was game time and I was ready to play. But nothing could have prepared me for what I saw.

BURIED

As we neared the opening, I could finally make out a group of men dressed in what looked like military gear but a uniform I did not recognize. They were dressed in all black and looked very stealth. They must have come to help those who were screaming. I was so excited that I almost threw caution to the wind and started hobbling as fast as I could towards them. I did not want them to go away before I got there. Surely, they would protect me too. It was then that I saw something that even to this day makes me ill to think about. I could finally see that the men were talking to the giant lizard creatures – half man and half reptile. It was clear they were in the middle of an intense discussion, a heated negotiation of sorts. The barter point was something I would never have believed had I not seen it with my own eyes. The men had a group of people, both men and women, with their hands tied behind their backs, hoods over their heads and shackles around their ankles. I could see their bodies shaking in fear. It was obvious that the men in black were not helping the situation. Quite possibly they were making it worse.

The next thing that happened shattered my world. The men, men from the surface, my species, handed the people off. The lizard men grabbed the rope that bound them together and pulled so hard that several fell to their knees. When one of them could not get back up, he was beaten mercilessly. I bowed my head down and covered my eyes. Having come from living in a place that could only be described as heavenly, to converge on hell at a point that should have been the apex of excitement, the culmination of a long journey, was beyond shocking and heartbreaking. No wonder my little angel was so afraid and wanted to hide. It was even worse than I had feared. *But why were these men doing this? Why would they be giving people over to the monsters?* It made no sense. I simply could not fathom a motive and there was nothing that I could do to change the situation. I remained quiet and concealed by my cloak as I listened to the captives being dragged off down the chamber, their moans growing more distant until they faded into complete silence. I sat there for a long time afterwards, until I was sure everyone had left. I was not going to take any chances with my potential freedom and my precious cargo. Meeting up with the lizards was not something I wanted and as for the men, I had no explanation for their behavior, only disgust. I did not want to run into them either. They too were monsters.

Eventually it was time to move forward. It had been quiet for long enough for me to assume the area was clear. I carefully stood and started limping towards the light. It must have been near dusk since the glow was starting to fade. As I came up to the open area, I could feel fresh air flowing in from my left. It would have been amazing to relish this moment had the stakes not been so high. The opening that led to freedom was close, but I did not care to look around. I certainly wasn't going to look to the right. I could not afford to react and seeing the monsters again would make it difficult not to. Instead I slowly stepped into the opening and turned towards the fresh air and dwindling light. What happened next was right out of a horror movie. There is a reason I always hated those kinds of shows but this was real, I couldn't simply turn off the television or leave the room.

"Who goes there?" The lizard man belted out his words as they tried to brutally beat their way into my head.

"I know you are there, stop now and show yourself!" The creature roared its evil command into the open air, hoping it would land on someone. Me. It hoped for ears to hear and then emotionally react into giving up the presence of the entire body. To survive I had to let its deadly serve go unanswered.

It was obvious that it could not see me. Otherwise it would have all been over in an instant or two, depending on how much it wanted to torment its prey. At this point it was only guessing at our presence. The light was drawing nearer as I looked up and saw the mouth of the cave and the dusk of a real setting sun. I took a deep breath and kept walking.

"You had better stop right now or I will certainly kill you. I will cut you up alive and eat you piece by piece. Bloody and screaming are the best snacks of all. Arrrr arrr arrr…" An utterly cruel laugh welled up from its vicious belly. The kind that makes you want to instantly vomit the noise out of your senses.

I kept walking forward, trusting that its threats were based in real preferences of what it would do if it saw us. I am sure it would have loved to dine on my still warm wiggling innards. If I allowed fear to come, in the slightest bit, it would all be over. It would sense it in the air and it would find us, Tinky and me.

"Just kidding. Show yourself now and I will spare your life." It cackled as it started moving in my direction. I could feel its massive body approaching. It was so obtrusive, even the most insensitive person would have known evil was on its way.

The taste of freedom was growing closer even as the giant lizard started closing in from behind. It was determined to flush me out one way or another. Testing the field with intimidation was not working so it thought cajoling might work better. Clearly it did not know me.

It was fast approaching, and I knew its threat was probably true. Tinky and I would make for a nice snack. I prayed that would not be the fate of those poor people I had seen earlier, even though it probably was. As the creature's temper started to boil, my countenance grew calmer. The impulse to turn around and to face my attacker was strong but I remembered Urda's warning – *do not look back. No matter what, do not look back*. I kept my head down and kept on walking.

"You've had it now..." It snarled at a fever pitch. Clearly its capacity for patience was quite limited and was at an end.

There was a sudden movement behind me, but I did not turn around.

CHAPTER VII

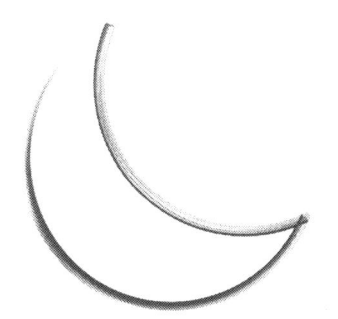

BURIED

Buried but Never Forgotten

Behind us the lizard creature started jabbing its giant spear wildly into the air as a last gesture of its vileness. It could not see us, it could not feel us, it just got lucky. One fateful jab, that was all it took. It caught me square in the back. Had I turned around my story would have been over. My first thought was thank goodness the books protected me but then I heard the faintest of cries. I had forgotten. That was where Tinky had taken refuge. I was supposed to have kept her safe. I failed to keep my vow to her, but she kept hers. She did not let the beast know that it had gotten her. She, above all else, wanted me to reach safety. Devastation pounded at the door of my heart. My world was about to come crashing in. Not wanting to acknowledge to this beast that it had inflicted a mortal blow straight into my heart, I kept walking. No satisfaction would be given on this day or any day. I kept my composure and walked right out of the cave. Right past the men in black as they stood guard on the other side. I kept walking right out into the cool desert evening. Fighting off all impulses of wanting to strike back and retaliate, I kept moving forward. I did not stop until I had safely cleared all their influences.

As soon as I could, I sat down and carefully opened the pack to find my sweetest friend clinging to life. The wound cut deep into her delicate flesh. She was slowly slipping away from me as my heart was also slowly slipping away with her. Nestled lovingly into my arms, I whispered calming words as I carried her away. We came to high ground, far enough away to safely stop and take refuge for a while. At the top I sat down and cradled her like I would a beloved child. She was my beloved child, the only one I would ever have. The stones around my neck had awakened and were gently throbbing a slow steady beat against my chest. My heart slowed to match them and to commune with hers, in one last act of harmony and love. Above us the heavens were on brilliant display with a million stars staring down with twinkling eyes.

"My angel, these are what you are named after." I had longed for the time to share with her a starry night. I had not imagined that this would also be our farewell. Ever so softly I sang to her, her special song…

>Tinky, Tinky, little star
>Why when we have come so far.
>Gone are you from my sight
>Gone are you from this night.

>Tinky, Tinky, little star
>In the heavens you now are.

>Tinky, Tinky… I will always love you…

I could go no further as grief clenched my heart and closed my throat…

As I looked up into the night, for just a fleeting moment I saw the stars blink off and then, as if nothing happened, they went on about their business as usual. Regardless that a precious piece of my world was being torn away, they kept shining and twinkling on into eternity, knowing the truth that all was well. The Heavens never forget the dance of life. I needed to remind myself as well. She was not gone. Urda said that she would always be with me. I had no idea that it wouldn't include her adorable furry form. The form I wanted right then. The form I had come to love and count on.

I sat there through the night cradling her broken body, her heart beating more and more slowly as she slipped past these Earthly bounds. At dawn, her tiny heart gave its last beat. This chapter was closed, this part of the story was over. There was one last thing I needed to do to honor her soul. I took off my cape and carefully laid it across the rocks. I was not going to need it anymore. I remembered. I knew without a doubt, it was all inside me. The power to transmute and transcend was my innate right and I did not need anything to help me hide. I would recover and life would move on, as difficult as it felt right then. For in that long painful now, it felt like all was lost. Then in a moment of graciousness, my heart was opened and I remembered my other beloved. The one that I left behind when I was torn from his arms in what seemed like a lifetime ago. Soon I would return to him. Life has a blessed way of coming full circle.

With gentle hands and a fractured heart, I took her still warm body and laid it on the cape. She always found comfort within its folds; it was only right that it enveloped her now. I placed the selenite wand Urda had given us in her paws to help light the way on the next part of her journey. There was a small opening in the rocks that I slipped my precious package in and tenderly covered it with stones. Her body would remain under the stars, carefully tucked away, as her spirit would dance among them forever more.

I stayed there mourning the next day and throughout that night. The changes in temperature did not matter. My body adjusted all on its own since I was a million miles away and not able to tend to it. My spirit was in the heavens with my precious friend. Keeping her company as she adjusted to her new reality. My life could wait.

Nights came and went as I stayed there in mourning and then finally, on the third day I rose again. Ready to face what was to come all alone.

It was time to go.

Standing up, I faced the east and the dawning of a new day. While I did not know where I was or even when I was, I absolutely knew who I was.

I turned and with the sun at my back, I looked to the west and bravely took the first step towards a new beginning. I wondered what had become of the world while I was gone.

Would it still know me?

EPILOGUE

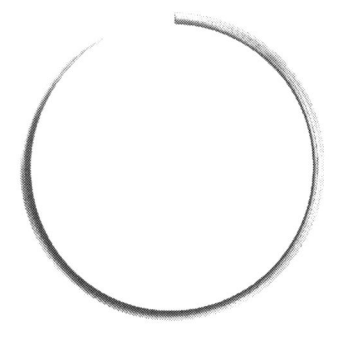

BURIED

Daniel

Daniel relaxed in his favorite leather chair enjoying a sip of sherry from an exquisitely cut crystal glass. It had belonged to his father and his grandfather and his great grandfather before that. Through many generations of men, this was a cherished nightly ritual. Even for Daniel the rather archaic routine held his heart, as not much else ever had.

The last thing Daniel remembered was the vibration of his cell phone.

The heirloom crystal slipped out of his hand and shattered into a thousand pieces just as his heart had shattered into a thousand pieces several long years ago.

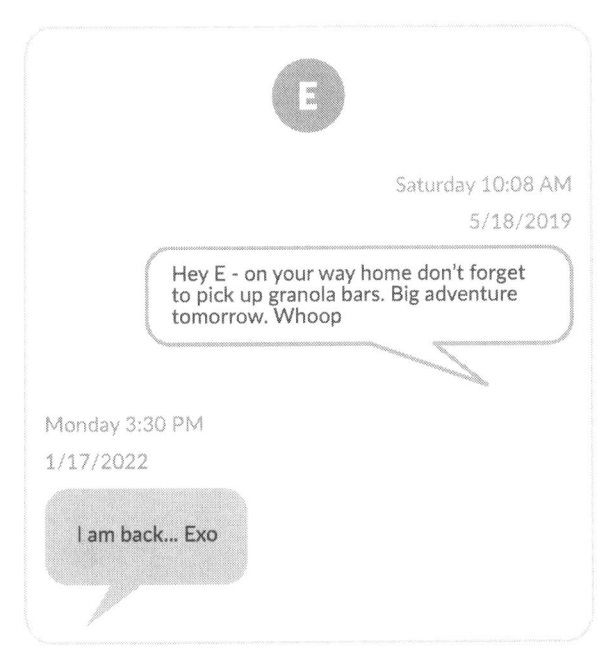

> **E**
>
> Saturday 10:08 AM
> 5/18/2019
>
> Hey E - on your way home don't forget to pick up granola bars. Big adventure tomorrow. Whoop
>
> Monday 3:30 PM
> 1/17/2022
>
> I am back... Exo

Author
Elisa Chastaine

The first time I left my body I was just seven years old. The world never looked the same to me after that experience. I realized in my heart of hearts that what I had been taught about life on this precious planet of ours was not the whole story. From that point forward, I knew without a single doubt that there was more going on than met the eye, especially behind the scenes. The rest of my life has been devoted to a quest to figure out that Truth. I have searched high and low, outside myself and inside myself. I have followed one guru after another, spent much time alone and lived in various alternative communities, all the while supporting myself as an entrepreneur and businesswoman. I have determinedly been on a vital path to somewhere, pursuing it as if my life depended on it. And it did. Finally, after many years of seeking and of exploring many rabbit holes, I have finally arrived at an understanding that has filled my heart with peace. While I would never say that I know the whole Truth, since it is a rather large subject that is constantly in flux, I can say that I have a solid foundation that has brought me joy, love and success.

A short time ago, if you had asked me if I would ever write a book - much less an award-winning one - I would have replied that you were either crazy or high on something! I was convinced from years of schooling that I stunk at writing and consequently I rather detested it. While I always knew I was an artist, being a writer is an entirely different endeavor, and one that I never imagined would come naturally to me. Fast forward to today and here I am, working on my next book after receiving over 11 awards on my very first novel, *Buried But Never Forgotten*. The part even crazier than realizing I am pretty good at it is that I have discovered I simply LOVE to write. Lesson learned, again: *never say never!*

Through writing, I have found a medium in which to share what I have learned as a result of all my searching, finding and losing… and then finding again. My hope is that through my stories I can help others along their journey. Perhaps if I clothe the lessons I have learned in exciting drama, then just maybe people will open their minds to a more expanded view of life, living and the Truth. And then, just maybe, the world will change into one that reflects the potential that we have as amazing beings – as human beings.

I hope you enjoy, reflect, question and learn!

My love to you… always and forever.

Elisa lives in Northern California with her husband and their feline friends. She spends her days enjoying the challenges of life and exploring the nature of reality. She also runs several businesses just to make sure things never get boring!

If you would like to correspond with Elisa directly, she can be reached at: elisa@metaphysicaladventures.com.
You can learn more about the book by visiting:
www.buriedbutneverforgotten.com

TRINKA
2015 – 2020

I miss my little angel every day...
Thank you for all the love you gave me.
Until we meet again. E xo

And finally, invite your friends to
join in the experience...

The more we work together,
the lighter we all become.

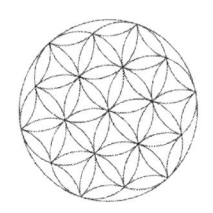

BURIED

Made in the USA
Middletown, DE
02 December 2021